ONE EXTRA CORPSE

ONE EXTRA CORPSE

Barbara Hambly

SEVERN
HOUSE

First world edition published in Great Britain and the USA in 2023
by Severn House, an imprint of Canongate Books Ltd,
14 High Street, Edinburgh EH1 1TE.

Trade paperback edition first published in Great Britain and the USA in 2023
by Severn House, an imprint of Canongate Books Ltd.

severnhouse.com

British Library Cataloguing-in-Publication Data
A CIP catalogue record for this title is available from the British Library.

ISBN-13: 978-0-7278-5079-9 (cased)
ISBN-13: 978-1-4483-1031-9 (trade paper)
ISBN-13: 978-1-4483-1023-4 (e-book)

MIX
Paper from
responsible sources
FSC   FSC® C013056
www.fsc.org

Typeset by Palimpsest Book Production Ltd.,
Falkirk, Stirlingshire, Scotland.
Printed and bound in Great Britain by
TJ Books, Padstow, Cornwall.

For Mom

Special thanks to the staff of the Margaret Herrick Library,
And to John Bengtson (silentlocations.com)

ONE

'Oh, Howie!' Emma Blackstone gasped, raising astonished eyes from the band of diamonds on its velvet bed, to the tender gaze of the man who sat so close at her side.

'It's *Harry*,' he whispered, and bowed his dark head over her hand in a passionate kiss. Two tables away, the dumpy, motherly-looking columnist for one of the Hearst newspapers looked aside quickly, feigning fascination with the dancers jigging to 'Shimmy Like My Sister Kate' on the Café Montmartre's highly polished floor.

'Oh, Harry!' Emma gasped obligingly.

'I want you to marry me, Emma.' Harry Garfield lifted the bracelet from its case, clasped it around her wrist. A lifetime of yearning, of promise, smoldered in the long-lashed brown eyes. 'You're the only woman I've ever known who—'

'I can't!' Face averted, Emma fumbled at the catch, startled as much by the declaration (it was, after all, only the second time she'd met the man) as by the probable cost of the jewels (which even to her inexperienced eye looked like real diamonds). 'You know I can't.'

The powerful fingers stayed hers, drew her back towards him. 'You don't have to answer me tonight.'

'I can answer you right this very—'

He rose from his chair, and with peremptory grace drew her to her feet. His warm hand in the small of her back, he guided her on to the dance floor under its fantastic canopy of blue satin.

The Hearst columnist (Mrs Barton? Preston? Emma had heard her name around the studio . . .) and her sleek and chinless companion nearly knocked heads, pulling themselves back into an upright position from where they'd been leaning to overhear.

The band switched to 'Who's Sorry Now?'. Pasadena

debutantes and the flapper daughters of railroad magnates devoured Harry Garfield with covetous eyes as he took Emma's slim, awkward height into his arms for a fox trot, the bracelet twinkling in the myriad brilliance of the chandeliers. A tall brunette girl in yellow satin – and half a galaxy of diamonds of her own – aimed a bosomy sigh in Garfield's direction as she was led out by a paunchy gentleman with a nose like a mangel-wurzel and a stare that would have made a cash register appear sympathetic.

Emma had to admit that her partner *was* a superb dancer. His lead was firm, his touch light, he knew what he was doing and it was no surprise that hundreds of thousands of women were passionately in love with him . . . despite having never met him in their lives. Such, she reflected, was the magic of Hollywood. Her mother, her childhood governess, and every single one of her aunts would have expired from outrage at the thought of her dancing with such a person . . .

Had they not all expired from the influenza, four years ago, that had followed in the wake of the war.

Later, on the way downstairs to where a studio limousine waited for her on Hollywood Boulevard, Emma touched the bracelet and whispered, 'I'll send this back to you . . .'

'Just slip it to me tomorrow at the studio.' Harry kissed her hand again with an air of tenderest affection, then raised his eyes to hers, chin tucked, to give him the air of a small boy. She'd seen him perform that particular gesture in reel six of *Hide-and-Seek Heart*. 'They read my mail.'

'I shall.' Emma wondered how one could inconspicuously 'slip' a handful of three-karat diamonds to anyone under any circumstances, much less when surrounded by several hundred actors, extras, wardrobe assistants, electricians, carpenters, property hands and guards. *Did Euripides ever have this sort of problem?* She supposed that having written a 'scenario' for Foremost Productions' leading female star – plot, action, and dialog cards – she could now claim the ancient Greek playwright (not to mention Mr Shakespeare) as a professional colleague.

Not that I would have the temerity to do so, on the strength of an opus entitled Hot Potato.

'You're a sport, Mrs Blackstone.' And with a quick glance over his shoulder – Mrs Parsons (*I knew I'd remember her name!*), her companion from the *Examiner*, Thelma Turnbit from *Screen Stories* and the 'cinema columnists' from *Silver Screen Magazine* and *Motion Picture News* were in the nightclub doorway behind them inconspicuously craning their necks – he drew Emma to him and kissed her passionately on the lips (*Wait! What? I hardly know the man!*). Someone in the gaggle of bystanders on the sidewalk took a photograph, a blaze of flash-powder and a white drift of smoke in the glare of the Montmartre's lights. Emma was too breathless with shock and confusion to speak as Garfield led her to the limousine and bowed as he opened its door for her. Another limousine, larger and lacquered a vivid crimson, blocked the studio vehicle's exit while the hard-faced man with the prodigious nose gave instructions to the driver. Emma was aware of the man's yellow-silk lady-friend at the edge of the crowd, holding hands and whispering something to a good-looking young man in checkered trousers and the most American shoes Emma had ever seen.

There were worse things, Emma supposed, as her escort helped her into the studio vehicle, than gentlemen who knew how to dance and how to dress properly, even if they did propose marriage and kiss one – and such a kiss! – on a public sidewalk . . .

And at least the head of Foremost Productions had arranged a limousine.

The actor sprang into his own sleek, snow-white Auburn, tossed fifty cents to the Filipino youth who'd brought it to him, and steered deftly away into the traffic of the Boulevard. Two other columnists and a photographer were crowding towards the studio car when its driver let in the clutch and followed.

Emma settled back into the velvet upholstery and reminded herself that Harry Garfield – né Howie Mellnick of Tumwah, Iowa – kissed women for a living, and the lurid intimacy was in fact less significant than a handshake. (*Si fueris Romae, Romano vivito more . . . had we been in Alaska I expect he would have rubbed my nose with his own.*) She turned the

diamonds over in her gloved hand, and hoped that the photograph wouldn't appear in any journal her sole surviving aunt
– or, God forbid, any of her late husband's family – would be
likely to read.

'Did Howie ask you to marry him?' inquired Kitty Flint –
known to the film-going multitudes of America as Camille de
la Rose – an hour later, coming into the kitchen of the villa
that perched like a fantasy Moorish castle in the Hollywood
Hills.

Emma, sustaining herself with a cup of tea at the kitchen
table, glanced in surprise at the clock. It was barely one in the
morning – *What on Earth is Kitty doing home so early?* – and
she asked, almost involuntarily, 'Is everything all right?'

'Oh, darling, of course.' Kitty turned toward the door that
led into the rest of the house, squatting with the supple
grace of a former Ziegfeld chorus girl as her three Pekinese
bounded into the kitchen in a great clattering of toenails and
flouncing of fur. 'Yes, yes, sweethearts, Mamma's home.'
She lifted and cuddled the pale-golden Buttercreme, while
Black Jasmine stood on wobbly little hind legs and butted
at her elbow, and big, rufous Chang Ming ran excitedly
around her feet.

'It's just that that pestilent *hag* Desiree Darrow came in.
Seth and I were at Man Jen Low in Chinatown, someplace
Frank wouldn't be caught *dead* in' – Frank Pugh, head of
Foremost Productions, was – as far as he knew, anyway – the
Man in Kitty's life – 'with Jack Gilbert, who must have been
hiding out from that awful wife of his . . . You know she's
hired detectives to follow him, with the divorce coming up?
Not that you'd need detectives to keep track of *his* love life
. . . But Desiree has been absolutely *hounding* Seth for *months*,
and it would be just like her to go tell Frank that she saw me
and Seth together, to get me in Dutch and Seth too, I bet, the
nasty weasel.'

Seth Ramsay – the blond Adonis currently starring in
The Thornless Rose – had been squiring Kitty to any number
of roadhouses, racetracks, and less-fashionable eating
establishments outside the immediate area of Hollywood for

some weeks now. On several occasions he'd turned up at Kitty's house at two in the morning, after Kitty had been brought home from dinner and romance with the obese, middle-aged studio head. When first Emma had arrived in Hollywood seven months ago in October of 1923 – to serve as her gorgeous sister-in-law's secretary, assistant, companion and dog-brusher – she had attributed Kitty's unflagging stamina to the cocaine that was so freely dispensed around the studio. But Kitty's decision to abandon the drug some months ago had had, so far as Emma could observe, no visible effect on her ability to dance and drink all night (Prohibition be damned) and act in front of the cameras under the blistering glare of the klieg lights at Foremost all day . . .

If, reflected Emma, *one could call what she did 'acting'.*

I suppose one can't have everything . . .

'And anyway –' Kitty blithely gathered Black Jasmine into her free arm and stood – 'Mickey's supposed to pick me up here at two, for drinks at Enyart's – that *gorgeous* boy who plays saxophone at the Coconut Grove . . .'

She scooted a chair out from under the table with one foot and sat, two dogs in her lap and Chang Ming continuing to bounce eagerly at her side. Storm-dark hair piled in loose curls around her face, dark eyes enormous and bright in their frames of kohl and mascaro, and Pekineses licking her chin, she looked nothing like the sinister *femme fatale* who routinely lured the heroes of her films to insanity, disgrace and tragic death. She reached around Black Jasmine, with some difficulty, to light a cigarette. 'So *did* Howie ask you to marry him?'

'He did.' Emma fetched another cup from the cupboard – old Mrs Shang the housekeeper never left so much as a spoon in the drainboard – and scratched a match to light the gas-burner under the breakfast coffee.

'Are you going to?'

Emma turned, startled. 'I can't imagine he meant it—'

'Oh, of course he did, darling.' Kitty regarded her with surprise. 'He asked *me*, last September.'

'But I thought—'

'Oh, *that*.' Her airy wave left a faint trail of smoke. 'Yes. That's why Frank asked me to get you to go out with him. And Mr Zukor over at Paramount told Roger Clint – that's Howie's friend, you know – that *he* had to start being seen with Clara Bow or Mae Murray . . . Could you get me that gin that's in the cupboard, dearest, while you're up? Thanks . . . I think they're trying to get him to marry Mae, as soon as *her* divorce goes through . . .' She poured equal parts cream and gin into the coffee Emma brought her.

And here I thought scandalous the discreet hand-holding between the wives of the dons and the younger tutors behind the library shelves at Oxford . . .

Latere semper patere, quod latuit diu, her father had always admonished, but she remembered her mother and her aunts whispering about such things the moment that scholarly gentleman left the room. And the recollection of her home – her home before the war, before marriage and widowhood and the death of them all – was like hearing the drowned ringing of Atlantis's bells, echoing up from the deep. A lost world – where a glance from the wife of the Dean of King's College toward a handsome lecturer at Merton would be the occasion for months – perhaps years – of averted glances, blushes, speculation, whispers, and discretion . . .

These people in Hollywood would make Caligula look quaint.

'That's why they had to quit living together,' Kitty went on. 'Howie and Roger, I mean. Which is *dreadfully* unfair . . . Oh!' She reached across Black Jasmine's insistent efforts to snuggle and drew the diamond bracelet to her.

'He gave me that.' Emma was still trying to digest that thought.

'How *sweet* of him!' cried Kitty. 'That's the one he gave me back in September. It cost over a thousand dollars at Cartier's. He's *such* a prince! It would be almost worth it to marry him, just to keep it. Just don't mail it back to him. That awful ghoul who writes for *Cinema World* pays somebody in the mailroom at the studio to read people's letters . . .'

'He warned me about that.'

'And you know that overage pocket-twister Darlene Golden writes love letters to *me* at the studio, signed from people like Ronnie Colman, who I only ever slept with just the one time . . . except for that time on location in Palm Springs. And that time after the Christmas party at Paramount.' She tallied quickly on ruby-nailed fingers. 'Just to get rumors in the screen magazines and stir up trouble for me with Frank. And from Charlie Chaplin, of all people, though anybody who knows Charlie would know I'm . . . um . . .'

She stopped herself, unwilling and almost unable to speak the words: *Too old for him . . .*

Emma finished drily, 'Over fifteen?'

Kitty sipped her gin-laced coffee with coy dignity. 'Not *that* much over . . .'

Emma refrained from shaking her head, well aware that the birth date in her friend's official studio biography was a solid nine years later than the actual year of her arrival in this world. Instead she said, 'No, I'll hand it to him, tomorrow, at the studio.'

'Oh, good!' bubbled Kitty. 'They moved my scene with Ken back to Friday – did I tell you? [She hadn't] Because Ken has a horrible toothache and can't see a dentist until tomorrow . . .'

The Thornless Rose, as a costume epic, was shooting on the much-larger Stage One at Foremost, *Hot Potato* on Two.

'But since Frank isn't going to be on the lot tomorrow, Seth's meeting me at nine, because his own scenes in *Rose* aren't going to be shot until after lunch . . . You *will* remember to wake me up at seven, won't you, dear? Oh!' she squeaked, scooping first Buttercreme and then Black Jasmine to the floor and springing to her feet. 'That will be Mickey . . .'

A car-horn blatted somewhere in the night, around toward the front of the house. Emma could only be grateful that Kitty's pink stucco Alhambra was one of the few dwellings this far up Ivarene Street. She followed her beautiful sister-in-law up the four steps to the dining room, down two steps to the dark cavern of the living room, with its gleaming chromium furniture and Chinese silks, and across to the door.

'Do you have your house key?'

'Oh – nertz . . .' Kitty set down her cigarette and fished in her handbag, while Emma doubled back to the kitchen to fetch the keys which still dangled from the back door. 'You're a darling, Emma!' she added, when Emma returned, carrying not only the keys but the extravagant concoction of silk and chinchilla that served in these warm California nights as a coat. Past her, through the now-open front door, Emma glimpsed moonlight glinting on a huge, humped shape, rather like a silver-trimmed dinosaur in the darkness of the yard below.

'Now, you think about marrying Howie.' Kitty turned in the doorway, her perfect oval face suddenly grave. 'You wouldn't have to give up seeing Zal, you know. I mean, Howie would understand – and so would Zal—'

'I have no intention of—' began Emma, though she knew how the sturdy cameraman would greet the news of the proposal. With a grin and a kiss – a *real* kiss, Emma thought. Lover, dear friend, sheet anchor in this gaudy maelstrom.

Like Harry, Kitty gestured her objection aside. 'And Frank would be *ever* so grateful . . . You could keep the diamonds and go out dancing every night.'

Emma tried to picture herself in the sort of baroque *menage-à-trois* (or *quatre*, or *cinq* . . .) engaged in by a number of Kitty's friends in the Hollywood community, and concluded that she simply hadn't the stamina. She was still searching for words to express this view of the matter when Kitty tiptoed to kiss her cheek, waved airily, and scampered down the steep, tiled steps in a clatter of diamond-studded heels.

Emma closed the door after her, and thought again of her mother and her aunts, her father and her brother Miles who lay beside them in Wolvercote Cemetery, and what they would have thought of their scholarly, responsible Emma adrift six thousand miles from home in this gaudy American Babylon.

But as she bent to gather up Black Jasmine and Buttercreme in her arms – the tiny Sleeve Pekes were too small to climb the stairs to the bedrooms – she heard, at the back of her mind, Jim Blackstone, Kitty's brother – the tall American soldier she had married and loved and lost in the closing months of the war – laughing with delight.

Diamonds and *an offer! Good for you, Em!*

She was smiling as she climbed the stairs to bed.

TWO

Naturally, Kitty wasn't home by seven the following morning.

Emma knew this because when she waked at five thirty, the dogs were still snoring gently on her own bed, Buttercreme's pink tongue protruding like a miniature welcome mat in front of her flat nose in a damp little circle of drool. Had Kitty come in, Emma knew, they would have waked her, Chang Ming by leaping to the floor and the two tinier Pekes by running about excitedly on the counterpane demanding to be helped down after him.

She nevertheless checked Kitty's room before taking the three little guardians downstairs and then down the back steps from the kitchen – leashed, because she had been warned of predatory coyotes back here in the Hollywood Hills and the two male Pekes feared nothing – for their morning constitutional. (*Wild animals attacking one's house pets are* not *something one would encounter in Oxford, or Manchester either . . .*) She had just returned to the service porch beside the kitchen for morning brushing when the telephone in the hall rang.

Kitty. Asking me will I please just bring her makeup and some clean things to the studio so she can meet Seth at nine, and don't forget the cigarettes and the latest copy of Secrets of the Stars *. . .*

For the four years between the deaths of her family and the appearance of her husband's sister in her life, Emma had been a not-very-well-paid companion to a manufacturer's widow in Manchester. Fond as she was of Kitty – and interesting as it was to live on what sometimes appeared to be the planet Barsoom and sometimes the Land of Oz – there were times when it was brought home to her that her duties here were in fact very much the same. (*Though I'd have given much to see old Mrs Pendergast being squired home at one a.m. by one lover only to sally forth with another thirty-five minutes later . . .)*

'Kitty?' asked a man's deep voice, with an accent of Central Europe.

'This is Mrs Blackstone,' replied Emma. 'I'm afraid Miss de la Rose is on her way to the studio already.' She glanced at the clock. *At least I hope and trust she is . . .*

'Tcha,' said the caller. 'This is Ernst Zapolya, madame; I am director at Enterprise Studios—'

'Oh, of course!' Emma recognized the name. 'I'm so sorry, Mr Zapolya. I'm not certain when Miss de la Rose will be arriving at Foremost, but I shall be there myself in an hour. I'll be delighted to tell her to call you.'

'Call will be difficult,' said the director. 'We are filming major sequence today – breakthrough of American troops into Ravenstark . . . *Crowned Heart*, you understand.'

Another name, more or less familiar. Emma had heard the 'extra' players at the studio, while standing around waiting to be called on to the sets of *Hot Potato* or *The Thornless Rose* – or one of the comedy two-reelers being filmed on Stage Three – talking about Enterprise Films' upcoming Ruritanian extravaganza.

'Ten thousand things must be seen to. Yet I must speak to Kitty – to Miss de la Rose – and is urgent that I do so this morning. Madame Blackstone, is there any way – any way at all – you could have Miss de la Rose to my office at Enterprise by eight this morning? It will not be long interview, I promise. But is imperative that I speak to her today.'

The urgency in the director's voice was unmistakable. When did Kitty say she was meeting Seth . . .?

She began, 'I don't know . . .'

'Please, madame. This is not some . . . some Hollywood intrigue, please understand. This is matter on which . . .' His words stalled for a moment. 'On which lives depend. Maybe many lives. Maybe future of country. Please. Do what you can.'

A little shaken, Emma said, 'I'll do what I can, of course, Mr Zapolya. Does she know what this concerns? Or is there anything more that I can tell her?'

'No. Nothing.' And as if the next moment he realized how brusque was his anxiety, he added, 'And if you would, madame, please – tell no one of this. I understand that it is not well seen, that Foremost's stars be seen at Enterprise. This stupid rivalry! But it is more than this. I beg you, speak to no one of this. Eight o'clock, if it can at all be managed.'

Through the flat tinniness of the receiver she heard – or thought she heard – desperation. Desperation beyond, as he had said, 'some Hollywood intrigue' . . .

'I shall do what I can, sir.'

'Bless you, madame, ten thousand times. I kiss your hands and feet.' He rang off.

Emma turned back into the kitchen, retrieved Black Jasmine from a rolling tussle with Chang Ming – the dogs seemed to feel obliged to fight one another before their lightly grilled chicken livers and buttered toast fragments – and carried him back to the brushing table, just as the telephone rang again.

'Darling,' cooed Kitty, 'I'm not waking you up, am I? I'm just on my way out the door—'

Whose door? Knowing Kitty, 'just on my way out the door' actually meant, dripping wet and wrapped in a towel.

'Would you be an *angel* and go down to the studio and have all my washing-up things in my room there ready? And bring my rose and burgundy Poiret and the shoes that go with it – the rose ones – and some clean stockings and step-ins and all that? Oh, and my cigarettes and the ivory holder . . . and the long pearls and the pearl earrings and the copy of *Secrets of the Stars* from my bedside table . . .'

'Of course. Mr Zapolya from Enterprise telephoned . . .'

'What, this morning? What on earth could he want? Ever since he married that man-trap Marina Carver he's avoided me like he owed me money! I hope you told him to run away and chase himself . . . and when you get there could you possibly get Tony at the commissary to make me some fresh coffee, three sugars, and some orange juice? Is there still some of that egg fu yung from the other night in the icebox? Would you bring it along?'

'He—'

'Oh, and see if Tony can give you some ice wrapped up

in a wash cloth, and some sliced cucumbers. My eyelids look like someone got at them with a bicycle pump. You're a darling, Em!'

The line went dead.

Emma glanced at the clock, estimated how long it would take her to reach Foremost Productions, and returned to the kitchen long enough to set the large tea kettle on the stove and light the burner. The house had piped water – her parents' had not, nor had Mrs Pendergast's Victorian brick mausoleum in Manchester – but it took nearly five minutes for the hot tap to actually run hot. Kitty had a bath tub worthy of Cleopatra upstairs, but for quick morning ablutions, both women relied on the spanking-new (and, Emma's Aunt Phyllis had always said, rampantly indecent) American innovation of a shower-bath. Even the stars' dressing rooms at Foremost boasted no such modern miracles.

She had, she calculated, just time for such an indulgence in indecency. Heaven only knew what facilities were available at 'Mickey's'.

At seven thirty, Emma guided Kitty's long yellow Packard through the wrought-iron gates on Sunset Boulevard, crossed the dusty quadrangle between the shooting stages, the commissary and the old adobe farmhouse around which the studio had taken shape, and disembarked in front of the 'Hacienda's' newer wing. Bud from the guard kiosk trotted up to her as she silenced the engine, grinned a friendly, 'M'am' as he helped carry makeup kit, satchel, dress-bags, and the wicker boxes in which the three Pekes were transported into the dressing room.

'Miss de la Rose hasn't by any chance arrived yet, has she?' inquired Emma, but felt neither surprised nor disappointed when the young man shook his head.

'It's not even eight o'clock yet, m'am.'

She sighed. 'One lives in hope.'

The muscular young guard's grin widened. 'They do say this town's built on dreams, m'am. I get you anythin', Mrs Blackstone?'

There was a time when she would have asked for a one-way ticket back to Oxford in 1914, but with occasional exceptions now, those days were mostly past. She was tempted to request a decent Latin edition of Caesar's *Commentaries on the Gallic Wars* – the studio's scenario writer, Sam Wyatt, having asked her to help him doctor the script of *The Gryphon Prince* – but guessed that at Foremost the one would be as unobtainable as the other. And she knew better than to request commissary tea.

'Thank you, no.' She smiled and Bud saluted her and left.

There was no way of telling when Kitty would actually put in an appearance. Turning back to lay out her sister-in-law's impedimenta – the dressing room was larger than the parlor of her parents' house in Oxford and far more expensively fitted up – Emma knew better than to prepare wash-water, or fetch hot coffee just yet. (*Is she going to have 'Mickey' drop her off at the gate, in full view of fan magazine spies?*) She knew herself to be, literally, a lady-in-waiting, and it was for this that Kitty had sought her out – having never met her before – at Mrs Pendergast's dreary establishment in Manchester.

At the moment she would have liked to walk across to Stage One, to watch Harry Garfield being stormily disowned by his wealthy socialite parents (Margaret MacKenzie and Nick Thaxter – Nick, in a silver wig and old-fashioned mutton-chops, was in truth only six years older than Harry himself). This was partly out of curiosity about how the scene she had written would look in action – and partly because one of the cameramen was Zal.

Emma closed her eyes briefly, and smiled.

As Shakespeare had written: 'Haply I think on thee, and then my state/Like to the lark at break of day arising/From sullen earth sings hymns at heaven's gate.'

Zal.

In rescuing her from Mrs Pendergast's establishment – from hopelessness and grief, as well as from the woman's petty bullying and the exhaustion of being constantly on guard against her employer's son and his friends – and in bringing her to Hollywood (a place Emma would never in her entire life have dreamed of ever visiting) Kitty had introduced her to Zal Rokatansky.

He'd be completely preoccupied, she knew, with checking

the lights and conferring with director Larry Palmer about angles and filters and rim lights. It always fascinated her, to watch Zal work with Doc Larousse and the lighting crew, with the director and the stand-ins, setting up precisely how the audience would perceive each shot, each scene, each event in the unfolding story being told.

Prior to being peremptorily enlisted as Kitty's 'companion' and hustled out of Mrs Pendergast's house seven months previously, the last cinema film Emma had seen had been in 1914; even to her unschooled eye, they looked much different now. 'They used to be shot in open stages, by regular daylight,' Zal had explained to her, on the first evening that he'd taken her out for coffee at Enyart's Café on La Brea Avenue. 'They're mostly done in closed stages now – "dark studios" – so you can manipulate the mood of a scene with lights. Makes it hotter than hell's boiler room and guys are always going out with sore eyes from the glare, but you can use a rim light or a baby spot to say, "Hey, this guy's the hero," or, "The villain is sneaking up so watch out!".'

'To say nothing,' Emma had carried on with a smile, 'of letting the director keep everybody at work until midnight if you're behind schedule.'

'Well . . .' Zal had returned her grin, a little shyly. 'That, too.'

In a world of gorgeous men and breathtaking women, Zal Rokatansky was a comforting anomaly, with his close-clipped rufous beard and his cap turned backwards, the way most cameramen wore them; a bespectacled teddy bear good at his job.

Emma walked the Pekes, laid out Kitty's fresh clothing and makeup, and ate her own picnic breakfast of boiled egg and bread and butter, with tea from her thermos bottle.

I suppose one could make Gaius a Neo-Platonist, she reflected, as she unpacked *The Gryphon Prince* scenario from her satchel.

Hot Potato had been Emma's debut scenario, but prior to that epic she'd been press-ganged into doctoring scripts when Sam Wyatt – Foremost's regular scenarist – was either unavailable, overwhelmed with other projects, or hungover. She still shuddered at the thought of the title card on a recent production which would read, '*King Lear* by William Shakespeare and Emma Blackstone.'

I really must *explain to Sam that there* weren't *any Christian legionaries in Julius Caesar's forces.* Her father – who had guided her studies in Classics and Latin and trained her as his own assistant – would turn in his grave . . . or burst into gales of laughter. *Maybe he's a Pythagorean? Though what would a follower of Pythagoras be doing in the legions in the first place?*

Los Angeles has to have a public library of some sort. She studied her own outline of the story to see what other parameters the heroic Gaius needed to fulfill in order to make Sam's story work. *I suppose he* could *be called Gaius even if he* is *secretly a Briton prince . . .*

Who else in the first century BC were pacifists, that Americans might have heard of?

She pondered the question, a task not made easier by the fact that Sam was in the process of switching over from the older method of numbering scenes in photoplays – whereby each sequence of events was numbered as a theatrical 'scene' in which it was assumed that the director would rearrange cameras and lighting for individual close-ups, inserts, reaction shots, and inter-titles – to the current identification of each separate camera shot as a 'scene'. The result was that half of Sam's notes referred to the beautiful Miriam – wearing chains and not a great deal else – being dragged before Caesar as Scene 12, and would switch without warning to Scenes 148–163 to cover the same action (and he would then forget and number much later scenes as 157, 158, etc . . .)

Her thoughts were broken into by a tapping on the panes of the French door that looked out on to the quadrangle. Turning in her chair, Emma hadn't even completed the question, 'Who is it?' when Seth Ramsay walked in, the Apollo Belvedere in exquisitely-cut flannels and an open-necked shirt.

'Kitty here, Duchess?'

'I'm afraid not.' Emma stood, as the New York actor looked around the big room. 'I spoke to her at about six thirty. She said she'd be here shortly.'

Ramsay chuckled mirthlessly, annoyance glinting in the dark-blue eyes. 'For Kitty, that means noon.' He was a tall man, like Harry Garfield powerfully built and like Harry, usually cast as the hero of the piece, where the hero was young and idealistic. Galahad, not Scaramouche. He glanced out the French doors that comprised the whole outer wall of the dressing room, then back at Emma, his gaze warming to a smile.

'I realize it must be a complete nuisance for you,' apologized Emma. 'Since she did say you were due at the Palace of Versailles after lunch.'

He grinned at her jest and stepped closer. 'Doesn't matter. I don't have to put on all that sissy rig for another hour and a half. You mind if I wait here, doll? Or . . .' Emma drew breath to point out that she herself had work to do. 'Why don't you come over to my room for a drink, while we wait? You can leave the rag-mops here.' He jerked his head towards Chang Ming and Black Jasmine, trotting out from beneath the divan to be made much of. His voice warmed. 'I hear you're a judge of champagne.'

At nine in the morning?

His hand slipped down her arm, to grasp her hand. 'The stuff I've got would be wasted on Kitty anyway.'

Emma drew back and he yanked her suddenly close. His other arm circled her waist, and before she could protest, his mouth was on hers, insistent and devouring and reeking of stale tobacco. When she tried to push free he only laughed, and his grip tightened. Kitty had instructed her in a technique supposedly effective in moments like this, but she hesitated to use it. *He's a star. He can get Zal fired. And what if . . .?*

Chang Ming rushed at his ankles, barking furiously, Black Jasmine right behind him.

Seth kicked them aside without loosening his grip. 'You know you want it, Duchess,' he whispered huskily, almost into her mouth.

'I certainly do *not!*'

He grinned, and thrust Emma back against the wall. Before she could pull away the French door rattled behind her. Seth shoved her from him and turned in a single smooth movement.

'Well, here's my little hot potato now!'

He scooped Kitty into his arms as she came through the door, kissing her with the same violence as Emma staggered back and caught herself on the back of the dressing-table chair.

'Ooo, and here's my Gryphon prince!'

Emma pushed long whisps of her hair back into the bun at the back of her neck, her hands trembling, her face burning. *Of course, if the man's used to doing fifty-seven takes of a . . . a* smooch *with Darlene Golden or Alice White,* of course *he can switch from me to Kitty without even wiping his mouth!*

The ferocity of the kiss made Harry Garfield's embrace last night look like a cousinly peck. Kitty dropped her head back, as if swooning with passion (Emma had seen her do fifteen takes of a similar swoon in Dirk Silver's arms in *Temptress of Babylon*).

That's why actors are always having affairs with other actors, she realized. *They all know the appropriate responses.*

Chang Ming and Black Jasmine retreated philosophically to either side of Emma and sat down. They had defended her, but were clearly resigned to their mistress' conduct.

'Dearest . . .' Kitty slipped from Seth's clutch and reached a hand to Emma. '*Please* tell me you've got coffee. I feel absolutely *ruined* . . .' But as she did so she threw the actor the seductive flicker of a glance, every line and curve of her body electric with promise.

Burning with rage and shock, Emma could not keep herself from reflecting that while Kitty couldn't act her way out of a wet paper bag, as the Americans said, with a man to fascinate she made Eleanora Duse look like a cigar-store Indian.

As she stumbled to turn up the heat on the little hot plate, she heard Kitty whisper, 'I'll be over to you in fifteen minutes, angelpants. Just let me tidy up a little.'

'You think I want to see you with your nose powdered?' He kissed her again, as if he would devour her alive. But as he turned toward the door he winked at Emma, conspiratorially, taking in her flustered breathing, her disheveled hair, with a glance that practically shouted, *You hot little minx, I'll have you begging for more . . .*

Then he drew Kitty after him, paused with her just outside

for one more kiss, and whispered something in her ear. Kitty glanced quickly back at Emma, then up at him again, eyes wide and lips parted with shock.

'Just so you know,' Emma heard him murmur. Turning away, he strode off down the long wing of 'star' dressing rooms, confident and graceful as a blooded racehorse.

'*Honestly!*' Kitty came back into the dressing room, picked up her burgundy cloche hat – which had fallen from her hair in all the excitement. 'That *man.*' She shook out dark, thick curls that fell to her shoulders. In a year when most stylish women bobbed and Marcelled their locks, Kitty – in keeping with her penchant for vamp roles – wore hers in a tumbled mane, or loosely gathered into a chignon, a style which didn't keep her from periodically urging Emma to get her own long, light-brown tresses cut.

Then she paused, seeing Emma sink down into the chair and turn her face aside, still shaking with anger and embarrassment and chagrin. She reached her in two steps, clasped her hands. 'Darling! You don't think *I* think you asked for that, do you? Whatever Seth said.'

'Is that what he told you?' Emma's back straightened, shame flashing into rage.

'Of *course* he did. What a liar that man is . . . But my *God*, he can go all night! And thighs like a Greek god!'

Emma suppressed the urge to inquire how many Greek gods had displayed their thighs to her friend (*Dozens, I expect*).

'I'm so sorry, I should have warned you.' Kitty squatted quickly and caressed first Chang Ming, then Black Jasmine, her eyes still raised worriedly to Emma's face.

'And to think I was blushing all night over Harry kissing me.' Emma sat back a little, collecting herself. *When you waken*, the philosopher emperor Marcus Aurelius had advised, *say to yourself: the people I will meet today will be meddling, ungrateful, arrogant, dishonest, jealous and surly . . . Go to the baths, and you're going to get splashed*, that wise ruler had warned. *Live in Hollywood, and you're probably going to get kissed . . .*

She wanted to write to His Imperial Highness and ask him how *he'd* like it . . .

Movement under the divan caught her eye, as Buttercreme peeked forth, to make sure the coast was clear. 'And some guard dog *you* are,' Emma added, which made Kitty laugh, hesitantly.

'And my mother warned me,' Emma added with a sigh, feeling the first rush of her rage subside. 'Or she would have, if she'd known I'd end up here in Hollywood. And all my aunts *did* warn me, constantly, about men . . . including your brother, I might add . . .'

'Dearest, I'm so sorry.' Kitty rose and put her arms around Emma's shoulders. 'And I can't even promise to tell him never to do that again, because he'll only think I'm jealous . . . I have a good mind to wait until quarter after one to go over to his room, and make him late getting to the set. Madge will kill him.' She named the director of *The Thornless Rose*. 'She can't stand it when someone holds up the shooting . . .'

And, reading Emma's expression when she looked quickly aside, added, 'He really is very good in—'

Emma sighed. His Imperial Highness was right, of course. Why expect Kitty not to be Kitty, or Seth Ramsay to be other than he obviously was? 'Do you want to freshen up?' she asked, rising and going to the hot plate where the kettle of water was now gently steaming.

'Oh, darling, *absolutely*!' Kitty shed last night's garnet silk like a dropped hankie and settled at the makeup table, opening a jar of cold cream though it was clear she'd made herself up before leaving 'Mickey's'. 'I feel *utterly* contaminated . . .'

You aren't the only one. Emma produced the perfumed Spanish soap from the luggage that she brought to the studio five days out of six (or seven, if shooting was behind schedule), a loofah, three sponges, and a thermos of coffee. While Kitty removed her makeup and retreated behind a screen to wash – the studio provided towels, thank Heavens! – Emma set out a third thermos of orange juice, a glass, a paper pail of egg fu yung (which had resided in the kitchen ice-box since Monday night), and Kitty's cigarettes and astrology magazine ('Your Stars and Your Man!')

'Mr Zapolya asked to see you when he telephoned this morning,' she said over her shoulder. 'Before eight, he said,

if that would be possible. But if not, it was desperately important that it be this morning.' She hesitated, remembering the
note in the man's voice. 'He sounded frightened.'

'If I was married to Marina Carver I'd be frightened too.'
Kitty put her tousled head around the side of the screen. 'When
she was married to Marsh Sloane she tried to stab him with
a bread knife because he was sleeping with . . .'

'He said it wasn't . . . wasn't what he called a "Hollywood
intrigue". It was important, he said. Something on which lives
might depend.'

'I like that! As if getting on the good side of Frank or
Adolf Zukor or Mr DeMille isn't important!' She disappeared
behind the screen again, like a half-grown bunny into a hedge.
'And the way Marina gets when she's high, you bet lives
might depend on it!' She popped her head out again. 'But
why would he call *me*?'

Emma shook her head. Kitty ducked back behind the screen,
and more light splashing ensued. 'Hand me my coffee, would
you, darling?'

'I wondered that, too.' Emma brought the cup into the
little sanctuary; Kitty was already in chemise and step-ins,
putting on her stockings. The little still-life of basin and
ewer, soap and sponges, brought back again to Emma the
recollection of her Aunt Phyllis's indignation at the news
that Uncle Ulysses had had a shower-bath installed – in a
separate room, of course – in his villa in Redding. *In this
household we take our baths before the fire in our rooms,
like Christians!*

That had been back when the family still had maids.

Back before Uncle Ulysses had been machine-gunned by
the Turks before he'd even reached the beach at Gallipoli.

And Aunt Phyllis had died of the influenza the same week
as Emma's parents.

'I really should have Pearl come over from Makeup and do
my nails.' Kitty stepped from behind the screen, all of five
feet tall, a rather delicate pocket-Venus in her slip and stockings, gathering the sable riot of her curls into a loose knot as
she returned to the makeup table. 'Jungle Passion is just a
little too red for the dress you brought. But I suppose Seth

. . . Oh, I know!' she cried, almost bouncing in her chair. 'Let's go over to Enterprise and see what Ernst wants that's so important, and leave Seth just sitting! He's so sure I'll come over wagging my tail he'll wait for me until the very *last* minute, and be late getting on to the set . . . and it'll serve him right if Madge *does* kill him,' she added, and gently smoothed almond face powder on to her cheeks. 'And besides – could you hand me the perfume, dearest? The Mitsouko, darling, not Trésor du Jasmine – I think Frank may have told Willers' – Willers was Frank Pugh's personal secretary – 'to keep an eye on Seth . . . the man's a poisonous spy!'

Delicately, she added the tiniest rumor of Persian Rose to her cheekbones. 'I think the only reason he isn't selling information to the gossip columns is because he thinks film magazines are sinful. Anyway, I want to see what Ernst thinks is so desperate and important!'

'It must be kept a secret, he said.' Emma brought her a cup of coffee, which Kitty proceeded to doctor from the bottle of bootleg brandy she kept in the makeup table drawer. 'He literally begged me—'

'Oh, good!' Kitty examined her face in the mirror, then cold-creamed the whole foundation off and began again. 'Palmyra Moonrise – that's the woman who writes for *Today's Astrology* – said that I would hold the key to a deep secret, that would open many doors. Or was that Madame Jalil in *The Mystic Almanac*?' Delicately, she applied first shadow, then eye pencil, then dark, sticky mascaro, between sips of brandied coffee and bites of egg fu yung.

'Oh, no, Madame Jalil wrote that Leos today would cross the path of secret love . . .'

Emma reflected, when at last she followed her beautiful sister-in-law out to the Packard again amid a fluffy whirlwind of Mitsouko and Pekinese, that *secret* was the last word she'd use to describe Hollywood *amours*.

Then she slipped the diamond bracelet into her handbag. *Well, maybe not the* last *word* . . .

THREE

'Well, nertz.' Kitty set the brake on the Packard, slithered nimbly from beneath the steering wheel and hopped to the ground. 'His car's not here.'

The guard at the gate of Enterprise Studios – a few miles to the east and north of Foremost, near the hills of the area generally known as Edendale – had warned them, 'Mr Zapolya's probably out at the *Crowned Heart* set by this time, Miss de la Rose.'

'If he has a secretary –' Emma gathered up leashes and Pekineses – 'she'll know.'

'According to Peggy –' Peggy Donovan (star of *Wednesday's Bride* and *Enough for Everybody*) was one of Kitty's closest friends – 'Lou Jesperson is so cheap there's only one secretary for all the directors on the lot, and how the poor woman manages that—'

She ducked aside as a company of American soldiers ambled by.

Extras, Emma realized in the next second, even as her heart leaped hard into her throat. *They're extras, that's all.*

The dull-green uniforms, the flat soup-plate helmets – even the rifles on their shoulders – were only costumes. Costumes for a play, like something in a children's game.

She made herself breathe steadily again as she let the Pekes jump down from the rear seat. Like the gorgeously-gowned ladies in evening dress emerging from a long, ugly building on the other side of the crowded studio 'street,' their thick yellow makeup glaring in the bright forenoon light.

Jim had worn that uniform. Jim had marched away.

Jim who had died in Belleau Wood, riddled with machine-gun bullets.

She closed her eyes.

Jim . . .

'I'll bet he *is* out on the set . . .' Kitty tripped up the steps of the bungalow as the soldiers moved on down the street, the men joking and trading cigarettes.

Doesn't she see *it?*

Emma picked up Buttercreme and Black Jasmine and followed her. *Jim was her* brother.

The two young women nearly collided in the doorway with the tall, square-shouldered man who flung the door open from within and strode out, shouting, 'Of course it can be done!'

He caught himself with a jerk on the door-frame. 'Kitty!'

The deep voice, the Mitteleuropa accent, were unmistakable. 'Ernst!'

He seized Kitty's arms, almost yanked her into the bungalow. Two other men, who had been in the act of following him out, sprang back out of his way.

Following them in, Emma had an impression of file cabinets, a battle-scarred desk and a handsome forty-ish woman in muted beige tweeds sitting behind it. A Kodak camera and half a dozen small tin cannisters of film balanced on top of a stack of correspondence files on a cluttered table; a yard-long tin megaphone and a bundle of green, red and blue flags stood in a corner. (To signal extras in a crowd scene, Emma knew: battle, riot, panic flight from dangers established in a previous shot, filmed days or perhaps weeks earlier . . .).

Framed photographs of several women – Emma recognized Mae Murray and Kitty's friend Blanche Sweet among them – graced one wall. Other than that, the room was nearly identical to the outer offices of the Foremost directors she'd been in during her seven months as Kitty's companion, secretary and dog brusher – only tidier.

'Go!' Ernst Zapolya waved to the two men and the secretary, as if sweeping them from the office like dust. 'Out. I follow in two minutes,' he added, to the men – dressed, like himself, in semi-military khaki trousers, shirts, and boots, the most comfortable gear for tramping around the back lot on a May forenoon that already promised to be hot. 'This I promise,' he added, when the older of the men paused in the act of scooping up the flags and looked as if he would have protested. 'Two little minutes. Go on ahead.'

The secretary – clearly used to her boss's commands – caught the men by the elbows and thrust them firmly before her out the door.

'Thank God you came.' Zapolya swept Kitty into his arms and kissed her as if Emma was invisible (*and as if this were his and Kitty's wedding night*, reflected Emma. *Or Reel 7 of* Hot Potato). 'My Kitty, I need your help.'

All the breeziness he'd shown moments before dropped from him like a discarded costume. The man radiated the proud strength of a lion, but in his face now Emma saw the shadow of desperation she'd heard that morning on the telephone. Lines of strain ground across those broad, Magyar cheekbones, the wide, sensual lips beneath the mustache were pinched tight. A handsome man, she acknowledged. But then, Kitty didn't sleep with any other kind.

No prodigious-nosed plutocrats for her . . .

'Swear to me – and you as well, madame.' He released one hand from Kitty's shoulder and gave Emma a formal Old World bow. But his dark eyes, looking into hers, were as intimate as a kiss. 'I beg of you, ladies, swear that none of this will go further. That you will come up with some . . . oh, some perfectly innocent reason for being here! Please.'

His gaze went from Emma back down to Kitty – he was six feet tall to her barely-five-feet – and then to Emma again. 'I give you my word, it is nothing dishonorable; nothing that will bring harm to anyone. But it is vital—'

The secretary's voice rose in protest outside the outer door. 'Mr Jesperson—!'

A fist hammered the panels.

'Ernst!' grated a man's voice. Not a shout, but flat as the crack of a leather belt on bare flesh.

'In one minute, Mr Jesperson!'

In her months in Hollywood, Emma had heard – mostly from Peggy Donovan – a hundred stories about Lou Jesperson's methods of keeping his employees in line.

The hard voice did not rise in volume. 'In one minute you're gonna be on the fucken sidewalk if you don't get your ass out to that fucken castle—'

Zapolya shoved Kitty and Emma (and the Pekes) into his

own inner office, closed the door on them – silently. Emma heard his boots creak on the cheap uncarpeted pine of the bungalow's floor, and then the opening of the outer door.

'It's ten twenty.' By the sound of it, Lou Jesperson started speaking as he stepped across the threshold. 'I got six hundred and fifty extras sittin' on their cans out on the lot, two hundred horses eatin' their heads off, another two hundred extras playin' pinochle on the other side of that goddam wall, six machine-gunners an' twenty sharp-shooters at seven-fifty a day, plus that mad-bomber Englishman, four cameramen, and Desiree Darrow in her underpants, and it's gonna take you how long to set up the shot?'

A squat, sand-colored man – Emma had seen him on the Foremost lot – and by the smell of it he was as usual smoking a cigar. The man stank of stale tobacco at thirty feet and through the office door.

'Your one minute is gonna cost me four thousand bucks, and believe me, there are guys all over town who can bring that shot in for less.'

She had seen Zapolya's pride – not to speak of what Peggy Donovan and Kitty had said of him. A man of arrogance, passion, and ferocity, both actresses had sighed on various occasions (and evidently copious libido as well). But Lou Jesperson was a man who had power, a man who understood to the core of his marrowless bones how to make other people sorry they'd offended him.

With the humble sincerity of a Barrymore vowing his loyalty to Prince Hal, Zapolya murmured, 'Of course, Mr Jesperson.'

Emma heard the slight scrape as he picked up the mega-phone, then the creak of his boots as he followed Jesperson out the door.

'Well, I like *that*!' Kitty straightened up from – Emma saw with exasperation but no real surprise – searching Mr Zapolya's desk drawer. 'First it's "thank God" and "this is too-too-earth-shatteringly-vital" and the next minute it's "anything you say, Mr Jesperson" and off he goes without even offering us a drink!'

She opened another drawer, pawed a little at its contents. 'I wonder what's got him so hot under the collar? It couldn't be . . . Oh,' she added, and bent again to retrieve something under the desk. 'Oh, *this* is where I dropped them!' She held up a strand of pearls, each pearl separated from the next by a tiny diamond. 'I couldn't think where . . . I've been looking for them for just *ages* . . .'

Hopefully, Emma reflected, since before Mr Zapolya's marriage, though one could never be sure.

'I wonder if that was what he wanted?'

'I don't see how it could have been,' pointed out Emma. 'He obviously didn't know they were still in his office. And why would it have to be today and not tomorrow? Why swear us to secrecy?'

'Probably so his wife's lawyer couldn't get the goods on him for the divorce settlement.' Kitty blew the dust off the necklace, and dropped it into her handbag.

'I thought he just married her—'

'He did.' Kitty checked another drawer, took out a bottle of bourbon and a glass. 'In February.' She held the glass up to the light of the window, then returned it to the drawer and took out another. This one was evidently cleaner.

'You want some of this, honey?'

Emma glanced at the clock above the file cabinet. Like Frank Pugh at Foremost, Lou Jesperson was evidently willing to lay out any amount of money to make sure that there was a large clock in every office and dressing room on the lot.

It was almost ten thirty. 'No, thank you.'

Kitty knocked back a generous slug, then replaced bottle and glass where she'd found them. 'Well,' she said, 'I'm not leaving 'til I know what this is all about.' She stepped away from the desk, sat lightly down on her heels, and caressed Chang Ming's golden head. 'How would my celestial creamcakes like a little walk?'

Like Foremost Productions, Enterprise had about ten acres of 'back lot' that stretched beyond the barracks-like ranks of costume shop, makeup, carpentry, nursery, film stores, editing rooms and prop warehouses. About half of this was 'standing sets' – New York streets, European streets that could be transformed into Paris or London when backed by appropriate matte paintings of the Eiffel Tower or Big Ben, medieval villages, part of a castle. The rest, in the case of Enterprise, consisted of bare scrubland and the foot slopes of the Hollywood Hills, where purpose-built sets could be erected for larger projects. For years, Zal had told her, the decaying walls of Babylon had loomed above Sunset Boulevard – a jaw-dropping construction of bronze gates, plaster elephants, monumental stairways, fading plaster, and peeling paint.

'That should be it.' Kitty pointed toward a line of Baroque domes and turrets, visible above the skeletal wooden framing that backed neat, brick, New York-style brownstone fronts. As they came closer, following a dusty track past shabby wooden building-fronts of the sort seen in cowboy films, Emma made out a more picturesque roofline of elaborately half-timbered gables and a few stair-step brick facades reminiscent of the older portions of Brussels. Twin gothic cathedral towers dominated the lesser buildings. The smell of dust drifted in the air, and the far-off hum of voices.

'There's the commissary tent,' Kitty added. 'So we can at least get coffee.'

A line of tents – vaguely reminiscent of a down-at-heels provincial circus – defined the rear edge of the medieval village set, with thirty or forty feet of clear ground before the palace square of Ravenstark, due to be liberated that morning by the American Expeditionary Force. 'Extra' players filled the enclosed space, gazing up at the balcony where Ernst Zapolya stood like a king, booted feet planted wide, head thrown back, megaphone in hand. Two camera cranes loomed like siege engines at the edge of the square; men in work clothes moved back and forth across the cobblestone pavement behind the crowd, planting nearly invisible markers here and there, presumably to guide the extras when it came time for their panic flight.

A line of saddled horses stood back from the set, and Emma shivered as she saw over a dozen of them equipped with lines and ankle rings of what was called a 'running-W'. She'd heard some stunt men swear that properly trained horses weren't hurt by being tripped at a gallop with the barbaric device, and had even seen many get up from the ensuing falls unhurt. But she knew that many didn't.

'You weren't expecting any of this,' she heard Mr Zapolya boom through his megaphone at the populace below in the square. 'Your government told you Americans were far off, Americans had been defeated by forces of your invincible army! And you believed them.'

He gestured, like Mussolini exhorting his followers to action. The extras, in vaguely Slavic folkloric attire, kept glancing around them, their attention torn between their director's instructions and the movements of the workmen behind them marking the pavement.

'This I want to see,' Zapolya continued. 'This panic, this disbelief. You have been betrayed! You flee for your very lives! And you are enraged, that Starkmann and the Countess von Raulen have lied to you! You clutch at your hair, you weep, you scream . . .' He pantomimed a demonstration. 'Watch for your flags and remember what group you're in.'

'Kitty, baby, what the hell you doin' here?' Peggy Donovan, red-haired, leggy and bedight in embroidered blouse and dirndl, emerged from the shadows of the commissary tent. 'Hiya, Duchess,' she added, with a grin at Emma.

'*Darling!*' Kitty turned and grasped her hands. 'If anybody asks, will you say you invited us? I need to talk to Ernst and I don't want to get him in Dutch with Marina—'

'Oh, shit, no . . .'

'Anything left to eat in there?' Kitty nodded toward the tent. Around the palace square, Emma saw the 'American Expeditionary Force' gathering, Zapolya now shouting instructions to them, where they were to come leaping through the houses. And beyond them, men were taking up their stations with machine guns and rifles – men not in uniform, but wearing the baggy trousers and cotton shirts of ordinary workmen.

'Not to speak of.' Peggy grimaced. 'Those sandwiches were day-old bread this morning, and I drained better coffee than that outta the radiator of my daddy's truck. Hey, handsome.' She knelt to ruffle Chang Ming's red-gold fur, gently scruffed

Black Jasmine and stood to caress Buttercreme, who was tucked under Emma's arm with her tongue hanging out half an inch as usual. 'You miss your Aunt Peggy, sweetpea? At least everybody's out on the set.'

She led the way into the tent. Lingering outside, Emma saw the extras shifting around beneath the now-empty balcony. Saw Zapolya emerge from the palace's gilded doors and stand for a moment, surveying the square with his megaphone in one hand and a long-staffed crimson flag under the other arm. His assistant – the young ginger-haired man who'd been in the office – dashed for one of the houses, green flag in hand. Through a window Emma briefly glimpsed the reflection of a camera's lens. Association with Zal let her pick out where the ground-level camera had to be. *Yes, in that doorway there. They'll have to shoot carefully not to get each other in frame . . .*

And it made her smile to think how much technical lore she'd picked up from Zal in seven months. Like her father's matter-of-fact skill at pointing out the differences between Etruscan and Sicilian pottery shards, or being able to distinguish at a glance a first-century inscription from a third-century one, by the shape of the letters.

And will I remember those differences in a year? Or will they fade with disuse?

A young woman emerged from the commissary tent, almost tripping over Chang Ming's leash. 'Oh, oops! I'm so sorry!' Her black-gloved hands were shaking with nervousness.

'My fault,' returned Emma contritely. 'I shouldn't be standing here daydreaming.'

'I hate this.' The woman – *girl*, thought Emma, she couldn't have been more than eighteen – took a deep breath, as if to steady herself. 'Shots like this . . .' She was costumed in what looked like a maidservant's uniform from ten years ago, the black, plain, old-fashioned sleeves and high-buttoned shoes made a startling foil for the fluffy halo of blonde curls, the immense, half-terrified brown eyes. The heavy camera makeup made her look even paler in the noon glare.

'You've missed most of his instructions.'

'Oh, that's all right.' The girl tucked a wisp of hair back

under her cap. 'All he needs me for is to be in the front row where the camera can pick me up when the shooting starts. I did all my close-up shots and got killed yesterday, except I really didn't get killed.'

Emma opened her mouth to make the obvious observation, but the girl went on breathlessly, 'But Paul thinks I did – Prince Stephan's friend, Ronnie Starr – and vows revenge . . . And I do get killed in the end.' She took another deep breath, and flexed her gloved hands, like a swimmer poised on the edge of the English Channel on a cold, rough day. 'Wish me luck . . .'

'Good luck.' And before Emma even had time to lift a hand in salute, the girl dashed off towards (presumably) her destiny in the square.

FOUR

*F*aithful Companion, guessed Emma, *to the Obligatory Plucky Damsel*. A role that went back to Celia in *As You Like It* – and in fact to Ismene in the *Oresteia*.

And like Ismene, she reflected with a sigh, *it sounds like she's going to get killed in the end, simply for effect*.

Across the heads of the crowd of extras, she saw Zapolya raise his hand and wave at that slim little black figure. The crowd parted briefly, swallowed her up.

A dark-haired villainess in a gorgeous evening gown came out on the balcony, followed by a tall man in formal dress with the blue ribbon of an order across his breast. Leo Craig, Emma recognized him from the Foremost Productions Christmas Party. The woman was Anita Tempest, undoubtedly plotting to take over the throne of Montebianco . . .

The ginger-haired assistant director gave instructions to one of the machine gunners, pointing.

'Oh, bring my little creamcakes inside, would you, sweetheart?' called out Kitty's voice from within. 'It's going to get really noisy out there.'

There were only a few people in the tall shadows of the commissary tent: mostly women and men from makeup, a handful of prop handlers and a stout gentleman checking over piles of embroidered blouses and dirndls and making notes on a clipboard. The garments were liberally splattered with stage blood. A bottle of the stuff, rather like ketchup in a cheap diner, stood at the stout man's dimpled brown elbow, along with a box of dirt.

Crumby cardboard boxes littered the other trestle tables, some still containing orange or banana peels, or bitten fragments of unappetizing liverwurst sandwiches. A few unopened boxes stacked one end of a longer table, beside a half-dozen paper cups. More crumbs marked the plate where the donuts had lain.

The last three of these confections rested on a paper napkin in front of Kitty at one end of the table nearest the wardrobe station. 'Was that Nomie Carlyle?' she asked.

'Ernst's been trying to convince Mr Jesperson she can act.' Peggy set three cups of coffee on the table, and made a face. 'He promised her he'll get a feature written for her.' Her opinion of the girl's talents – and of the source of Ernst Zapolya's belief in them – sounded clear in her voice.

'You should have seen the little bimbo yesterday trying to convince Desiree not to try to rescue Prince Stephan. Thirty takes! Desiree was ready to kill her. And Ernst was all . . .' She made her mouth hard at the corners, and cooed in an exaggeration of the director's Slavic basso, '"Now weep just a little, my dear – one brave little tear . . . Look up in hope, as if you see the little bird that you thought was dead begin to stir in warming sunlight . . ." Like she wouldn't pluck a little bird she thought dead for its feathers, if she thought she could sell 'em for a hat.'

She sipped her coffee, and pulled another face. 'And watching her make cootchy-coo at Ernst . . .!' Her exaggerated shudder flapped her entire body. 'If you need to talk to Ernst, you better be ready to catch him as soon as the shot wraps. Ever since he "discovered" Nomie, Marina's been showing up wherever he's filming – you know she threatened to shoot Desiree, when she caught them smooching in the summerhouse in their garden? Like Ernst hasn't made a pass at just about every— Oh!' she added, waving. 'There's Desiree!'

A dark-green kimono billowing elegantly over an extremely abbreviated satin brassiere and step-ins – these garments artistically torn about their hems and sides – Desiree Darrow made her entrance into the tent. A few dabs of stage blood and a great deal of dirt augmented her makeup; her dark golden hair had been carefully disarrayed (and embellished with several false switches, presumably because the attack on the palace was taking place sometime during the war and before the popularity of short haircuts); and her lipstick looked awfully fresh for a woman who was struggling in advanced deshabille through the front lines to come to the aid of the man she loved.

'You ready?' Peggy held out a cup of coffee to the star as she crossed to their table.

Both she and Kitty produced flasks – Miss Darrow poured dollops from both into the brew, and slugged the whole cocktail down as if it were medicine, which, Emma supposed, it was. 'Ernst goddam better get this in one take.' She twisted her body, like a runner warming up.

'Oh, he has to,' agreed Kitty. 'It'll take a week to re-build the set . . .'

'And that sharpshooter better be sober.'

'It's Smitty,' Kitty reassured her. 'You don't need to worry about him.'

A very youthful assistant in plus fours and a plaid shirt appeared in the tent entrance. 'Miss Darrow?'

'Everything set up?'

The young man nodded. 'Follow the red marks on the pavement. They're kind of hard to see. Stay clear of the cart, that house with the turret, the area in front of the palace steps, and the fountain. There's charges buried in front of the fountain, and about ten feet to the right as you're crossing the square.'

'Thanks, Tommy.' She flexed her feet in their alligator-skin pumps. 'And I bet Little Miss Nomie gets to run under cover in the first ten seconds, doesn't she?'

'That's why you're the star, honey,' Peggy soothed.

Desiree made a vulgar gesture at her, and followed the obliging Tommy from the tent.

Emma turned inquiringly to Kitty. 'Sharpshooter?'

'Well, yeah.' Kitty sipped what was left of her coffee, and looked around for the sugar. 'I'm glad they got Smitty. He's really good. I don't think he's ever even hit one of the horses. I'm a little surprised Jesperson put up the money to get him, because he isn't . . .'

'Wait a minute,' said Emma. 'You mean they're firing real bullets?'

'They pretty much have to.' Peggy looked surprised at the question. 'Blanks just don't look the same on film. And everybody would look pretty silly running around screaming, if you didn't see bullets hitting the walls. But they really are pretty good about aiming between the groups of extras, or over their heads. And the extras are used to it.'

She grimaced again, and shoved the tin cup away from her.

'They scare the hell out of me.' Rising, Kitty brushed the dust off her skirt. 'Back when I was an extra, everybody knew which directors you had to watch out for, and Ernst was one of the worst. You want to go watch? Teddy . . .?' She turned to the stout wardrobe man, still counting over costumes and now and then adding dabs of blood and dirt, finicky as a laundress in reverse. 'Will you keep an eye on my little sweetnesses?' She collected the leashes from Emma. 'Poor darlings, the noise will scare them outside.'

Emma reflected in dismay, *The noise will scare* me . . .

No wonder that poor little actress had been terrified.

'And if Marina Carver's going to show up and jump on him,' added Kitty, herding Emma towards the entrance, 'we'd better be ready to get to him before she does.'

'Nothing to worry about.' Peggy hitched up her dirndl to adjust a garter. 'She's over on Stage Two shooting *Broadway Bluebird.*'

'Well, if she does turn up,' said Kitty, 'would you be an angel and head her off? Ernst said it was important and I'm *hours* late . . .'

From the commissary tent Emma watched Zapolya's tall form spring lightly down the palace steps, cross to the deep, gothic portico of the cathedral's facade, megaphone and flag still in hand. The extras stirred – *And well they might*! thought Emma, appalled – then closed ranks, and Emma had a brief glimpse of Nomie Carlyle's silver-blonde curls and sable dress. A cameraman appeared on the balcony beside the Evil Countess and her Still-More-Evil Henchman, put his eye to the viewing-lens at the back of the camera box, and the young gentleman in plus fours darted up beside him, hung over the balcony railing to hold a slate in front of the lens: scene and take numbers, Emma knew, having held a lot of slates herself in seven months. He vanished as Zapolya appeared moment-arily in the carven embrasure of the cathedral door, and slashed with the red flag.

A flicker of green from the palace doors under the balcony

– another flag – as all the extras cowered back, looking around them as if they heard the shots (which had yet to be fired), realized they had been betrayed and that the righteous vengeance of the Americans was upon them . . .

Emma saw the doors open and the girl Nomie snatch up her dark skirts and bolt for safety behind them as the gunners opened fire. Bullets tore chunks from the steps, shattered the long windows on either side of the door. Emma's heart turned to water in her breast.

She'd driven young men from the Oxford train station to Bicester Hospital during the war, young men who'd come from this. Her brother Miles, her husband Jim, both had spoken of the noise of the guns, the heartstopping din of battle. How it froze you, disoriented you, the first time you heard it, the first time you were *in* it . . .

Dear God . . .! Her mind simply stalled on the words.

It wasn't like the single shots one heard going out with the dean of New College to murder pheasants, something Emma had only done once.

It was nothing like it.

Dear God . . .!

She saw, to her horror, machine-gun bullets stitch the palace wall, over the heads of the extras but not all that far over their heads. Another line of shots slashed across the cobblestones, almost at their feet ('that sharpshooter better be sober,' Miss Darrow had said), and at the same moment, explosions shattered a corner of the palace steps, and a nearby house-front, filling the air with smoke and dust. The extras fled, screaming, (*'This panic, this disbelief – you flee for your very lives!'*) crowding up in a surging mass when another explosive charge went off right in their path. Some tried to break away in the direction of the camera cranes and genuine safety, but that was where the machine-gunners were posted. Others dashed for the shelter of the house facades, only to have more explosions drive them back.

A white flash in the smoke caught her eye. Desiree Darrow – through her horror Emma wondered what plot twist required the Obligatory Plucky Damsel to be thus skimpily attired – raced across a momentary gap in the chaos, rifle bullets kicking

geysers of dirt and rock-chips just behind her heels ('It's Smitty
. . . You don't need to worry about him'). An explosion only
a yard away threw her to her knees, and she scrambled to her
feet and ran in earnest as a second charge went off only a foot
from where she'd been downed.

Others weren't so lucky. Through the thickening smoke
Emma saw two extras down, who neither moved nor struggled
when others tripped over them, kicked them . . .

Dear God!

The one cameraman she could see, high on the tallest
crane, kept cranking with a light, steady movement of his
wrist. The extras milled, now genuinely confused by the
smoke and noise and shoving, losing whatever instructions
they'd been given about which way to run. Instants later the
American cavalry came leaping in over a ruined wall seconds
after its explosion and collapse, the horses seeming to spring
out of the smoke, the sabers flashing like dragon claws in
the smoldering light. The cameraman on the balcony had
vanished, camera and all, and there was no trace of either
Miss Tempest nor Mr Craig; an explosion ripped most of the
balcony from the wall, stone and bricks and beams cascading
on to a knot of terrified extras just below.

Up on their cranes – one high, one lowered almost to
ground level – the two cameramen cranked away. Desiree
Darrow had long since disappeared – *If she hasn't been shot
down by a stray bullet!* – but the chaos continued, horses
and soldiers milling among the extras now, dust and smoke
thicker and thicker . . .

When is it going to stop? They have their shot.

The air was rank with the stink of cordite, churned-up dirt
and smoke.

Dear God, somebody yell cut . . .

She wasn't sure when or how the signal was given to cut.
Maybe the gunners just ran out of ammunition. They sat back
from their weapons; men ran towards the mob, waving yellow
flags. The cavalrymen reined their horses out through the gap
where the camera cranes stood; one man ran over, gently got
a struggling horse to its feet, led it away, the trip-lines trailing.
Another horse lay motionless.

Three men who'd been standing a little distance away, near one of the other tents, now strode toward the battleground. Emma saw they were carrying satchels. Four others emerged from the smaller tent, stretchers over their shoulders. She strode after them, blazing anger and horror almost choking her. She'd known that extras were sometimes hurt in the course of crowd scenes, but had never actually seen something like this being filmed.

They knew this would happen, she thought furiously. *They knew people would be hurt. If they arranged stretchers, they knew there would be some hurt badly.*

She passed Mr Zapolya's ginger-haired assistant, in conversation at the foot of one of the cranes with Miss Darrow, who had re-acquired her kimono and was sipping from a silver flask. 'I only count four down,' she heard the assistant say cheerfully. 'Not bad, for a shot like this.' And to the cameraman climbing down from his perch, 'I hope to hell you got all that, Benson . . .'

Two men lifted a woman in a blood-stained dirndl on to a stretcher. She was twisting and crying; one of them gave her a morphia pill. Another extra – in one of the torn and blood-spattered costumes Teddy had been counting out in the commissary tent – moved up to take the hurt woman's place. The assistant yelled, 'OK, everybody down! We're gonna take some pick-up shots.'

The cameramen were already shifting their tripods, the gaffers moving reflectors.

Emma wanted to go over and strike the man.

Where she stood near the injured woman – as the two bearers lifted the stretcher and the new extra lay down ('On your back, honey . . . pull your skirt down a little . . . not too much . . . head a little to the side . . . hand over your head . . . a little higher, we gotta see the blood . . .') – Emma turned her head toward the cathedral steps, wondering how Zapolya was taking this.

Shocked at what he'd done? *Not a hope . . .*

Ernst was one of the worst, Kitty had said . . .

Like Agamemnon surveying the carnage on the plain of Troy?

Or is it just a day's work to him?

But she saw no sign of him at the top of the cathedral steps. Then something black moved within the shadows of that gothic archway. An extra taking refuge? *The man would probably have pushed her out*, reflected Emma bitterly, striding up the steps. *If he thought he could do it without being caught on camera and spoiling the shot . . .*

The cathedral had clearly been modeled on Notre Dame de Paris, with enough borrowings from Chartres and Rouen so that the plagiarism wouldn't be too obvious. The portal was straight Notre Dame, an embrasure some ten feet deep under a gradually descending sextuple archway of saints, with a twenty-foot bronze double door at the back. Only where the jarring of explosions had cracked the curved side of the embrasure on the right did the illusion break down: beyond the 'stonework' (studio plaster whose dust and fragments littered the pavement) the framing of hastily-nailed two-by-four lumber was visible, like telltale underwear beneath a torn frock, bathed in the bald light of the early-afternoon sun.

All that, Emma noticed later.

What she chiefly saw at first was Ernst Zapolya's body lying just behind the chalk mark on the floor that indicated where he'd become visible to the cameras outside – and Nomie Carlyle stretched across the threshold of the bronze doors in a dead faint.

FIVE

'We shouldn't touch anything—' Emma started to say, as the ginger-haired assistant director flipped Zapolya's body over and three of the four medics, two stretcher-bearers, two cameramen, Desiree Darrow, Kitty, two marksmen, and twenty extras crowded into the portal and clustered around the body.

'Shit,' said the assistant. 'He's been shot!'

'Well, *there's* a surprise.' Desiree helped herself to a flask from the cameraman Benson's pocket and took a drink.

'That ain't no rifle wound.' One of the marksmen – a freckled, sandy-haired bean-pole who turned out to be Smitty – unbuttoned the director's blood-soaked shirt and drew it down off his left shoulder. 'Nor no machine-gun ricochet neither.'

'He dead?' asked one of the cavalrymen.

'Oh, hell, yes,' said a medic, something Emma could have told him as well, given the corpse's staring eyes, the amount of blood in the shirt and puddled on the floor, and the fact that the unfortunate director had voided himself at death.

Kitty had already crossed to Nomie, knelt at her side. 'Nomie, honey,' she whispered, and the girl stirred, opened those childlike brown eyes – stared for a moment as if she couldn't recall where she was – then burst into hysterical sobs.

'Oh, my God,' she choked. 'Oh, my God—'

She clutched Kitty's arms, and Emma saw that her fingertips were scratched and bruised, her nails torn, as if they'd scrabbled and twisted at unyielding metal or stone. 'The woman,' she sobbed. 'It has to be her! The woman in black . . .'

'There,' Emma heard the cavalryman say in his harsh Texas twang. 'Look where the shirt's powder-burnt. Somebody got right up next to him . . .'

Everybody fanned out all over the space within the cathedral

portico, looking for the gun and obliterating any tracks there
might have been.

'The woman in black,' whimpered Nomie again, and indeed,
when Emma looked around, she saw, lying on top of the plaster
debris from the collapsed ceiling section, a pair of black gloves,
like deflated spiders.

'Get him on the stretcher,' said the medic.

'Shouldn't we leave him for the police?'

'Somebody run get Mr Jesperson . . .'

'Miss Carver on the lot?'

More extras poured into the confined space of the portal,
all of them talking at once.

'We can't just leave him layin' . . .'

'It was the Communists! I bet it was the damn Russki
Communists!'

'Get those people out of here!' yelled the medic, and the
assistant director got to his feet, snatched up the red flag that
somebody had kicked aside and waved it back and forth.

'Now, everybody get back . . .'

The cavalryman, more sensibly, picked up the megaphone,
bellowed, 'Y'all move back to the foot of the steps!' And,
when they at least hesitated in their milling, he looked
around him and yelled, 'Buck! Cartwright! Montana! Get
'em back—'

Three other cavalrymen – members, Emma guessed, of the
tight-knit community of former cowboys who'd drifted to
Hollywood with the closing of the American cattle ranges –
moved up, authoritative in their US Army uniforms. The
assistant director came to Nomie's side, knelt. 'What
happened, Miss Carlyle? What did you see?'

She sobbed, gulped, and shook her head, face still buried
in Kitty's shoulder. Kitty helpfully produced a thin silver
flask from her handbag, helped the shaken girl to drink.

'Oh, Mr Nye!' Nomie looked up, seized the assistant's hands
– which, Emma observed, were shaking almost as badly as
the girl's. 'Oh, it was . . . He told me to meet him back here,
that he had something important to tell me. I came in
around the back, through the doors.' She gestured to the huge
bronze portal (though Emma could see, close-up, that though

actually made of sheet-metal of some kind they weren't really bronze). 'As I was coming around under the scaffolding from the back of the palace I saw a woman in a black dress walking away ahead of me, coming out of the doors and going in the same direction I was, away from me. I didn't think anything of it – I thought she might have been someone from wardrobe or makeup or something . . .'

She shook her head, brushed the flaxen curls from her forehead with her bruised hand. 'But when I came in here I saw Ernst – Mr Zapolya – lying there, with blood under him. I ran up to him, and I heard the doors slam shut behind me. I saw he was dead. His eyes were open – horrible! And I-I ran back to the doors. There was shooting and explosions out in the set, I knew I couldn't get out that way, and that nobody would hear me scream. I tried to open the door, and all the time poor Mr Zapolya was lying there . . .'

She began to weep again, buried her face in her hands. 'It must have been that woman,' she sobbed. 'That woman in black . . .'

Movement caught Emma's eye. With everyone gathered, kneeling or crouching, around Miss Carlyle, Kitty had gone back to the body of her former lover, kneeling at his side.

And systematically going through his pockets.

'What the *fuck* is all this?' Lou Jesperson's voice scraped like a file on granite – not loud, but with a harshness that would cut through anything.

Young Mr Nye scrambled to his feet. 'Mr Zapolya's dead, sir—'

'I can see that, you cretin. Who shot him?'

'Point-blank range,' said Smitty. 'Small caliber – looks like a .32. Probably a Savage. Shot him up under the left shoulder blade from behind, like she was standin' next to him an' behind a little.' Pointing his finger like a child playing cops and robbers, he grabbed the nearest extra and demonstrated.

'She?' Jesperson's eyes, like bleached-tan marbles, flicked towards Nomie.

'A woman,' whimpered the girl. 'A woman in black. She

came out the doors, just as I turned the corner back at the end
of the set.'

A lumpy-faced little man in an execrable tweed suit –
by the briefcase under his arm Emma guessed him to be either
the studio's lawyer or publicity chief – strode to the bronze
doors, shoved them – then shoved them again harder. 'Shit,'
he said, and rammed the portal with his shoulder. Had he been
Tarzan of the Apes the gateway would probably have given
way. As it was, the lawyer (or publicity chief) bounced off it
like a tennis ball and backed up, holding his shoulder. 'Shit,'
he said again, and glanced up at the gaping holes in the
archway above. 'Probably jammed when the charge went off
at the corner of this wall.'

'It was horrible . . .' Nomie covered her face.

Jesperson, standing above Zapolya's body, cursed again,
and glanced over at young Mr Nye. 'You get scene 704 shot,
Mike?'

The assistant stammered, 'We – that is, we found his body
right after we wrapped 703—'

'Then get the hell on with it! What the fuck are you waiting
for? We got the square full of ruins an' smoke, we're not
gonna set it all up again tomorrow.' He jabbed at Nye with
his cigar. 'Tell Teddy to get them extras down here an' laid
out . . . Scorp,' he snapped, waving to a tall man in the forefront of the line of extras, resplendent in a much-soiled and
bloodied American officer's uniform. 'You get on your horse
and do your ride through the square.'

'With him layin' there?' demanded Scorp, shocked and
deeply offended.

'He'd be the first man to tell you to finish the shot while
we got the scene set up,' retorted Jesperson. 'Somebody tell
Benson and McIntyre to get back to their cameras . . . Vachek,
you get those doors open and take him out that way. Sellers, you
search his office – but first you round up every goddam one
of those extras and tell 'em if one word of this gets out
before six o'clock tonight, not one of 'em is going to get
called from this studio again, or any other studio in town if
I have anythin' to say about it. And that goes for you, too,

Dee.' He glared at Miss Darrow. 'And you, Nomie. *Then* you search his office,' he continued, to Mr Sellers, who was still rubbing his shoulder.

'And don't you call the cops 'til I phone you. I'm goin' over to his place. He still live on Vermont, Mike?'

'I'll close down the switchboard,' promised Mr Sellers.

'Good. Anybody know . . .?'

'Oh, God!' screamed a woman from the sunlit arch of the cathedral portico. The extras parted before her out of sheer instinct, as the woman clasped her hands to the base of her throat as if unable to breathe: medium height, she looked smaller, almost childlike, masses of light-brown ringlets framing a perfect oval face that was exquisite despite the garish camera makeup. 'Ernst . . .' she whispered, staring at the body stretched on the artificial flagstones. 'Oh, *Ernst* . . .!'

Emma recognized her at once. The Angel Next Door, the fan magazines had named her, after the 1920 film of the same name in which she had starred.

Marina Carver. Ernst Zapolya's most recent wife.

Casting up her eyes to heaven – with one quick glance to make sure that a riding extra was close enough to catch her – the Angel Next Door crumpled into a photogenic faint.

Jesperson said, 'Shit,' as the cowboy knelt to lay the swooning girl on the ground.

Not a girl, really, thought Emma, hurrying toward them. Closer up, and in the soft shadow of the set, Emma guessed her age at thirty or more. Nonetheless she was costumed as a Victorian schoolgirl: a sailor dress with a calf-length skirt, wide collar, hip-sash, a ribbon with a huge bow in her hair.

A Victorian schoolgirl in mourning. Dress, ribbon, cotton stockings and bow – even the trim on the collar – were black.

The studio chief snapped at Mr Nye, 'You waitin' for an engraved invitation or somethin'?' and strode to the un-conscious woman's side, putting himself firmly in front of Emma – almost shoving her aside – to do it. Over his shoulder he yelled, 'Get goin'! An' get Panky to pump in some more smoke . . .'

People crowded in between them, forcing Emma back. She

retreated to the bronze doors where Kitty was still holding Nomie in the circle of one arm – she met Emma's glance, and rolled her eyes.

'We better scram before he decides he needs to lock us up. He's right about scene 704, though. It'll take two days to repair and re-dress the set, if they don't use it now.' She looked anxiously at Nomie. 'He didn't say what he wanted to see you about, Nomie, did he?'

The girl shook her head, tear-filled dark eyes wide.

'Were you screwing him?' Kitty's voice was gentle as she eschewed euphemism; Nomie shuddered, clasped her scraped fingers tight on Kitty's shoulder, and began to weep again.

'Come on,' said Emma gently. 'Let's get you out of this . . .'

Kitty produced her flask again, pressed it into the younger girl's hands. 'You have a dressing room here, honey? Or someplace where you can lie down?'

She and Emma helped Nomie to her feet. Nomie turned her head, to where only Zapolya's booted feet stuck out from among the crowd of extras and medics still kneeling around him. Trembling, she whispered, 'Ernst . . .'

'She did it!' Marina Carver sat up in Lou Jesperson's arms, her face twisted now with desperation and grief. She jabbed a trembling finger at Nomie. 'She did it, the jealous little whore—'

'Marina!' The sharpshooter Smitty, among those kneeling at her side, spoke pleadingly. 'You can't go sayin'—'

'That white-haired bitch shot my husband because he wouldn't love her!' Marina Carver declaimed. 'He loved me! Only me!' Her flailing hands slapped at her chest, then flung out wide. 'He spurned her—'

She lurched to her feet, her countenance like Medea's in the girlish tousle of her curls. Hands outstretched, she stumbled towards Nomie as if she would have strangled the girl – though noticeably not so quickly as to make it difficult for Smitty and Benson the cameraman to catch her arms. With a scream of despair that seemed to rip the soul from her body she flung her arms heavenward, and collapsed again, this time gauging her fall so that she landed on her knees at Ernst Zapolya's side.

Hurling herself across his corpse, she clutched him to her, and fainted again.

'Nomie . . .' Mr Nye scurried to catch them as Emma would have led the silent young actress away. 'You can't go yet, baby, we need you in this scene.'

'Surely you can't—' began Emma indignantly.

The young man faced her, and in his eyes she saw his own struggle to keep going. *Please don't make this harder for me, lady.* 'We got to, ma'am.' And to Nomie: 'This is your big scene, baby. And Ronnie's big scene. We got to do it while the ruins are still smokin'.'

Nomie straightened her shoulders, stepped away from Emma, and nodded, a tiny gesture. Now, at least, she looked as if she had come through the carnage and ruin of the square outside. At the back of the set, someone had managed to pry open the cathedral doors, revealing a backstage maze of 'balloon framing': ramshackle ladders, dangling ropes, a cluster of reflectors, a light-tree, and the back of another set nearby, all strewed with rocks, dirt, debris, and broken pieces of plaster and two-by-four shattered loose when a too-close explosive charge had rocked the set and jammed the door.

'You!' Jesperson strode over to Nomie, resembling nothing so much as an animate barrel of nails. 'When you're done this scene I want you.' He rounded on Kitty and Emma, jabbed at them with his cigar between his fingers. 'And you girls, I'm gonna wanna talk to you . . . Nomie, I don't want to hear one single word about you.'

Kitty took Emma's hand and drew her, without appearance of hurry, past the line of plaster saints towards the smoke-fouled daylight of the ruined palace square. The air burned with cordite. Panky – presumably the properties manager – had not only kindled discreetly-hidden smudges to wreathe the ruins with further smoke, but had lit a dozen concealed fire-pots as well. Small blazes flickered behind the palace windows and amid the broken walls, like the outliers of hell.

At the edge of the square Emma saw two extras lying on blankets, groaning softly and moving a little with pain. An open truck, of the sort usually used to transport props, trundled the few hundred feet back towards the main studio buildings, already loaded with the injured. Other extras, in the exaggeratedly torn and bloodied garments that Teddy had been counting out earlier, were taking up poses of artistic mortality amid the devastation. Two or three horses lay in the palace square, very still. A prop man was just pulling the straps of the running-W off one of them. Where a wall had been blown up near the palace, a little group of cavalry waited, the man Scorp at the forefront, an officer's peaked cap on his head and his face like stone. Mr Nye, who had hurried out before them, was saying, 'I want you to ride slowly around that side of the fountain, just looking down at the dead. Nomie's going to be lying by the ruins of that house there. You stop beside her . . .'

From behind them by the cathedral doors, the sweet voice of Marina Carver shrilled, 'Ernst! Oh, God, Ernst! She killed him! I know she did! She was jealous of our love . . .'

Emma stopped, turned to go back, and Kitty's grip tightened on her wrist. 'We need to get out of here *now*.'

Emma moved to twist free, seeing everyone preoccupied with Marina Carver, and the body, and Jesperson snapping orders . . . It would be an easy matter to cross behind them and pick up the gloves she'd seen, lying on top of the debris next to the set's rear wall. Nomie's, she assumed – at least she'd been wearing gloves when she'd spoken to her – had it only been two hours ago? – outside the commissary tent.

Black kid gloves with a thin line of lace at the cuff.

But she saw that they were gone.

They stopped at the commissary tent long enough to collect the dogs. 'Is it true the Communists shot him?' asked Teddy from Wardrobe – the whole table before him was now heaped with dust-caked, dirtied sarafans, trousers, embroidered shirts and boots, many of them spotted and streaked with genuine blood. He'd pushed up his sleeves over plump arms, and a small pan of soapy water and a pile of rags lay at his elbow. A dozen extras clustered at the trestle tables around the tent, swilling coffee or Coca-Cola and talking eagerly, emphatically, hands swooping. Emma counted a dozen flasks on the table among them. Others were slumped like people who really had survived battle. Others, Emma judged from the table before Teddy, had simply changed their clothes and gone.

'Myself,' Teddy added, in plummy Oxford accents, 'I'd put my money on Miss Carver. She's threatened to, more than once, you know – drunk, of course, and couldn't hit the side of a barn . . .'

'Communists?' Emma tucked Buttercreme under her arm, followed Kitty down the track that led back through the streets of New York, Paris, *Praecipua-Via Oppidulum* and across a rather scruffy Middle Eastern marketplace, toward the main buildings of the studio.

'Darling, ever since the Bolsheviks took over Russia, the Bureau of Investigation has been looking for Communists under peoples' beds. A few years ago they arrested just *hundreds* of people and deported them, and raided the offices of anybody they even *thought* looked a little bit pink. And I'm sure Mr Jesperson's going to like that explanation a whole lot better than that Ernst was shot by one of his girlfriends. The Hays Office is still twitchy over whoever it was who plugged poor Bill Taylor . . .'

She held up a cautionary finger, as they approached the cramped bungalows under the shadows of the stages. The door to Zapolya's was open, and Kitty's car stood in full view of it. A studio guard smoked at the bottom of the steps, looking up through the door with great interest at whatever was going on inside.

Emma whispered, 'Wait here,' and Kitty obediently stepped between two of the close-set little cottages, setting Black Jasmine down and taking the disapproving Buttercreme in her arms in his place. In her plain, slightly old-fashioned tweed skirt, cotton shirtwaist, and sensible shoes, Emma looked pretty much like every clerk and seamstress on the lot, and would be, she knew, virtually invisible. It was Kitty's job – as well as her delight – to be recognized everywhere she went, ablaze in her diaphanous rose and burgundy and trailing three Pekinese in diamond collars.

Emma didn't know whether Mr Jesperson had a telephone connection from the back lot to the guard shack, nor whether he actually would tell the gate guard not to let Camille de la Rose off the Enterprise lot until he had himself returned from searching Ernst Zapolya's house and finally called the police. From everything Peggy Donovan, Kitty, Zal, and everyone else she'd talked to at Foremost had said, she wouldn't put it past him.

She backed the car along the narrow studio 'street' until she came level with Kitty, then drove, with circumspect calm, to the gates. The guard let them through without comment.

'Did Miss Carver – or Mrs Zapolya, I should call her – really attempt to shoot Miss Darrow?'

Kitty glanced up from digging through her handbag, an effort enthusiastically assisted by both Chang Ming and Black Jasmine. 'Well, fortunately for everybody at the party, by the time Marina's drunk enough to start shooting, she can't aim worth the north end of a southbound goat. She's *frantically* jealous—'

'I thought she was divorcing him?' Emma frowned, concentrating carefully on staying on the right-hand side of Sunset Boulevard.

'She is, darling.' Kitty shrugged. 'I think she thought that marrying him meant something to him. It was a way of making sure he was hers – like any man *ever* pays attention to a wedding ring. She was that way about Clive April.' She named an actor (*Or is he a director?*) whom Emma had heard mentioned around the Foremost lot. 'She tried to pull out Blanche Sweet's hair just for talking to him . . . Clive, I mean. He was her first husband. Or maybe her second – well, before Ernst, anyway. Her mother's been claiming for about six years that she's twenty-two but I don't think she was that when she came to Hollywood, and God knows how many husbands she had before she got here.'

Emma schooled herself not to even think about Kitty's three husbands or the date on her birth certificate. Instead she asked, 'Was that what you were looking for? In poor Mr Zapolya's pockets? Something to tell us what he wanted – and why it had to be kept such a secret?'

'This is a matter on which lives depend . . .'

'It was.' Kitty sat back, withdrew a fat envelope from her

handbag – bearing the letterhead of Enterprise Motion Picture Studios – and sat frowning at it as the car wove its way through the traffic towards Ivarene Street. 'And whether it was the same something that he needed to talk to Nomie about.'

'And what did you find?'

'Only this.' She held out the envelope. 'It's got seven thousand dollars in it.'

SIX

DIRECTOR SLAIN ON SET, shrieked the headline of the next day's *Sunday Times*.

And, only a few points smaller: DETECTIVES UNCOVER CONFIDENTIAL CLUES.

'You should have seen old Seth's face when Darlene Golden told him you'd left the lot ten minutes after you said you'd "be right up".' Harry Garfield grasped Kitty's hands, stared with frantic yearning into her eyes.

Kitty turned her face aside, sobbed, 'Served the putz right for making a pass at poor Emma.'

He laid a gentle hand to her cheek, drew her gaze tenderly back to his. 'What a chiseler!'

'CUT!' Larry Palmer yelled.

If anyone in Hollywood had ever heard of the Fourth Commandment, Emma reflected, they probably thought it referred to a film by Cecil B. DeMille.

The tender strains of 'Til the Sands of the Desert Grow Cold' stopped mid-bar. Emma looked up from the *Times* article as the director – tweedy, bearded, and slightly stooped – corrected the angle of 'Buddy Livingstone's' tender gesture of insistence that the beautiful showgirl 'Cincinnati Wilder' – whom his socialite parents despised – tell him the truth about why she tried to run from him . . .

As usual, it looked nothing like what Emma had pictured when she wrote the scene. Certainly the dialog title card expressed sentiments entirely different during this heart-rending encounter.

Not that it mattered a great deal. At the best of times Kitty's acting challenged comparison with primary-school Christmas pageants.

Herr Volmort from Makeup scuttled on to the exquisite garden terrace to dust Kitty's face with an artistic hint of powder – sweat from the glaring klieg lights did not belong in a scene purportedly taking place outdoors at night – then turned to likewise correct Harry's appearance. 'And be a little more reluctant when he turns you back,' added Larry to Kitty. 'It cost you everything you had, to run from him once. You know his love for you will ruin him with his family – your heart is breaking . . .'

Kitty nodded earnestly, her dark eyes wide. Herbie Carboy dashed to hold the chalked scene number in front of Zal Rokatansky's camera lens, the Rothstein Boys struck up 'Til the Sands of the Desert Grow Cold' at the exact point they had left off, Harry grasped Kitty's hands again and stared with frantic yearning into her eyes. 'Will I see you at Doug and Mary's tomorrow night?'

While Doc Larousse and his team re-arranged the lights for scenes 520 to 531 (the outraged incursion of 'Buddy's' parents into his declaration of love for 'Cincinnati') and second camera-man Chip Thaw set up for another angle on the master shot, Zal joined Emma at what Emma generally thought of as Kitty's base camp to one side of the vast, dim interior of Stage Two. The semi-circle of canvas folding chairs, portable makeup table, portable gramophone (and stand), wicker carry boxes for the dogs, silk cushions, an elaborate Chinese lacquered basket for Kitty's astrology magazines, three mirrors of varying sizes, and several floral tributes from admirers included also a folding table for drinks: a thermos of coffee (Zal's), a thermos of tea (Emma's) and a thermos of coffee liberally doctored with gin (Kitty's). *Or*, reflected Emma resignedly, *of gin moderately flavored with coffee* . . .

Zal bent to kiss her lips. 'You holding up?'

It was just after six. The shooting that morning at eight (after nearly two hours in makeup) had gone on longer than planned owing to the near-fatal hangover of Nick Thaxter – 'Buddy's' father – and the Big Confrontation between Buddy, his parents and the heartbroken-but-scrappy Cincinnati would probably not 'wrap' (as they said in Hollywood) until well past ten. 'I got sandwiches from the commissary,' said Emma. '*Nervos Hollywood, prandial infinitam*, as Cicero would have said had he ever visited a film set.'

Zal laughed, and turned the *Times* around so he could see the headline. 'Doesn't look like the cops wasted any time.'

'I'm curious,' said Emma, a little drily, 'as to when someone finally thought to summon them. Something I notice no one mentions in the article.'

'Well . . .' The cameraman propped his glasses more firmly on the bridge of his nose as he studied the columns of print. 'Since the article seems to be mostly about what a great picture *Crowned Heart* is going to be, they probably didn't have room to mention much else. You can only ask so much of the poor guys, Em.'

'Hollywood.' Emma sighed. The photo under the headline was, of course, of Desiree Darrow and Bruce Allan – a.k.a. Prince Stephan. Only further down the column was the piece illustrated with an image of the deceased – and he was pictured, slightly out of focus, standing at the side of the angel-faced Marina Carver, currently starring in *Broadway Bluebird.* That part of the article which didn't detail the perfections of *Crowned Heart* concerned Miss Carver's agonized grief at her husband's murder and her courage in going on with work on what was certain to be the greatest hit of her dazzling career . . .

'I wonder if they found anything at Zapolya's house?' Zal paged through the rest of the paper – which included full-page Sunday advertising spreads, a much-expanded section of illustrated comics, and a supplement entirely devoted to tractors – looking for a follow-up. 'It says here just that "confidential clues have put the police definitely on the trail of the mysterious Woman in Black . . ."'

'No mention,' remarked Emma, 'of the frock Miss Carver was wearing. The gloves I saw were black,' she added. 'I thought at the time they could have been Miss Carlyle's, because they didn't have any debris on top of them, but they were awfully close to the back wall of the set.' She removed a smaller thermos-jar of milk from her picnic basket, offered it to Zal and then dosed her own tea. 'She'd have taken them off to try to pry her fingers under the edge of the door.'

'They find the gun?'

She scanned the column for the place. 'It was in the area

immediately behind the back wall of the set, about ten feet from the doors. But if—'

'Oh, thank God!' Kitty scampered over in a firestorm of sequins and fringe. 'Just one little sip before they put more lipstick on me . . . You want some coffee, Howie?'

'Thank you.' Harry Garfield, unbearably snappy in sleek, double-breasted gray, inclined his head.

'With or without gin?' inquired Zal, and Emma brought a clean cup.

'There's tea,' she added, and Harry bowed again.

'I kiss your hands and feet, Duchess. If you can spare it, I'll take the tea – and a sandwich, if you have any extra there.'

'Larry will shit bricks if you get mayonnaise on your jacket,' pointed out Kitty, spoiling the elegance of the hero's ensemble by tucking a napkin, bib-wise, into his shirt collar. 'Darling, Frank's here, and he asked . . .'

Harry bowed to Emma again, as she fished in her cardigan pocket for the little tissue-paper bundle of diamonds. 'I have a great favor to ask, Mrs Blackstone. And I guess of you, too, Zal . . .' And his hand forestalled her wrist, as she would have drawn the gift forth.

'Frank told you to take Emma to this hoedown at Pickfair tomorrow night?' guessed Zal, himself devouring ham and swiss as if it were the first food he'd had since breakfast (which Emma suspected it was) and the last he'd get until midnight – another thing she'd learned in her first few months was as characteristic of Hollywood as bright lights and film magazines. A few feet away, cameraman Chip Thaw was trying to simultaneously eat a donut, drink a cup of coffee, smoke a cigarette and explain undercranking to young Herbie Carboy, with limited success in any of these endeavors.

Garfield glanced over his shoulder at Frank Pugh, studio chief and part-owner of Foremost Productions, looming over the slender director like an overweight, still-dangerous corrida bull. 'Mrs Blackstone,' Harry apologized quietly, 'I realize it is unforgivable to treat you like a prop – but I'm honestly a little bit against the wall here. Pictures of us at the Montmartre made it into *Silver Screen* this morning, and Frank . . .'

'I told Frank,' declared Kitty righteously, 'that he has no

business ordering you to do anything you don't want to do. But I know Zallie's going to be checking test strips tomorrow evening, and he can take you out for coffee afterwards, and Doug and Mary always serve the absolute *last* word in *scrumptious* food. Besides, Connie Talmadge will just tear her hair out with jealousy. She's been just *passionate* about Harry since—'

Emma turned to Harry with raised brows.

'Can't.' He sighed. 'She's going with Jack Gilbert. Since *A Man's Mate*, Connie's mother thinks he's a more prestigious escort, divorce detectives or no. Have pity on me, Mrs Blackstone.' He took her hand again, fell to his knees before her, and tucked his chin to look up through his eyelashes again à la *Hide-and-Seek Heart*. 'At least have pity on Roger.'

'Roger?' It took her a moment to identify Harry's 'friend'.

'He knows you're Zal's girl. Miss Talmadge is serious.'

'And Kitty's right. The food'll be better than you could get at the commissary helping me do test strips,' Zal pointed out.

'The same could be said,' Emma reminded him, as she held out her hand to let Harry kiss it, 'if I stayed home and shared dinner with the dogs.'

'*Do* you mind?' she asked, as Zal steered his elderly Bearcat off Sunset Boulevard on to Vine, and started the climb up into the hills. It was, as she had foreseen, nearly midnight. The neighborhood of the studios was dotted with coffee shops and small restaurants that remained open until all hours; seven months in Los Angeles had still not accustomed Emma to the sight of businesses routinely open on Sundays, much less this late on Sunday nights. Frank Pugh had insisted that Emma and Zal join himself and Kitty for a late supper at Musso & Frank's, and the big man had spent a part of the evening telling them both how much he appreciated the 'romance' between Harry and Emma and how good it was going to be for *everybody's* careers (he had looked pointedly at Zal).

Pugh had driven Kitty back to the studio to pick up her car. Emma – with Chang Ming and Black Jasmine snoring in her lap and Buttercreme's wicker box at her feet – wondered whether Kitty would spend any part of tonight at home, or whether she should pack yet another change of clothing and shoes for her for the morrow. In that case it would be both prudent and efficient to do so before bed tonight.

'Only if it bothers you.' The streetlamps flickered across the lenses of his glasses, picked reddish gleams in his hair and the tangle of his close-clipped beard. Against the stars, the tall palm trees rose like silhouetted feather dusters, an incongruous world, reflected Emma – rather like a film set itself.

'It bothers me that he's treating you like a pimp,' she said. 'Other than that . . . I know it's not serious—'

'It is, in a way. He may ask you to marry him.'

'He has.' From the pocket of her cardigan, Emma brought out the diamond bracelet again, turned it in her hand. 'Is this a genuine gift, by the way? Or only to impress me – and *Screen Stories* magazine?'

'Depends on whether you accept it . . . and him.'

'I wouldn't,' she said after a time, feeling the touch of his glance. 'Not even knowing I could use his money to go back to Oxford, to take up my studies seriously again. To do genuine field work, to actually finance my own expeditions to the Apennines and Egypt and the ruins of Babylon. To actually use the skills I was trained in . . .'

'Is that what you want?'

'Yes – I don't know. I think so.' She put her hand out, touched Zal's arm in the darkness. 'But what I *don't* want is to be part of that world as . . . as a curiosity. As a film star's eccentric wife who'd rather go digging up crumbly old tombs in central Italy than attend parties at Pickfair Mansion and drink bootleg champagne. I want it to be real.' She glanced across at him, a lumpish silhouette as the dark of the hills embraced them. A gentle voice in the night, and – even more than the memory of his kisses – the sense of safety that she always had with him. Of peace.

'You can still do genuine research, even if it's being paid for by a Hollywood studio.' She heard in his matter-of-fact voice the note of his regret. 'And *real* is not what you're going to get in Hollywood.'

'I think it is.' She touched his arm again. Black Jasmine

woke in her lap, and sleepily caught her wrist with one paw. 'And it would mean that Frank Pugh would still be a part of my life – or the head of whatever studio Harry was contracted to. Mr Pugh would insist that I remain most of the year here in town, so people won't go round printing pictures of Mr Garfield holding hands with Roger at the local nightspots while I'm away.'

'You're probably right about that, Em. But if he goes over to Paramount or Universal—' He broke off, turning the wheels on to the steep drive of Kitty's ersatz Moorish castle, and the headlights flashed across the figure of a woman standing in the porch, at the top of the tall flight of tiled steps.

No car, Emma noted automatically. *She must have come by taxi . . .*

She would have thought it was Kitty, at this distance, but for the woman – girl – stepping forward down the first of the steps, so that the moonlight showed up the soft halo of her blonde hair.

Not Peggy either . . .

'Oh, thank goodness!' cried the girl, as Zal and Emma climbed out of the car where one fork of the graveled drive leveled itself off in front of the house. She came running down the rest of the flight, and Emma recognized Nomie Carlyle. Nomie stopped at the bottom, looked from Emma to Zal and then to the little two-seater's now-empty body, as Emma lifted out first Black Jasmine, then Buttercreme in her wicker box. Chang Ming, tail threshing with delight, bounded up to greet Nomie as a long-lost benefactress on the strength of a single brief encounter in the Enterprise Studio's commissary tent yesterday, and rolled adoringly on his back before her dainty sequined shoes.

'Is Kitty not with you?'

'She may be along.' Zal glanced back up toward the road above the little dell that comprised the villa's front yard. 'God knows when, though.'

And despite her vexation – Emma had hoped to spend at least some time in the dim-lit parlor, in the comforting circle of Zal's arms – Emma heard the note of dismay in the blonde girl's voice. 'What is it?' she asked gently. 'Come inside, dear

– what's wrong? You wouldn't have taken a taxi all the way
up here if it wasn't—'

'They're saying I did it!' Nomie clutched her hands together,
as if to physically defend herself against a threat. 'Marina told
the police – and Mr Jesperson is backing her up because
she's one of the studio's biggest stars! And I don't know
what to do!'

'*Was* he your lover?' Emma came down the few steps to the
kitchen – Kitty's villa was a conglomeration of rooms on
different levels, to accommodate the slope of the hill – with
a glass of light wine in one hand, the bottle in the other. Zal
was just pouring hot water into Emma's teapot, and then
into a mug containing (Emma shuddered) a tablespoon
of Washington's Instant Coffee, something Kitty kept for dire
emergencies, such as hangovers that couldn't wait for the
percolator to run its cycle.

Nomie accepted the wine gratefully, her face turned aside
from the question. Sat for a moment, silent. Then nodded, a
tiny gesture.

'Did you love him?'

'He was ever so kind to me,' said the girl. 'Men . . .' She
shivered. 'Men in this business . . . casting directors and-and
producers . . . Ernst was different. Or at least,' she added, as
Zal's brows skated towards his hairline, 'he was different
to *me*.'

Emma ignored the opinion that was stamped so clearly
on Zal's face. 'And I take it Miss Carver – Mrs Zapolya –
found out?'

'It'd be hard to ignore,' remarked Zal, 'with Ernst trying
to talk Jesperson into starring Nomie in her own feature.
Marina's best buddies with Willa Jesperson – who's the real
bucks behind Enterprise Pictures. Mrs J's dad's the head of
Moonbeam Soap and owns about two-thirds of the real estate
in St Louis.'

Nomie sipped her wine, raised tear-filled eyes to Emma's.
'Ernst . . . hated all that,' she whispered. 'All that behind-the-
scenes string-pulling. He had to do it, he said. The same way
girls – and men, too – have to . . . do what they have to do,

to get seen by casting directors. He despised money. And he despised the men who run the studios. All he wanted to do, he said, was tell great stories, in the greatest way possible . . .'

Zal opened his mouth to make some comment, then closed it. Something in his eyes made Emma think again of the horses lying dead in the smoking ruins of the Ravenstark palace square, of the extras fleeing in genuine terror as explosions ripped the ground around them and the shattered balcony collapsed on their heads. ('Not bad for a shot like this . . .' young Mike Nye had remarked.)

And Lou Jesperson's harsh voice grating out instructions for Scene 704.

But at that moment Chang Ming, dozing at Nomie's feet beneath the table, sat up, silky ears lifting, and looked toward the back door. Buttercreme and Black Jasmine appeared in the doorway through to the living room, ears cocked and tails threshing. In the yard below, Emma heard the scrunch of tires on gravel, the sudden silence as a powerful engine stilled.

Then the brisk tap of diamanté heels on the wooden stair up to the kitchen door, and the rattle of a key. 'Dearest, I hope I'm not interrupting you in the transports of passion or anything—'

Kitty halted, startled, in the door between the dark scullery and the kitchen itself. 'Nomie!' She hurried in, hooked a teacup from the shelf as she passed and made a beeline for the wine bottle. But there was real concern in her voice as she said, 'Is everything all right, honey?'

'I guess Jesperson and the Angel Next Door have cooked it up between them to tell the bulls Nomie done it.' Zal set the coffee cup in front of Nomie, the teapot in front of Emma, then perched on the back of one of the kitchen chairs with his feet on the seat.

Kitty's mouth popped open in shocked indignation, despite the fact that the pearls which even now adorned her throat she had retrieved from beneath Zapolya's desk.

'They've been at the studio.' Nomie's voice sank in despair. 'Asking about me. And a man who I swear was a detective was talking to the woman at my apartments. Kitty, please. I

know you don't know me very well, but . . . when my sister
was in the business, she said you never turned your back on
someone who needed help. And I need help. *Please . . .*'

Kitty stood for a time, cup in one hand and the other still
resting on the wine bottle's green shoulder, her eyes on the
younger woman's face with a kind of sad compassion. 'You'll
have to tell the truth,' she warned after a time.

'About Ernst?' The lovely face lifted to hers. 'I know I . . .
I put myself in his way. I know there are people who call me
a gold digger, who say I . . . I was only with him because he
could help me get ahead in pictures. Is that what you mean?'

Kitty hesitated for a long time, then nodded. 'That's what
I mean, honey.'

Nomie looked away again. Emma saw the lines of tears
track silently through her makeup; saw how her hands shook
around the stem of her wine glass.

Kitty filled her own cup, bent for a moment to reassure
Chang Ming that she really loved him best in the whole
wide world, then went to the inner door to fetch the two
Sleeve Pekes before they hurt themselves clambering down
the kitchen steps.

'Do you need to get out of town?' Emma asked.

Nomie's huge eyes flared wide. 'Oh, *no*, Mrs Blackstone!
I couldn't leave in the middle of shooting! I'd never get work
again!'

'Not to mention it's the best way to get the cops to think
you did it,' added Zal. 'Unless you want to take out an ad in
the *Times*.'

'Besides –' Kitty turned back, her arms full of animate fluff
– 'you know Lou Jesperson isn't going to have Nomie arrested
until after shooting wraps. He just *hates* re-shoots. They all
do. So that gives us – how long?'

'There are the scenes on the Isle of Love next week,' said
the girl. 'We'll be filming on San Clemente Island Wednesday
and coming back Saturday. And then maybe three days back
here in town, for me to get killed . . . Plus whatever time it
will take Mr Jesperson to find a new director . . .'

'Is there a way we can delay the filming?' asked Emma.
She looked uncertainly from Kitty to Zal, visions of poisoned

cameramen and Graustarkian sets in flames. (*Honestly,* this *is what I need to be writing a scenario for, not some silly romance between Julius Caesar and a virtuous Trinovante maiden.*)

'Sure,' said Zal cheerfully. 'At that party tomorrow night, get hold of Willa Jesperson and convince her to get Lou to hire Erich von Stroheim to replace Zapolya as director. Goldwyn's just merged with Metro and Louis Mayer's outfit, and the new production chief pulled Stroheim off *Greed,* that he's been working on for a year and a half. I know Stroheim's strapped for cash, so I'm pretty sure he'll work cheap. And he's big prestige, and one of the top directors in the business. He's also a twenty-four-karat guarantee that any production he works on is going to run months over schedule. That should give us all kinds of time to point the cops at whoever really pulled the trigger.'

'Are you sure Mr Jesperson will hire him?' Emma recalled those cold little eyes, like tobacco-stained pebbles. *Your one minute is gonna cost me four thousand bucks . . . there are guys all over town who can bring that shot in for less . . .*

'Oh, Willa'll make sure.' Zal leaned his folded elbows on his knees. 'You ever seen that house of theirs, out in Pasadena? She had a Renaissance palazzo dismembered in Florence and brought over here in boxes, with solid gold doorknobs and hand-polished marquetry floors. Makes Pickfair look like a Bowery flophouse. Furniture from six different chateaux in France, first editions in the library, not that either she or Lou has ever read more than a film scenario . . . To get von Stroheim's name on *Crowned Heart*? She'd put a gun to Lou's head. And serve him right.'

SEVEN

As Nomie had no idea who the Woman in Black might have been ('I'm sure Marina was over on the set for *Broadway Bluebird*') – and as it was by that time nearly two in the morning – little more was accomplished that evening. Emma spent much of the next day – Monday – when she wasn't asleep on the divan in Kitty's dressing room – working on *The Gryphon Prince*, and considered herself lucky that Frank Pugh would be escorting Kitty to the Beverly Hills mansion of Douglas Fairbanks and Mary Pickford that night; Kitty's scenes ceased filming at three.

'I'll still be here at ten,' said Zal resignedly, over commissary coffee. 'Alvy Turner's been sick for a week' – he named one of the other Foremost cameramen – 'and his assistant hasn't got his cranking speed even yet. Half his footage is either faster or slower than mine or Chip's, and it's driving Larry crazy, because he likes to have at least three angles on a scene. He can't really spare either me or Chip to keep an eye on the kid. The Pacific Electric diner'll be open late, if you're not dead on your feet after the party.'

'*You're* the one who'll be dead on his feet,' protested Emma, but she gripped his hand quickly, as one of the prop men leaned in through the long dining-room's door and yelled.

'Mr Rokatansky? Mr Palmer says they've got the shot set up . . .'

'Mr Palmer can catch fire and die,' muttered Zal, with unabated cheer. He stood up, kissed her hand, grabbed his cap and strode away, leaving Emma amid a welter of newspapers.

WHO IS THE WOMAN IN BLACK?

DIRECTOR'S MURDERESS SOUGHT

HAVE YOU SEEN THIS WOMAN? – which was a cab-driver's description of a 'mysterious woman' picked up on Hollywood Boulevard 'in a great state of agitation', her clothing 'smelling strongly of gunpowder'.

There was also a letter to the editor of the *Herald* denouncing the growing presence of 'socialist agitators' in the 'golden empire of film' and demanding the detention and questioning of all such persons in connection with not only 'this most recent savage outrage' but also with the murder two years ago of director William Desmond Taylor. 'Two such mysterious crimes – and who knows what others previously ascribed to accident or misadventure? – must they not surely be the work of the same fell hand?'

Emma shook her head. It wasn't only Kitty who was composed of equal parts wild make-believe and genuine warmth. Everything in Hollywood seemed to be a weird cocktail of real events – real people – and glittering towers of nonsense in which it was sometimes almost impossible to see where truth lay.

This division between reality and fantasy was on prominent display that evening, as Harry Garfield walked her up the long brick pavement from the gates on Summit Drive. Lights shone golden in the big L-shaped house called Pickfair. Music lilted on the air. Studio musicians, Emma guessed, like the Rothstein Boys at Foremost, supplementing the fees they got for playing to get actors 'in the mood' on the sets. There was something of the film set in the lawn that spread before the house, and the Chinese lanterns glowing like luminous fruit in the surrounding trees and transforming the covered terrace into a box of amber light.

We have lots of money! trumpeted the acres of parquet and oriental carpeting inside, the ceiling frescoes and mahogany paneling – not to speak of the swimming pool Emma had glimpsed at the bottom of the slope below the curving drive, dug into the ground like an artificial lake. And yet, the good taste and genuine welcome glowed just as brightly as Harry escorted her in. Their coats were taken by a black-suited butler who looked himself like something ordered from a casting agent (and perhaps he had been). *If you can call them coats*, reflected Emma – lightweight garments of silk and fine suiting that wouldn't have lasted ten minutes on a May night back home. Kitty had cheerfully lent Emma one from her enormous collection – cut-velvet and fur – even as Kitty had bought her the gown she wore (*Darling, you just* can't *go to parties here looking like somebody's maiden aunt*!).

After five years of first war and then destitution – followed by another four of Mrs Pendergast's grasping household – a new gown of night-blue silk held an almost magical delight. Maybe the diamonds on her wrist would have to be handed back to Harry at the earliest possible moment (reporters and photographers clustered the sidewalks outside the gates of Pickfair's grounds), but they were real diamonds. Harry had said, 'Oh, please wear them tonight, Duchess.' And, with a wicked grin, he'd added, 'Think how pleased Frank'll be.'

And after she'd greeted Harry with a kiss, Miss Pickford (*Or should I call her Mrs Fairbanks?* Her name had originally, Kitty had said, been Gladys Smith) had clasped Emma's hand in welcome, taken one look at the diamonds, and met Emma's eyes with sympathetic amusement dancing in her own as she shared the joke: *I know what* those *mean, honey* . . .

And Emma had smiled back, feeling immediately at home.

Frank Pugh, with Kitty on his arm (*the fourth Mrs Pugh must still be out of town*), stood near the bar, in earnest conversation with a powerfully-built, smooth-faced, balding man whom Emma recognized as Mr DeMille of Famous Players. Gorgeous in pistachio-green and silver, Peggy Donovan shared gales of laughter with the sweet-faced Gish sisters; like a very well-dressed faun and unrecognizable out of costume, Charlie Chaplin fetched lemonade for an angel-faced little brunette girl whom Emma personally thought should have been home doing her homework. Emma even glimpsed Seth Ramsay, talking a mile a minute to a clearly-bored Mae Murray.

And as always, she was struck by how small they all looked in person. How thin. Almost fragile.

And very human, when they weren't being the larger-than-life archetypes that audiences clamored to see. Curious to see Gloria Swanson discussing lawnmowers with Ramon Novarro rather than languishing in his arms; to see Buster Keaton's grave, steely beauty break into a grin at one of Jack Gilbert's jokes.

'Hollywood Memorial, I heard,' said Rudolf Valentino to a

sleek-haired young man whom Emma vaguely recognized – from the Foremost Productions Christmas party – as her hostess' scapegrace brother Jack. 'Tomorrow at two, I think. I hear old Jesperson offered the minister a hundred dollars to mention in the service how wonderful *Crowned Heart* and *Broadway Bluebird* will be . . .'

'Be worth it to go just to see if he does!' grinned young Pickford. 'You read in the *Examiner* it was Clive April who did it?'

'The Angel's second husband? Dressed as a woman in black?'

The young man shrugged elaborately. 'Well, you saw him in *Garden of Fortune*. He looks great in a dress!'

Valentino rolled his eyes.

Another complaint overrode the star's next comment: '. . . so I told him, if I had to wear another damn bedsheet I was walking; I'd look like a damn sissy!'

And a few steps further away, the square-faced, elaborately-dressed mother of the Talmadge sisters leaned close to Elinor Glyn and half-shouted over the strains of 'I Cried For You', 'I don't believe it was the Communists at all! Everybody knows poor Betsy April was diagnosed with . . . well . . .' She leaned closer to whisper to the slim, vampish writer in her black velvet and jet.

Miss Glyn raised elegant brows. 'Well, that sounds like a visit to one's gynecologist is in order, not a homicide. And from what I've heard of Betsy, there was no reason to think Ernst in particular was the culprit . . .'

Lou Jesperson came in from the garden, glaring around him as if the money being spent on lobster patties and caviar was coming out of his own pocket. His elbow supported the hand of a tall, queenly woman whose red-and-golden gown, with its intricate bias drapes and layerings, shouted *Worth*! She was younger than Emma had pictured her, and slimmer. But she had the small, calculating eyes that appraised the cost of her hostess's frock and took comfort in the fact that her own was more expensive.

The sort of woman who *would* have gold doorknobs in her house.

'So I says to him' – a woman's voice surfaced like a breeching whale over the party din – 'if I have to either get wet or ride a horse, the deal's off . . .'

Mr Fairbanks crossed over to Jesperson at once, with his lithe, springy stride, and started what was clearly a business diatribe. Mrs Jesperson turned aside from it, wrinkling her nose, a look in her eyes that might have been pain. She glanced towards the clock.

She's just waiting for an excuse to leave . . .

Emma looked around quickly for Kitty. But her sister-in-law – who never left a party before dawn – was still flirting with the clearly-enchanted Mr DeMille. On impulse, she pressed her own escort's hand, and he obediently followed her. *Like Talthybias the Herald in Book III of the* Iliad, reflected Emma. Or a sandwich-board man with a sign that said, *This Is Someone Connected With the Studios . . .*

'Mrs Jesperson . . .' She held out her hand to the studio owner's wife. 'Please excuse me for being forward – I'm Mrs Blackstone, from Foremost Productions.' (*Well,* that's *true, anyway – I did write the scenario for* Hot Potato.) 'I can't tell you how shocked I was over what happened Saturday, and I wanted to ask you – do you mind talking about this? If you do, please say so, but I was on the set when it happened . . .'

The sharp hazel eyes altered, from annoyed distaste (*How do I get rid of this woman?*) to wary interest. 'Not at all, Mrs Blackstone.' Her voice, though low and well-bred, still retained the flat ghost of a mid-South accent. She put an opera-gloved hand on Emma's elbow, and glanced at Harry.

'If you'll excuse us for a moment, Harry,' said Emma, and felt the fingers gripping her arm relax.

They retreated toward the foyer, and Harry strolled off to join Gilbert and Keaton at the bar.

'You were on the set, you said?' The tension in Mrs Jesperson's features did not ease. (*Because one of Enterprise's stars is a suspect? Or more than one?*) 'My poor dear, no wonder you were shocked! You were a guest . . .?'

'I'd come with Miss de la Rose' – she gave Kitty's *nom du cinema* – 'who had personal business with Miss Donovan. It was nothing important. But I know how dreadfully the film magazines spread rumors, and twist facts, and will take the smallest remarks out of context.'

She saw her companion flinch, and glance toward Miss Glyn and Mrs Talmadge, the words, '. . . well, of course everyone knew he was sleeping with the girl . . .' floated across to her.

'And I know it's just going to be a matter of time before they start hounding Miss de la Rose and myself.'

'Mrs Blackstone, if you only knew!' The words were those of sympathy and commiseration, but the watchful gleam in the eyes did not alter.

'I'm afraid, since I've been – well – keeping company with Mr Garfield, that I *do* know.' Emma sighed. 'So – I realize this sounds like a terrible thing to ask, but is there anything that you want me, or Miss de la Rose, to say, or not to mention, if we're asked? We can't really deny we were there – too many people saw us. And we had to leave before Mr Jesperson started – well – *briefing* the crew and extras as to what to say about the crime . . .'

'Mrs Blackstone, how considerate of you!' A tiny bit of the rigid control went out of the other woman's shoulders, and something altered, just slightly, in the stony eyes. 'I'm afraid Hollywood is truly a frightful place for rumors.'

'Worse even than the academic circles of Oxford,' agreed Emma, at which her companion gave a genuine chuckle.

'I'm afraid both would have to go far to outdistance the St Louis Women's Club in the month before the debutante ball.' Mrs Jesperson shook her head. 'I think discretion is the watchword in these circumstances. Did you know Mr Zapolya?'

Emma shook her head. 'I read in the papers yesterday that the police have a suspect in mind. And I must admit I am horrified,' she added quickly, as Mrs Jesperson drew back. 'So far as I could see of the filming that day, and what I read was . . . it sounds like such a brilliant story!' Following Kitty's technique of imagining what she'd sound like in similar circumstances, she threw into her voice the terrible regret she'd felt, when first she'd heard of the destruction of the last remaining Etruscan–Latin dictionary in the fifth century AD. 'Such a beautiful piece of drama – so far beyond the usual run of costume melodrama one sees from other studios . . .'

She glanced significantly toward the bar, where Pugh and DeMille had been joined by a thick-faced, nondescript man whom Emma guessed was one of the studio heads.

'It's what I keep telling my husband!' Genuine sorrow – and frustration – suddenly cracked Mrs Jesperson's voice. 'We *can't* be like the rest, cost what it may. A true artist never counts the cost! There *is* a market for these films among the better class of people, but one can't sell cheap plush and pretend it's velvet! People – people of education and taste – can tell the difference . . .'

'Exactly!' agreed Emma. She sighed inwardly; like Prince Hal, *I'll gild this one with the happiest terms I have . . .* 'And I found myself hoping – I know Mr Zapolya *was* that sort of director. I've seen his work' – she hadn't – 'and it's head and shoulders above . . . Well, it has something that very few other directors working in Hollywood have. It sounds terribly callous, considering the tragedy of the man's death' – Mrs Jesperson's perfectly painted lips flinched – 'but it would be almost as tragic for his final work – the true soul of the man – to be turned into something less than the vision he had . . .' (*Honestly, scenario writing seems to affect the brain . . .*)

'That is exactly my feeling, Mrs Blackstone!' The gloved hands gripped Emma's with sudden emotion. 'It just about drives me *crazy*, to hear Lou go on about, Who can we find who's cheap? He doesn't understand . . .'

'Good Heavens, no!' Her glance flickered into the main room, hoping Mr Jesperson wasn't going to come stumping into the conversation with a demand that they needed to be going home.

No, he was still deep in conversation with Mr Fairbanks and a nondescript gentleman wearing a diamond stickpin the size of a quail's egg. *An investor?*

'The film – well, all films, really, but historical drama of that scope – needs a special touch, a special vision, to match Mr Zapolya's . . .'

'There are few who can.' Her companion's tight mouth hardened again. 'Certainly not in this town. So few comprehend that no . . . no small-minded nit-picking must come between the vision of a genius and its realization.' Her brows pulled together, an expression that curiously made her face seem younger, not older. 'And he *was* a genius! He had that breadth of vision, like Griffith used to have – I'm sure you've seen *Birth of a Nation*, Mrs Blackstone. So superb . . . inspired! All the quibbles of petty men about it . . . I understand Mr DeMille is working on filming *Across the Border*, or I would tell my husband to hire him to finish *Crowned Heart*. I cannot imagine another whose vision—'

'What about Erich von Stroheim?' asked Emma, with a sense of having thrown a dart, with perfect timing, into the gold. 'I understand he's been taken off his Metro project . . .'

'*Has* he?' The small, sharp eyes flared with interest. 'Are you sure? Louis would know,' she added, with a nod towards the nondescript gentleman with Pugh and DeMille. 'He's just combined with Metro and Goldwyn. If we can get them to lend us "Von", as they call him . . .' She wheeled unceremoniously from Emma and clove her way through the scattered groups with the purposefulness of a gourmand in pursuit of the caviar tray. Emma trailed behind, wondering how to catch Kitty and discreetly warn her that the suggestion had been delivered and accepted. A second bubbled encomium of Mr von Stroheim's – 'Von's' – suitability might appear suspicious.

She needn't have worried. The little group of filmmakers parted like well-trained extras at Mrs Jesperson's approach, and Kitty, beaming, stepped forward.

Willa Jesperson halted in her tracks at the sight of her. Emma, catching up with her, saw her face flame beet-red, her eyes ignite with fury . . . For a moment Emma thought that the older woman was actually about to snatch a glass of champagne from the tray of the nearest waiter and hurl it at Kitty.

But after a long, glaring moment she only turned on her heel, stormed to her husband – still in conversation with Fairbanks – grabbed him by the arm, and thrust him towards the foyer and, clearly, the mansion's outer door. Mr Fairbanks and the man with the diamond looked startled; a caviared toast-point in hand, Jesperson dug in his heels, opened his mouth in protest.

'We're leaving.' His wife's voice wasn't loud, but she sounded suddenly breathless with rage.

Jesperson took one look at her face, gulped down his toast-point, and followed her. The man used money as a threat, Emma had observed in Zapolya's office: like a gun aimed at the director's heart. Money was not only power – it was a weapon, that could be used to make life hell for those who thwarted the will of those significantly wealthier than themselves.

This wasn't just a woman in an expensive dress who loved cinematic spectacle. *Her dad's the head of Moonbeam Soap,* Zal had said, *and owns two-thirds of the real estate in St Louis . . . The real bucks behind Enterprise Pictures.*

Licking his fingers, Jesperson stalked out of Pickfair Mansion at her side like a man who has chosen to depart. But had she yanked him by a leash it could have been no clearer.

'Well!' Kitty set her empty champagne glass on the tray of the nearest waiter – Emma recognized him as one of the extras who had stormed the walls of Ravenstark on Saturday – and took another. 'What was *that* about?'

Emma glanced uncertainly after the departing couple, then back toward Frank Pugh, already re-absorbed in conversation with DeMille. 'You haven't . . .?'

'Oh, *please!*'

'I think you just been insulted, doll.' Peggy Donovan lounged over to them, eyes dancing behind a scrim of cigarette smoke. To Emma, she added, 'Willa doesn't care who waxes Lou's boots for him – all she's ever done to *me* is give me a big dose of stink-eye.'

'Well,' opined Kitty, 'if she fired every woman Jesperson ever popped Enterprise would have to make men-only Army films, and nobody's going to those anymore.'

Peggy hooted. 'If you ask me—'

A woman called, 'Peggy, honey!' The middle Talmadge sister, Emma thought. *Constance?*

Peggy chirped, 'Be right back, doll!' and turned to scamper away. The oldest Talmadge had her own film production company, and Emma knew better than to think that Peggy was going to 'be right back' any time soon.

She touched the red-haired actress' arm, staying her. 'May I come see you tomorrow? I know you won't be filming—'

'Make it Wednesday, doll. Everybody's got orders to be at that funeral or else. Wednesday Mike'll be doing pick-up shots in the courtyard . . .' She gripped Emma's hand quickly, gave her a bright grin. 'You come by the set around one. One thing you can say about Mike, he makes sure everybody gets a lunch break. I'll tell the boys at the gate.' And she darted away like a green-and-silver hummingbird through the crowd.

A firm hand slid under Emma's elbow and Harry Garfield murmured, 'You had enough of this, Mrs Blackstone? I sure have.'

Emma sighed, relieved. 'Please.' The level of noise in the rooms was rising, as more people arrived; someone had wound up the big cabinet-model gramophone, and the scratchy foxtrot booming from its horn competed jarringly with the little orchestra on the terrace. As the actor led her out into the blazingly illuminated night, she murmured, 'Thank you. I may actually kiss you for that.'

The star grinned. 'Save it for when we get to the gate, Duchess. That's where the press are.'

Of course they are. This is Hollywood.

In tenui labor, Virgil had written, *sed tenuis non gloria . . .* The fame was greater than the labor that elicited it. Quite true, given what she'd seen so far of the dailies from *Hot Potato.*

At the foot of the lawn, some of the more free-spirited members of the Hollywood community clustered boisterously around the swimming pool. Presumably, given the quantities of liquor in evidence, it was only a matter of time before someone got baptized. Flash-powder erupted like toy lightning as Emma's escort handed her into the snow-white Auburn that a uniformed attendant brought to the curb, and a boxy black Ford with one defective headlamp – presumably bearing a contingent of journalists – followed them down Summit Drive through the velvet dark of the hills, and thence to Benedict Canyon Boulevard and down to Sunset.

'You get used to it,' said the actor with a shrug, when Emma pointed this out. 'Roger's waiting for me at the studio, and we'll take his car home when I drop you off.'

If there's anything, reflected Emma, *that would definitively cause me to turn down the prospect of matrimony – diamond bracelet and all – with this man, it would be the thought of being followed by reporters and photographed every time one put one's nose out the door.*

Well, she added to herself . . . *other than the prospect of Zal Rokatansky . . .*

EIGHT

Zal was in the film lab, shaking his head over a strip of celluloid held up to the glow of the light-box before him. On the other side of the little room, row after glistening black row of test strips dangled, like alien stockings hung to dry. 'We're gonna have to re-shoot,' he sighed, when he'd locked up his cabinets, switched off the light box, washed his hands and joined Emma in the lab's tiny outer office. 'Miles of it. His speed's all over the place. He'll learn,' he added, and fetched his crumpled corduroy jacket from the chair where it was draped. 'He's got a nice sense of movement in the tracking shots. But everything's either a little bit faster or a little bit slower than the rest of the action, so we can't use a foot of it.'

He took Emma's hand, gave her a quick, warm kiss on the cheek. As always she felt steadied by his presence, and the edginess produced by the glare and noise of Pickfair faded.

'Have fun at the barn dance?'

'It's always interesting to see the ways people can come up with to spend a great deal of money,' said Emma. 'Kitty was quite right: the food was excellent. And Kitty managed to outrage Mrs Jesperson without saying a word – I've no idea how. She never even glanced at Mr Jesperson, her dress was perfectly decent – for Kitty – and I can't imagine she did it on reputation alone.'

'Not with all the competition she's got in this town . . .'

'Before that happened, I did manage to speak to Mrs Jesperson about Mr von Stroheim being at liberty. She seemed delighted . . . I only hope she remembers that enthusiasm when she gets home and calms down about whatever Kitty did that offended her.' She followed Zal down the rickety staircase of the building devoted to film stock: editing rooms, undeveloped 'roughs' and can after can of last year's

productions waiting to be melted down so that the silver
nitrate could be retrieved. The smells of dust, of glue, and
the pervasive smoky sweetness of raw film.

'Oh, she'll remember.' Zal ducked through the door that
opened from the vestibule at the bottom of the stairs, which
led – Emma knew – into the editing room. She had a brief
glimpse of plank tables, light boxes, tiny hand-crank viewers,
splicing machines, glue pots, and yet more reels of film. While
she waited in the closet-sized cubicle she glanced down at
that morning's *Examiner* on the table there: ENTERPRISE
STAR COLLAPSES ON SET (Yes, it was Marina Carver,
'overcome with grief'. *Is it possible to be 'overcome' with
that degree of grief for someone you're divorcing?* She wasn't
sure.) But it was the picture below it that caught her eye, and
the smaller headline: CLUB OWNER QUESTIONED IN
STOCKBROKER'S MURDER.

The man shown sprawled on a bloodied sidewalk wore
the checked trousers, baggy raincoat, and saddle shoes that
Emma had seen before, Friday night outside the Café
Montmartre.

The young man who'd been holding the hand of the long-
legged dark girl in yellow silk while her fearsome-nosed escort
spoke to his driver.

And there was Mr Prodigious Proboscis himself in an inset.
Jake Ricelli, said the caption. *Owner of the Alibi Club downtown and associate of Los Angeles Mayor George Cryer.*

Zal returned to the vestibule, locked the editing-room door
behind him. 'Willa Jesperson knows how much dough there
is to be made from films, but God forbid anyone should see
her grabbing for it. She wants to see herself as the muse of a
new art. And she's right, in a way.'

He followed Emma outside, locked the door of the building
behind them. 'You compare the stuff that's being done now
– by Lubitsch, or Ingram, or Griffith when he's not being
preachy – with the stuff Sennett was cranking out six or seven
years ago, and you can see how far film can go, and what it
can be. Zapolya was right in the forefront of that. When people
are willing to pay for depth, and spectacle, and to take the
time to get it right.'

It was after ten, but the 'streets' between the studio buildings – the three 'stages', the bungalows where directors had
their offices, the long, low barracks of Makeup, Wardrobe,
and construction shops – were far from deserted. Lights
shone around the doors of Stage Three, and up through the
muslin sheets that comprised its open roof. From a fog of
cigarette smoke around the stage's door the voice of Jerry
Stubbs – half of the studio's slapstick comedy team – bawled
outlines of the next gag to his cameraman. Generally the
less expensive one- and two-reelers were shot in daylight:
Larry and Jerry must be behind schedule . . . Four porters
walked by, each bearing a potted fan-palm like a tropical
Birnam Wood.

'Did you know Mr Zapolya?'

'I worked with him.' Zal's voice was dry.

'On one of those big spectacles of his?'

'Oh yeah.'

She walked in silence for a time, pulled the fur and glitter
of her borrowed wrap closer around her bare shoulders,
suddenly chilled. She saw again the horses lying dead or
broken among the ruins and drifting smoke, the bleeding extras
being carried to the trucks. The terrifying din of explosions
and guns. *Not bad, for a shot like this* . . .

'Isn't there any way,' she asked at last, 'of filming gunshots
that's less . . . potentially lethal? I know Mr Zapolya was shot
deliberately, but any of those poor extras could have been
killed. I was a volunteer ambulance driver during the war, I
know some of them were seriously injured . . .'

'That's Hollywood.' His voice, usually cheerful, was
suddenly hard as flint. 'That's what they'll tell you.' They
reached his dilapidated Bearcat, parked behind Wardrobe
amid a crowd of other vehicles, and he handed her in – the
little car having been manufactured with neither doors nor
a roof. 'The directors, and the studio owners. If they're
shooting at you, dodge. If you can't dodge, find some other
line of work.'

'Peggy Donovan told me they pay extra to hire sharp-
shooters, thank goodness. But couldn't they—'

'Blanks don't show up as well on film,' said Zal. 'And

they're more expensive than live ammo. The cowboys do what they can to keep the horses from getting hurt, but you've seen what a running-W does. And it's even odds that the rider won't walk away from a really spectacular spill, either. Jack Stevenson, one of the stunters over at Pathé, got killed doubling for Pearl White here a couple of years ago.'

A man in a rose-colored chauffeur's uniform emerged from Wardrobe, started up an equally rose-colored Daimler a few feet away and drove slowly toward the dressing rooms to pick up Darlene Golden. Emma recognized the chauffeur as one of the most comely extras she'd ever seen on the lot.

'It's not just the extras, either,' Zal went on. 'Lillian Gish still can't use three of her fingers, from filming that ice-floe scene in *Way Down East*. Looked great on film. Back in 1914, one of the girls in *Across the Border* drowned on location. So did one of the cameramen who dived into the Arkansas River to save her. And I can't tell you how many bones Buster Keaton has broken. Pretty much every big battle scene DeMille shoots ends up with horses dead, and extras being carried off the set on stretchers. Zapolya, same thing. He's had more than one extra die of injuries. And he's not the only one. And if they gotta go on working with a broken wrist or broken toes . . .' He shrugged bitterly. 'Heroin's not that hard to get. Not in this town.'

Her voice was a whisper. 'That's horrible.'

'That's Hollywood. That's part of the deal. That's three-fifty a day.' He let in the clutch, and steered carefully to the gate. 'Two bucks, at places like Monarch and Silver Star. You risk your life the same way if you work in a steel mill, or a coal mine, or a stockyard, you know. And if you're an extra, you have exactly the same chance that anybody'll give a damn if you collapse or lose your foot or your eyesight. If I were a Buddhist,' he added, with a wry grin as they passed under the archway and turned a cautious left on to Sunset Boulevard, 'I'd say Zapolya getting shot on set was karma.'

They worked their way down Grand Street, then Main, brick buildings looming dark against dark sky, between hills already brown and shaggy with the onset of summer. High overcast turned the night misty, the air moist. The lights were off in shabby hillside bungalows and then in the square bulk of office structures. Night and silence, the elf king's jester had said. Wind flicked Emma's hair and she huddled deeper into her gaudy coat; as they turned the corner past the long, Spanish block of the cathedral something caught her attention from the corner of her eye. A car with one headlamp out . . .

She smiled. *Miss Parsons – or whoever it is – is going to be very cross indeed when the person who gets out of the car isn't Harry Garfield . . .*

Coles' Pacific Electric Buffet – in a sort of half-basement on the ground floor of the Pacific Electric Railway building – was quiet at this hour, but nobody spared a second glance at Emma's night-blue evening gown and glittering coat, nor the shabby attire of her far-from-elegant escort. As one of the few places in Los Angeles that was open at midnight, the staff was past being surprised.

'French dip sandwich,' ordered Zal, as they took their seats. The tabletop was the varnished door of a cable car, the wallpaper nearly invisible under an assortment of photographs of Pacific Electric cars, bathing beauties on Venice Beach and local notables whom Emma didn't recognize grinning beside fancy new automobiles. 'You want anything?'

'I supped at the king's table,' returned Emma. 'As Mr Homer says, "Viands of various kinds alure the taste/of choicest sort and savor . . ." Tea, please.' She smiled at the waitress. 'And they had quite good wine . . . particularly considering it can't legally be made or sold here.'

'Never let it be said that Los Angeles cops take graft for cheap goods.'

'I'm going out to Enterprise Wednesday,' she went on, after they'd talked and joked about Prohibition and bootleggers and the extremely efficient delivery service that ran from the San Pedro wharves to every nightclub in town. (As she had suspected, Mr Jake Ricelli of the formidable proboscis was a participant in that operation – and she shivered again at the recollection of the photograph.) 'I gather the entire personnel of Enterprise is expected to attend Mr Zapolya's funeral tomorrow – with the exception of Miss Carver, I should hope, if his death has truly hit her that hard.'

Even at six years' distance, she remembered the pain of reading that letter from Jim's commanding officer as if it had happened yesterday . . .

And the pain of getting through every day thereafter.

'Are you kidding? The guys in the film lab are taking bets on how many times she faints during the service.'

Emma felt her face heat, and wondered why it hadn't occurred to her that even grief would be used to publicize *Crowned Heart* and *Broadway Bluebird*. She remembered the grave steles she had seen – Greek, Roman, the lively, tender sculptures of the Etruscans. The love that glowed across all those centuries, undying.

Then she sighed, and let the thought go.

Hollywood . . .

Go to the baths, and you're going to get splashed.

'I shall have to ask Peggy if the pastor does in fact slip an advertisement for *Crowned Heart* into the funeral oration.'

'"I come to bury Caesar, not to praise him",' Zal intoned in his plummiest imitation of John Barrymore, '"but I can and must praise the spectacle, grandeur, and excitement of his final work, and urge you to . . ."'

'Beast!' She kicked his shin sharply under the table. 'I don't really see how a woman – even one who was in the process of divorcing her husband – can use his death . . .'

'You obviously haven't read enough Euripides,' pointed out Zal. 'You going to have a look at the back of that cathedral set while you're there?'

'I don't suppose there'll be anything left there to see. Half the studio must have trampled it yesterday and today, to say nothing of Mr Jesperson's lawyers. Heaven only knows who will be poking about there tomorrow.'

'Not the police, anyway . . .'

She sighed. 'But yes, if I can . . .'

'I'll write a message for you to take to John Benson – he's the main cameraman on *Heart* – so if anybody stops you, you can say somebody told you he was out there on the set and you're looking for him. And since it sounds like the cops have already been told who to arrest—'

'Duchess!' A tall, sturdy form wove her way between the diner's tables; dark eyes sparkled beneath a black pudding-bowl haircut. 'Am I glad to see you! Gorgeous dress,' director Madge Burdon added, eyeing the night-blue silk approvingly. Then, with a second glance at Emma's wrist: 'Howie ask you to marry him?'

Emma rolled her eyes, only half jokingly.

'You finally get Emily rescued from that torture chamber?' inquired Zal – referring to Scenes 800 to 837 of *The Thornless Rose*, and it was Madge Burdon's turn to make a silent appeal to heaven.

'I'm gonna frikkin' drown that Ramsay one of these days,' she said with a sigh. 'I don't care how pretty he is in a torn shirt. How hard is it to kick your way through a prop door? Twenty takes, and we had to replace that frikkin' door every other time . . .'

She slumped into the chair that Zal pushed into position for her, looked across at Emma. 'And then Pugh comes in, lookin' like a zeppelin in a tux. And he says, can I get hold of you and get you to change scenes 248 to 270? He says it doesn't have enough oomph.'

Emma tried to recall what happened in Scenes 248 to 270 of *The Gryphon Prince*, but wasn't obliged to. The director went on: 'He says, can Caesar rescue Miriam from a tiger? He says Universal is going to have Rin Tin Tin fight with a wolf in his next picture, so he wants to get in ahead of them and have Caesar rescue the girl from a tiger—'

'There weren't tigers in Britain in 54 BC,' Emma pointed out.

'There could have been,' returned Miss Burdon, unanswerably. 'They were just down in Africa, and the Romans knew about Africa. And Gren Torley's bear is sick, or molting, or pregnant, or something. And besides, a tiger looks better on film.'

Emma opened her mouth to protest that tigers were no more native to Africa than they were to Britain, and closed it. Miss

Burdon – and Frank Pugh – would only argue that the Romans had known about India, also. Nor, she supposed, would either of them accept the information that the Roman general had been forty-five at the time of his invasion of Britain and had never been known to wrestle a tiger in his life – and she was fairly certain that neither Mr Pugh nor Miss Burdon would accept Caesar prudently shooting the predator from the safety of a blind in a tree.

'Shouldn't it be Gaius who wrestles the tiger?' she ventured. 'He is after all the hero.'

'Yeah, but Seth refuses even to be on the set with a live tiger. Even poor old Oswald, who's about thirty years old and has to eat mush because he's only got three teeth left, poor old guy. And anyway Gaius duels Caesar to rescue Miriam, and we've got to show what a mean tough bastard Caesar was, Pugh says. I hope Marsh doesn't hurt Oswald.'

Emma sighed again. 'I shall do my best.'

'I knew we could count on you, Duchess!' Miss Burdon thumped Emma stoutly on the shoulder, gave a jaunty grin and a salute to Zal, and returned to her own table at the other end of the room, where the waitress was just setting out plates of soup, sandwiches, and donuts before the reptilian Herr Volmort from Makeup and two of the ladies from Wardrobe.

'Ain't it great to be counted on?' asked Zal, following the direction of Emma's suddenly-thoughtful gaze.

'*At pulchrum est digito monstrari et dicier, hic est.*' Emma sighed. 'You don't suppose . . .' She turned back as the waitress brought a cup of tea, a small tin pot of hot water and a thick sandwich of meat and cheese whose crusty bread seemed to have been pre-soaked in beef broth. She started again. 'You don't suppose that Herr Volmort – or maybe Millie Katz' – she named the wardrobe mistress – 'would know someone at Enterprise who'd be willing to tell me what scenes from *Broadway Bluebird* were being filmed Saturday, and at what time? Even leaving out the issue of the black costume, Miss Carver was right there on the Ravenstark set within minutes of Nomie finding the body.'

'You could ask,' said Zal, assaulting his dinner like a

starving man. 'Everybody in town pretty much knows every-body else.'

He pushed the tiny pitcher of cream in Emma's direction. 'But it might not prove anything. Divorce or no divorce, Marina kept a pretty sharp eye on Ernst, and she knew Nomie would be on the lot that day. She's a big enough star that she could just tell her director she wanted to take a walk the minute she heard the artillery stop. How far is it, from the shooting stages at Enterprise out to the set?'

'It's one of the things I hope to see Wednesday. I'm sorry to say I didn't notice what sort of shoes Miss Carver had on Saturday, though if she was dressed as a schoolgirl – a schoolgirl in mourning, no less! – they have to have been fairly sensible.'

Zal sighed, and mopped what remained of the bread in the excess gravy. 'Even if you find out,' he pointed out, 'even if you trace the gun they found to Marina's underwear drawer – the police may not care. It sounds to me like Jesperson thinks Marina did it, and he's not going to let The Angel Next Door swing for murder if he can pin it on some poor little jazz baby who he isn't making any money off of. I'm guessing he told them Nomie made threats because she thought Ernst was stalling the divorce – and I'm guessing he's put the word out that nobody's going to mention Marina taking potshots at Ernst while she was drunk at a party, if they ever want to work again. Or anyway they're not going to be called to take the stand.'

Cole's closed at one. In the hard glare of the streetlamps, Sixth Street had the bleak look of a steel engraving. Even the street-cars seemed to have fallen silent. Emma found herself wondering if Kitty would be at the house when Zal dropped her off there, or whether she'd arranged to meet 'Mickey' (or Seth, or Dusty from Paramount, or that handsome young man who worked in Wardrobe . . .) for late-night drinks at some secretive little speakeasy on Marchessault Street. 'I won't ask you in,' she said, as Zal pressed the starter. 'I know you have to film Kitty being arrested for murder at eight, and I'll be on the lot.'

'I look forward to seeing how you explain how that tiger got to England in 54 BC. And to seeing who they get to actually wrestle poor old Oswald. The last stunter who tried it, Oswald fell in love with, and they had to throw a bucket of water over him to remind him he wasn't on his honeymoon. If you stay . . .' There was a note of hesitancy in his voice. 'I mean, if you stay and don't marry Harry Garfield, you're always going to be dealing with studio time and studio demands and one weird thing after another. It won't be like cataloging inscriptions at Oxford.'

'I enjoyed cataloging inscriptions,' Emma said with a sigh. 'It was like fitting together a jigsaw puzzle, only with time and space and the voices of people long gone. But I'm afraid when my name appears on a film in which Julius Caesar saves the life of a Briton slave-girl by wrestling a tiger in the New Forest, I'll be barred from the Bodleian Library for life.'

'Why do you think everybody in Hollywood changes their names?'

She laughed, and the Bearcat pulled away from the curb, keeping neatly to its proper lane despite the fact that, unlike nearly every other car in America, it still had right-hand drive.

And in the empty darkness of the street, Emma could have sworn that for one moment, she saw another car pull out a block behind them.

A car with one headlight.

It turned a corner almost at once, but three times during the drive up Vermont Avenue and thence up into the hills, she glimpsed it again. *Or maybe it's three different cars, all missing one headlight . . .*

But there was no sign of it when Zal steered the little Bearcat down the steep drive and into the blackness of the shaggy lawn before the house on Ivarene Street. The lamp had been left burning on the high porch, and another glowed behind the living-room windows, grateful golden warmth in the dark. Zal walked Emma up the high, tiled steps, and kissed her on the doorstep. No brotherly peck this time, his arms strong around her. Past his shoulder, the steep little street was dark. The high, rounded shoulders of the hills, whispering with the harsh rustle of sagebrush and manzanita, guarded their secrets. And when Emma opened the door, Chang Ming was already on the threshold, plumed tail wagging furiously, eyes bright with welcome and delight.

NINE

'Jealous?' Peggy Donovan's famously mobile eyebrows climbed halfway up her forehead. 'Honey, that's like asking if Calvin Coolidge can keep his mouth shut. You look up "jealous" in the dictionary, and the only reason you won't find Marina Carver's picture there is because it's back in the Cs, under "crazy".'

She glanced in the direction of the throne room, a glaring box of bluish-white light at one end of Stage Two. Velvet curtains swagged back from an immense baldachin – which reminded Emma forcibly of the canopy over the dancefloor at the Café Montmartre – to reveal the royal arms of Montebianco, three white bulls cabosse on a sable field. Beneath this emblem of the de Taureau dynasty, Ollie Withers, a bit-player muffled to the chin in the ermine cloak of Montebiancan royalty, sweated in the glare of the klieg lights on his gilded Biedermeier throne.

Twenty gentlemen-in-waiting, likewise sheathed in satin, lace and powdered wigs, and thirty guardsmen, cinched excruciatingly into form-fitted uniforms, flanked the ersatz monarch, while riggers and gaffers adjusted the kliegs, reflectors, and light-trees, and the new director continued his meticulous consultation with the three cameramen. Zal was right, Emma judged. The towering canopy, the severe velvet cascades of the curtains, gained a gravitas from the shadows that plain daylight would never have given them. 'This is royalty,' proclaimed the chiaroscuro of darkness and rim lights. 'Kneel.'

Satisfied that this symposium had at least another thirty minutes to run, Peggy perched on the edge of one of the trestle tables along the shooting-stage wall, produced a flask from the pocket of her dirndl, dosed her Coca-Cola, and generously offered Emma a drink. Even in the barn-like vastness the heat of the lights was insufferable.

'Watch out for the peanuts, honey,' she advised, nodding toward the small bowl of them nearby. 'They've got cocaine in them.'

'Oh,' said Emma. 'Er . . . thank you.'

Emma had intended to go straight to the issue of Miss Carver's alleged potshots at Desiree Darrow – presumably Peggy had been present on that occasion – but asked instead, 'If Mr Zapolya's *amours* bothered her that much, why on earth did she marry him? According to Kitty, the man was notorious all over Hollywood. She can't have thought she'd change him.'

The actress shrugged. 'No?'

Emma recalled her friend Dennis Boothe back at Oxford. That plumpish, fussily-groomed lecturer at Merton had fallen in love repeatedly, sincerely, and ultimately painfully with a whole succession of unsuitable town girls. More than once he had declared to her, over tea at The Queen's Lane, 'I know she isn't like that, really! All she needs is the love of a good man, a man who understands her . . .'

'She's in love with being in love.' Peggy squirmed herself around so she was sitting tailor-fashion on the table, and sighed. 'So's Kitty, kind of, but Kitty knows that kind of thing wears off in about six weeks. Less, if the guy doesn't brush his teeth. But Marina is always lookin' for The One.'

Emma said, 'Oh,' again. Dennis had married two of those gin-swilling Dulcineas in succession, she recalled, with predictable results. And had gone to his death in Flanders' Fields still believing that he – and they – could be saved if he just loved hard enough.

'And she thinks she's just great enough, just wonderful enough, to make a man change his whole way of life to please her.' Peggy's glance returned to the set. It was one in the afternoon and evidently lunch had not yet been called. The new director – a medium-sized man with close-cropped hair, the stiff carriage of a Prussian aristocrat ('Which he's not,' Zal had informed her), and a grin like a Satanic pixie – had gone over to supervise yet another shift in the place-ment of a baby spot. The stand-in for the King of Montebianco appeared to be about to melt into a royal puddle on the throne.

'She wears people out. She won't let anything go,' Peggy went on. 'Not criticism, not a piece of gossip, not a compliment, not a fight. She'll keep coming back to it and coming back to it until you want to tell her to take a long walk off a short pier. Poor Clive just about had a nervous breakdown when he was married to her. When she wasn't claiming she was pregnant, she was in hysterics, threatening suicide – two or three times a month, sometimes. I remember once they'd had a fight or something, and he got in his car and drove off, he was so mad. She got in her car and drove after him down Franklin Avenue, cut him off in front of the studio, got out of the car, and continued the argument, for another hour and a half on the sidewalk in front of the gates. She's the kind of person who'll call you up at three in the morning with some crisis or other in her life, and how you're the only person she has to talk to. If you hang up, she'll call you back. If you're a man and you hang up, she'll show up on your doorstep fifteen minutes later. She did on Clive's, even after the divorce and he was married to Betsy Colby. She did on Ernst's.'

Emma glanced at yesterday evening's *Herald*, which lay on the trestle table beside the peanuts. The front page displayed a picture of Marina Carver draped in a dead faint across Ernst Zapolya's flower-smothered coffin in the chapel of the Hollywood Memorial Cemetery, her outspread arms embracing the lid. The article in the *Examiner*, which had described the funeral, had related how the bereaved widow's shrieks had stopped the service and 'pierced the hearts of every person present'. Emma could not help noting that in the *Herald* picture, the lid of the coffin was closed. In the *Examiner's* headline photo, the lid was open, and Miss Carver's unconscious body lay in a different position. Presumably she had fainted twice.

'Fainted my ass,' Kitty had sniffed, viewing the picture over breakfast that morning. 'People don't fall like that when they faint. Their legs go every which-way and if you're a girl, your skirt rides up.'

'He whispered my name,' Miss Carver had cried when revived (said the *Examiner*). 'I heard him, as clearly as I hear your voices now!'

The *Examiner* had further described how Miss Carver had been so prostrated by grief as to need the services of a physician and a nurse.

'Did she really shoot at Mr Zapolya and Miss Darrow?'

'Oh, shit, yeah. She's got about six handguns – Ernst said it was six, but I'll bet there was more of them that he didn't know about. When she first came to town – she was an extra over at Lasky in '17, though she swears that wasn't her – a bootlegger she was seeing went crazy over *her* and broke into her apartment one night and threatened to kill her because she dumped him. After that she carried a purse-gun. She has about three of them hidden in her dressing room. Poor Clive used to go through the house the day before they'd throw a party, unloading all of them.'

'Why did Mr Zapolya marry her?'

'Oh, Ernst was nuts too. He was passionate – and impatient. That's why his films had that energy. Things gotta be taken care of *now*, and they're all that matters *now*.' She grabbed Emma by the arms and shoved her face almost into hers, her eyes, and her mouth, taking on for an eerie second the appearance of Ernst Zapolya's; the same lunatic intensity Emma had seen in his face, when he'd been setting up his extras for the simulated carnage in the Ravenstark town square.

'Like that.' And she was Peggy again. 'I don't think he thought for a minute what it would be like to be married to somebody like that.'

'Oh, dear.' Emma wondered briefly if the Greek hero Jason had considered what it would be like to be married to a woman who'd think it reasonable to chop up her younger brother so that pursuit would be delayed while her father picked up the pieces.

'Yeah.' Her hostess nodded and munched thoughtfully on a peanut. '*Oh dear* big time. So when he starts seeing this mystery woman—'

'You mean Nomie Carlyle?'

'Oh, hell, no.' She dismissed the younger girl with a wave. Behind her, Mr von Stroheim was now demonstrating to the guards the proper way of stopping and turning at the end of their march-in. 'Everybody knows about Nomie. She's been in more laps in this town than a napkin.'

Emma recalled the number of Peggy's lovers and carefully assumed an expression of well-bred interest, like Cleopatra listening to yet another of Antony's tales of his own heroism with a straight face.

'No, there was some other woman that he never talked about. Not a whisper. *That's* what drove Marina crazy. That he was seeing somebody more important than her – so important that he couldn't breathe a word about who it was.'

'Sharply! Turn with the whole of the body! My captain in the Imperial Guard would have you flogged fifty lashes for a turn like that, and I will too! Go back again . . .'

'See, Marina could look down her nose at other girls at the studio, and make snide cracks about them, because she knew she was the star. If things got too serious, she'd just get Jesperson to can 'em. This other woman . . . Thank God!' she added, as the glaring lights by the throne snapped down and the whole corps of courtiers and guards retreated behind the curtains. Mike Nye scurried to the little circle of folding chairs where Guy Jeffries – the true king of Montebianco – his heir, and the plucky American female journalist with whom Prince Stephan had fallen in love were playing pinochle, then darted towards Peggy.

In the shadows at the other end of Stage Two, the rest of the delegation of peasants – due to be insulted by His Majesty and defended by the plucky American female journalist – got wearily to their feet. The slate lying on the other end of the trestle table was chalked, TAKE 27.

No wonder the peanuts seem appealing.

'*Broadway Bluebird*'s filming over on Stage One.' Peggy twitched the wrinkles from her brightly embroidered skirt. 'Marina's probably over in her dressing room.'

So much for being prostrated by grief. Emma wondered if the widow had a physician and nurse in attendance on the set.

'It's next to mine, that barracks behind Stage One . . .'

And she hurried away, to join her peasant followers who were already being instructed – with illustrative pantomime – on the proper way to cringe.

Emma sat still for a moment, trying again not to remember that letter from the colonel of the 9th Infantry. She recalled she'd been due on shift with the Volunteer Ambulance Corps, driving the survivors of the fighting from the Oxford train station to the hospital, and she'd gone.

It isn't for me to judge. Work may be her way of healing, as it was for me.

She doubted she would have fainted (or pretended to faint) for newspaper cameras, though. Much less twice.

Finishing her soft drink, she paused in the stage's curtained doorway only long enough to orient herself. As Peggy had said, the dressing rooms of the 'featured players' could be glimpsed beyond the open framework of Stage One, a walk of about two minutes from where she stood. The back lot lay in the opposite direction. Emma glanced at her watch, checked that she had Zal's note in her skirt pocket, and set off for the ruins of Ravenstark.

It took her slightly over eight minutes to reach that end of the back lot. The tents still stood; one crane hovered over the broken pavements and the remains of the fountain. But work had clearly been done yesterday. The shards of plaster, brick and framing were gone from the front portion of the square, and someone had taken down the wrecked remains of the balcony. Ladders stood against the palace wall. Stocks of fresh lumber cluttered the area below, and tire-tracks crisscrossed the dust.

Good heavens, are they going to re-build the entire set for re-takes? She'd been around the studios long enough to guess what that would cost, and bethought herself again of Mr von Stroheim's reputation for maniacal accuracy.

No one, however, was here today. Crows flapped into the high, gray sky at Emma's approach; what looked like a weasel fled, gripping the discarded heel of somebody's sandwich in its jaws.

Plaster fragments, torn-up dirt, broken hunks of paving still strewed the ground in front of the palace, the quaint brick houses, and the cathedral's mighty parvis. Emma picked her way between the building supplies before the palace doors, up the marble steps, and through the gilded portal, re-tracing

Nomie's route. There was a sort of vestibule behind the doors
– presumably to keep a shot from being spoiled if a camera
happened to be lined up when they were opened. But beyond
that lay only a maze of framing – such as she had glimpsed
through the cathedral's doors on Saturday – that supported the
palace's front wall.

A wooden stairway ascended to the canvas-and-framing
vestibule behind the balcony's French windows. Light trees,
reflectors of various sizes, and boxes of clamps stood in the
shelter of the wall as if seeking shade there; nearby lay a stack
of sections of track, and a broad, low cart for moving the
camera. Emma followed the wall to her right, noting where
another small tent had been pitched, its rolled-up sides showing
it empty save for a couple of picnic tables. For the gaffers and
riggers, between shots? The set wall curved, and around the
corner she saw the rear of the cathedral set, larger and deeper
than the flat-fronted palace, the supports for its towers and
roof like tumbled jackstraws overhead. It was like being inside
an impossibly vast, ruined barn.

Because of the depth of the entryway, a section of the
portico set extended back, as if a huge box had been erected
behind the main wall of the cathedral front. Behind that extension the damage from the nearby explosion lay untouched,
plaster fragments, broken bits of scaffold, splashes of sunlight
where pieces of wall had been blown out. There was one such
about ten feet beyond – and just above – the cathedral doors;
two others, where the wall of the main set continued towards
the platform where one of the camera cranes reared into the
jumble of tower framing. The explosion that had jammed the
cathedral door tight had, she saw now, warped and skewed
the framing of the set itself. Someone had opened the great
door to take Zapolya's body out (they'd still been filming
Scene 704, presumably), but the aperture was barely eighteen
inches. With all her strength she couldn't push it further
against the pressure of the damaged frame. The killer, she
thought, must have shot the director and emerged just as
Nomie came around the corner.

*Did she see her? Was the black figure I glimpsed the killer,
or Nomie herself? Had the killer dodged behind the farther*

*corner of the set extension, waited till Nomie went through
the door, then slammed it – maybe braced it somehow? – and
fled? If the gun was found a few yards beyond the door –
probably just under that hole in the wall – that would have
meant the mysterious Lady in Black would be fleeing towards
the explosion that jammed the door . . .*

Walking a little further on to look at the camera crane
platform, Emma stopped in her tracks at the sight of the
damage there: broken supports, flooring tilted, the maze of
two-by-fours, plaster and canvas overhead leaning perilously,
ready to drop. *Did that cameraman really continue cranking
the film through the gate, as the boards moved under him,
thirty feet above a concrete base with hundreds of pounds of
construction framing twisting uneasily above his head?*

Another explosion would have precipitated the whole
avalanche.

Zal . . . She remembered his words about Zapolya's carelessness about his extras and crew. Remembered, too, that Zapolya
wasn't the only one who put getting the shot above the safety
of those who did the actual getting.

And then she thought again: *Zal.*

*I wonder if there's any way Zal could have a look at the
raw footage of the scene? That way we'd know exactly how
much time elapsed . . .*

She backed cautiously away from the deadly house of
cards, looked over her shoulder again at the corner where
the set curved around from the palace. From the cathedral
door *someone* could have seen a slight, blonde-haired girl
emerge around that corner, hurrying in terror of the explosions or in concern about how much time she was going to
have to speak to her lover. And that *someone* could retreat,
around the far corner of the extension, until Nomie went
through the door . . .

*How long between the time Nomie went through the palace
doors, until she came to those of the cathedral? And from
there, how long until the explosion that jammed the door? It
was filmed from all three directions . . .*

Once Nomie was through the door, the killer could have
returned, closed the door on her, and gone straight back, away

from the set and the explosions, rather than following the set wall toward the camera crane. *It would make more sense . . .*

But when Emma followed that possible route of retreat, she found that anything that could have been interpreted as a woman's track had been well and truly obliterated by the comings and goings of the clean-up crew loading up the reflectors themselves to take them back to storage in the studio shops. Nor had the killer conveniently dropped anything: handkerchief, monogrammed pen, lipstick tube (*Remember, Watson, no one in the studio wears Djer Kiss but Madame X!*), incriminating note luring Mr Zapolya into the cathedral set . . .

Except, of course, those gloves . . .

Following the wall of the set away from the cathedral extension – and making a wary detour around the damaged crane platform and the framing nearest it – Emma found much the same situation. Everyone in the studio, it seemed, had been over this ground, sagging crane platform notwithstanding. If the mysterious Woman in Black had passed this way – either coming or going – her tracks had been eradicated, and neither the studio nor, it appeared, the Los Angeles Police Department had seen any reason to pursue the matter.

They had their culprit.

It was fortunate indeed, then, that when Emma returned to the Enterprise Studios commissary – to find that lunch had only just been called (it was now four in the afternoon) – the first thing that Peggy Donovan told her was that Mr von Stroheim had declared that none of the ballroom footage shot by his predecessor was usable because no pre-war European royalty would wear such gowns, and the ballroom set itself resembled a cheap nightclub.

It would all have to be re-shot.

So, she reflected, at least they had plenty of time.

TEN

'Is there a chance you can get a look at the footage of the battle?' asked Emma, later that evening, as she carried two magazines of exposed film along Foremost's glaringly-lit studio street to the film building. 'So we can see how much time actually elapsed between Miss Carlyle going through the palace door, and the explosion that jammed the cathedral door shut after Miss Carlyle found the body? And goodness knows what else might have been caught on film, depending on which way the killer actually left the area behind the set.'

'It's a thought,' Zal agreed. He led the way through the vestibule of the film building, and into the film room itself, where a half-dozen of the black, double-circle aluminum magazines had already been stowed on the rack labelled H.P. – 05-07-24, with scene and take numbers chalked on to their sides. 'John Benson would probably let me into the Enterprise film warehouse – we could sneak in through the back lot and meet him. With a shot that expensive you can bet Jesperson can't get rid of it.'

'Get rid of it?' She looked up, startled, from sorting out the shot notes.

Zal shrugged. 'If it does show Marina Carver lurking somewhere around the set, you can bet *that* footage is gonna end up on the cutting-room floor. But he can't just ditch the whole reel. The last thing Jesperson – or anybody in Hollywood – needs is the Hearst papers getting hold of yet another big-name star involved in lethal shenanigans.'

He collected his jacket from the back of a chair and locked the door of the film room, then the building itself, behind them. 'Personally, I'd like to have a look at the *Broadway Bluebird* dailies from that morning as well. It'd tell us what time Marina was actually in front of the camera. You clock yourself from the back lot?'

'Eight minutes,' provided Emma. 'If she started as soon as the shooting began . . .'

'Or as soon as it ended.' Zal handed her into the Bearcat, again parked behind the Makeup and Costume shops. 'But it won't hurt to have a look.' He guided the little car carefully across the quadrangle between Stage Two and the Hacienda, halting by the arcade that shaded the fronts of the star dressing rooms. Lights still burned, not only in Kitty's, but in those of Nick Thaxter and Harry Garfield on the second floor, where the impassioned 'Buddy Livermore' and his disapproving father – after the quarrel that preceded the older man's murder – were cold-creaming off the layers of Motion Picture Orange and powder preparatory to going and having a drink together at the Hotel Christie bar.

Kitty's voice chirped at them as they crossed to her door. '*Absolutely*, darling! And you know it's going to be at *least* another week while he gets the set re-built! Not to mention how long it takes to build a gondola . . .'

Telephone, Emma deduced.

'. . . insisted that the franc notes in the casino scene be actually photoengraved, and he and the engravers all ended up being arrested as counterfeiters . . . and I don't know *how* much they spent on building entire *streets and casinos* from Monte Carlo up in Monterey . . .'

Kitty, still in her film makeup and draped in a shimmering kimono of peacock-hued silk, half-turned from the telephone, pressed the mouthpiece to her chest, and explained in a whisper, 'It's Nomie, darlings! She's going to meet us at the Coconut Grove for dinner . . .'

Zal knelt to ruffle Chang Ming's fur as the little dog rolled at his feet with a blissful idiot grin.

'No, sweetheart, we'll be there in just a few minutes. I'm just getting ready to go out the door. Nick took just for*ever* to get the shot right . . .'

Emma went to Buttercreme's wicker carry box – from which the tiny empress had to be dragged forth bodily – leashed all three Pekes, and led them outside for a final inspection of the straggly beds of verbena and penstemon that grew along the edge of the dressing-room wing, preparatory, she assumed, to an evening spent at the Coconut Grove. The management of that establishment had in the past admitted not only Camille de la Rose's well-mannered little lapdogs, but John Barrymore's pet monkey, a cheetah owned by Pola Negri, and any number of Mack Sennett's Bathing Beauties.

'Duchess!' Footfalls scuffed the gravel of the path, and the light falling from Harry's dressing room above showed Madge Burdon's sturdy form striding out of the darkness, a folded mass of notes in hand. 'You got a second, honey? I was afraid I wouldn't catch you. Hi, lover boy,' she added, bending to pat first Chang Ming, then Black Jasmine. 'You haven't finished the chase scene, have you? Pugh says it's got to be changed. Blue Walsh – the stunter who was going to double Darlene – got thrown over at Mixville this afternoon and broke his shoulder and his leg in two places, and now Darlene swears she won't get on a horse even for the close shots. Pugh says, can we have her trapped in a canoe being swept downstream, so Seth can gallop along the bank and jump in and save her—'

They didn't have canoes in ancient Britain. Emma knew better than to object.

'Oh, and can you switch Seth back to being a Christian? Fishy' – Conrad Fishbein was the studio publicity chief – 'says nobody knows who the Pithatarians' – *Pythagoreans* – 'were and nobody cares, and we're going after the Sunday School market here.'

'Julius Caesar died thirty years before Jesus Christ was born,' Emma pointed out.

'No kidding?' The director looked surprised. 'I'll tell Fishy that, but I bet he's going to ask you to change it anyway. I mean, how many people know when Julius Caesar died? Yeah?' She turned as someone called to her from across the quadrangle, then looked back, and gripped Emma's hand.

'Do what you can, honey. Give it the Little Eva touch, you know. The damsel in peril . . .'

And she dashed off towards the little knot of assistants

beside Stage Two – 'I'm coming, goddammit, hold your
bladder' – leaving Emma to wonder where in Britain one
would encounter either an onrushing river or one frozen over.

'Oh, darling, *thank* you!' cooed Kitty, when Emma returned
to the dressing room, to find her rubbing cold cream on to her
face. 'Would you take my little cream cakes along and meet
Nomie at the Grove? I'll be there in just a few minutes, but
she's there already. Her scenes today were canceled, because
Von says they'll have to re-shoot because Bruce doesn't have
the right kind of medals on his uniform, or something . . .
Zallie, you can take Emma to the Grove, can't you? Tell them
to charge my account.'

Meaning, Emma knew, the studio's.

Zal bowed over Kitty's hand. 'Who am I to turn down a
free steak?'

'Thank you!' Nomie Carlyle's voice was barely a whisper, but
almost shook with emotion, as Zal and Emma edged their
way among the gilt tables, Moorish pillars and papier-mâché
palm trees to the table in the box that Frank Brown kept
permanently reserved for Kitty.

'Kitty'll be along in a minute,' reported Zal, taking the
leashes of the three Pekes and holding a chair for Emma. 'She
was taking off her makeup as we left the studio—'

The girl's distress vanished and she giggled, then said, 'Oh,
the little darlings!' and bent to pat Chang Ming and Black
Jasmine, Buttercreme having vanished at once to the most
sheltered position beneath the table. 'They're saying now it'll
be a week before we start shooting the Isle of Love scenes,
and it sounds like another couple of weeks—'

'With von Stroheim behind the camera,' prophesied Zal,
'it'll be a couple of *months*. Plenty of time. And that's not
counting re-takes.'

'It would take Miss Carver eight minutes to walk from her
dressing room to the Ravenstark set,' reported Emma. 'If we
can find a way to see the dailies of *Broadway Bluebird* – what
on Earth was she doing dressed as a schoolgirl in mourning,
anyway? – we might get some idea of whether she had time
to get to the set.'

'Oh, I asked Gina Zink about that,' said Nomie. 'Marina's stand-in. She says Marina claimed a headache and retired to her dressing room at twelve thirty. But when Tommy Chalmers came running with the news that . . .' Her voice faltered.

Then she drew a deep breath and went on, 'Tommy says he met Marina on the path between the set and the dressing room.'

'And I suppose she'll faint again if anybody asks her why she decided to set off for Ravenstark before the shooting stopped.' Zal sipped his beer.

'Her mother said Marina had a premonition of doom,' Nomie reported. 'Her mother was on the *Bluebird* set most of the morning. She left Los Angeles Saturday night . . .'

'I wondered why I didn't see pictures of her at the funeral.'

'She left her daughter "prostrated by grief"?' asked Emma, startled. 'The night her daughter's husband was murdered?'

Nomie shook her head, and Zal said, 'I've heard a rumor – which might or might not be true – that Mama Carver – whose real name is Eggwall, by the way – is trying to round up European backers to form her own film company. She may have snuck off to meet them. It's something she isn't likely to want Jesperson to know, and from everything I've heard of the lady, she'd leave her daughter dying of grief on the kitchen floor rather than pass up a meeting with backers.'

Emma looked inquiringly at Nomie, who only shook her head again. 'Her mother lived with Marina,' she added. 'At least she did, when Marina was married to Marsh Sloane, and then to Clive April. Ernst refused to have her live with him and Marina.'

'Marina got the old bat a place up on Normandie Avenue,' remarked Zal. 'And a car and chauffeur, to bring her to Enterprise every day.'

'She hated Ernst' – again Nomie's voice faltered on the name – 'like poison; an awful woman.'

Then she looked from Emma's face to Zal's raised eyebrows, and added firmly, '*No.* The woman I saw wasn't her. She walks with a cane, for one thing. For another, she always dresses –' she made swirly gestures with her hands

– 'like Elinor Glyn, except it's always in "native fabrics" and Mexican embroideries and silk harem trousers. She makes all her clothes herself.'

'You know if she was dressed that way Saturday?'

'I wasn't on that part of the lot.' The girl's cheeks flushed a duskier hue under rice-powder and Indian Rose. 'I stay away from Marina as much as I can. And her mom.' Whatever Peggy might have said about Mrs Zapolya's scorn for rivals lesser than herself, Emma read fear in Nomie's eyes. 'Her mom was always telling the fan magazines things about me – about any woman Ernst . . .' Again the break in her words, the averted eyes.

'I'm sure that's why Ernst asked to see me on the set,' she went on after a moment. 'So she wouldn't follow him and make a scene about the divorce.'

Emma recalled what Peggy had told her about Marina Carver's fondness for 'scenes'. 'But I thought she wanted the divorce.'

'Well, she did . . . sometimes. Her mother egged her into filing, see. And sometimes Marina was all for it because Ernst . . . well, Ernst . . .'

The strand of Kitty's pearls, retrieved from a corner of Zapolya's office, returned to mind.

'Other times . . .'

'The woman you saw,' Emma said. 'How was she dressed? In black, you said. Was she tall? Short? Fat?'

Nomie widened her dark eyes. 'Oh, there aren't any fat people on the Enterprise lot. Mr Jesperson thinks nobody's going to pay money to see a fat person on screen.'

Zal sighed grimly, and remarked, 'Not anymore, anyway. What kind of clothes?'

'I don't . . .' Nomie gestured helplessly. Her own frock – silk, expensive and cut to display her slim charms – had a mourning note to it, dark blue spangled with black and gold. Marina Carver's, Emma recalled from the newspaper photographs of the funeral, had included black veils that hadn't obscured a single detail of her face or form.

'I really can't remember. I only saw her from a distance, and to tell you the truth, I was too scared to take much notice.

I know the sharpshooters fire over peoples' heads, or into the ground, but those set walls aren't very sturdy.'

Emma shivered, recalling the maze of framing, guy ropes, partitions behind the set. She'd only seen the carnage from the safety behind the gunners and the camera. With only the flimsy walls of plaster and canvas to protect her from the gunfire and explosions, it was no wonder the girl's memory of all that long distance behind the palace set was unclear.

'Was he going to give you money?'

Nomie looked genuinely startled. '*Money*? No, I – Ernst didn't . . . didn't give out money to . . . He said love had to be free. That money destroyed it.'

Zal carefully refrained from rolling his eyes.

'And you didn't happen to hear,' Emma went on, 'any studio rumors about Mr Zapolya having an *affaire* with someone else, did you? Someone important? Someone whose name couldn't be bandied around?'

Nomie looked away again. On the dancefloor beyond her, Emma glimpsed the bootlegger Jake Ricelli and his long-stemmed brunette beauty; saw how the girl's discontented gaze followed the wide-shouldered form of a minor Paramount contract player swaying the dazzling Mae Murray in his arms.

'I was afraid,' Nomie murmured at last. 'Afraid that was the reason he asked to see me so secretly. Because he wanted to . . . to tell me that he wasn't going to see me again. Not because of Marina. But because of . . . *her*. Whoever she is. And I . . . I couldn't just let that happen. Not without . . . Well, I wanted to ask him not to send me away. My contract is only for a year, and . . .'

She glanced first at Emma, then at Zal, then down at her gin fizz again. Emma sipped her wine, and thought of all the would-be stars who came flocking to Hollywood every year, desperate to work their way up through the ranks of extras to 'bit players' and then to featured players. Who inhabited every boarding house and cheap hotel and shabby courtyard apartment between Glendale and the sea. Who waited tables or cleaned houses or worked on charter boats, only to pay their rent – and did other things besides. Who believed directors

and casting directors and producers and stars who said that
love had to be free . . .

The music ended. Ricelli pushed his diamond-studded
partner back toward their table and crossed the floor to join a
couple of grim-eyed men seated on the other side of the dance
floor. The girl's eyes followed the Paramount player from the
room.

'I really did care for him,' added Nomie defensively, still
not looking up, as waiters brought artichoke cocktails and
consommé Andalouse.

'Could that be what that seven thousand dollars was for?'
asked Emma, as the Bearcat pulled once more out of the
Ambassador's stylish entryway and into the thinning traffic
on Wilshire Boulevard. 'It seems an awful lot for what sounds
to me like . . . Well, if not precisely a casual affair . . .'

'You can get an abortion in Chinatown for under twenty-five
dollars,' said Zal grimly. 'I doubt Nomie's paying as much as
nine dollars a week for rent. So yeah – I can't see Zapolya
giving her seven grand, even if he was trying to talk Jesperson
into giving the girl a feature contract – which he may not have
been. She's beautiful, but she couldn't . . .' He fished for a
simile. 'She couldn't out-act Kitty.'

'Oh, dear. That bad?'

'I'd be surprised if she was getting more than a hundred
and a quarter a week, and a one-year contract isn't what you
give somebody you expect to be in your life for very long.
Not seven thousand dollars' worth.'

The lights of Los Angeles fell behind them as they turned
on to Western Avenue, toward the hills. Westward, the oil fields
lay, a sprinkle of pinpricks and the musty stink of the pumps
in the blackness. 'Nomie Carlyle's spent the past four years
doing whatever she feels she needs to do, to stay in pictures,
and the fact remains she hasn't managed to be more than an
extra. She just didn't have Kitty's good luck in finding a sugar
daddy like Frank. God knows she tried. A girl that young
doesn't have a lot of choice if she wants to stay in pictures,
but from what I've heard there isn't a producer or a casting
director in town she hasn't had a pull at.'

In the silence as he thought again of that pretty, fair-haired girl they'd put into a cab outside the Ambassador, one of the dogs wuffed sleepily in his box, pursuing elk or dragons in his tiny dreams.

'She put in time as one of Sennett's Bathing Beauties,' went on Zal, 'with all *that* entails. She was fourteen then . . . she claimed sixteen, but nobody was fooled. I think she had a try at Chaplin, but he was just getting out of one marriage and tangled up with another engagement, and,' he added, with a trace of sadness in his voice, 'she may have been kind of obvious about what she was after by then.'

'She had no parents? No one to . . . to look out for her?'

'Lot of 'em don't.' The headlamp of a car behind them caught the edge of his glasses as he moved his head. 'They follow the rainbow to LA, like I did, like Kitty did . . . Everybody comes to Hollywood from someplace else. The lucky ones have someplace to go back to. You'll never meet so many orphans and strangers in one place again in your life.'

They passed an adobe church, a streetlamp illuminating a sign written in both Chinese and other odd characters that Zal had told her once were Korean. *Orphans and strangers indeed . . .*

He finished grimly, 'And it might not have done her any good if she had.'

Emma considered some of the things she'd heard of the parents of child stars: blithe acceptance of life-threatening stunts, extravagant new houses in Beverly Hills bought on the expectation of future earnings. To say nothing of the very odd circumstance of leaving Los Angeles the night of their son-in-law's murder . . .

Hare-brained investments, handsome 'financial advisors' and shouting matches with producers. 'You'll have to tell the truth,' Kitty had said, with sadness in her voice . . .

She turned her head, as the lights of Hollywood glimmered before them, along the feet of the hills . . .

And saw, in the dark of Western Avenue behind them, the bulk of a car with a single headlamp.

ELEVEN

'Well,' said Zal reasonably, 'let's find out.' From Western he turned on to Franklin, but instead of proceeding along to Ivarene and Kitty's Moorish paradise – Kitty had finally arrived at the Grove at ten thirty on Seth Ramsay's muscular arm and had barely waved at their table – he turned north again into the dark of the hills themselves.

The single headlight followed.

'What on *earth* . . .?'

'Howie ever talk about anybody following him?' asked Zal.

Emma shook her head. 'Even the most rabid columnist wouldn't . . . And they'd be following *him*, not me. I've met Roger Clint, and he said he'd buy me a corsage the next time Howie takes me out . . .'

'Oh, hell, Roger wouldn't hire a detective to shadow you. Or stay up til all hours – he's working on *North of Thirty-Six* for Famous Players, he has to be in the saddle at seven. Again, besides . . . *Why*? If he thought Howie and you were making nookie, he'd ask you. Or Howie.'

He turned on to another road, this one unpaved and steep, winding back into the hills. In 1896, a man named – of all things – Griffith J. Griffith (*One would almost suspect his parents of watching too many movies!*) had donated over three thousand acres of these rugged California hills to the city of Los Angeles. *California as it once was*, thought Emma. Sagebrush, gullies, caves, and rock formations where former cowboys robbed the stagecoaches from Lasky and National and FBO, cloaked now in silver-blue moonlight.

And undoubtedly generations of children will go to their graves thinking that this is what Central Europe looks like – and China, and the first-century Holy Land, as well as Roman Italy, the entire United States from Maine to the Pacific, Russia, and Scotland.

More than once, loading dog boxes and astrology magazines into the Packard in the stillness of pre-dawn, she'd seen coyotes from these hills exploring the upper reaches of Ivarene Place, or lines of neatly-marshaled quail scurrying down the pavement. On one occasion she'd seen deer.

Zal glanced at the side mirror and swore.

'*You* don't have a secret wife somewhere . . .'

'I killed the last one,' Zal confessed, shamefaced. 'And the one before her is still sending me money to stay away.'

'How much?'

'Two fifty a month. More than I make at Foremost.' He turned up yet another trail, tires scraping at the rocks. 'And if we get a flat out here I'm gonna track those bastards down if it's the last thing I do.' He switched off the engine and the lights, hopped out of the car and came swiftly around to help Emma down. Holding her hand, he scrambled up the small embankment above the trail, and into the blackness of spice-smelling brush.

Darkness like indigo velvet. Stars down to the hilltops, as if they were at sea.

The faint ticking of the engine as it cooled.

After a long while, a car passed the end of the trail and continued – innocently – on up into the hills.

Zal whispered, 'Who, me?'

He helped her down the slope again, her shoes skidding in the loose dirt.

'Here.' He handed her a clean white handkerchief, one of the half-dozen he habitually carried to keep his camera lenses – and glasses – spotless. 'You go down to the bottom of the trail – carefully, stay on this side of the trail and don't let yourself be seen from up the road – and look out and see if you can see anything. There's not a lot of moonlight, so you may not. But if it looks clear, hold up the hankie. I'm gonna be backing down without lights.'

She whispered, 'All right.'

'I don't know who these people are,' he went on softly. 'Or what's up. But they can't possibly be mistaking you for Kitty, and the only thing I can think of is that it's something to do with whatever Ernst Zapolya needed to tell Kitty. Something that maybe they think he told you, too. Maybe seven thousand dollars worth of something.'

'Kitty hasn't mentioned anyone following her.'

'Kitty gets followed all the time,' said Zal. 'Fans, photo-rag writers, photographers . . . If she saw a car full of guys in black cloaks and slouch hats all waiting for her outside her dressing room she wouldn't think a thing about it. Or she'd figure it was some PI Frank's wife hired. Or the wife of God knows who. If I know Kitty, she'd send 'em out coffee on a cold night, and end up going dancing at the Biltmore with the best-looking one.'

Emma giggled ruefully. 'I'm afraid you're right.'

'But I think,' he added, 'we'd better warn Nomie to watch her back as well. At least until we figure out what's actually going on.'

No mysterious dark vehicle lurked where Emma could spot it by the thin moonlight. No shadow followed them home. 'Doesn't mean they aren't back there someplace,' said Zal, as he steered the Bearcat carefully down the rutted gravel toward Beechwood Drive again, and thence to Franklin. 'They've got to know where you live by this time, if they've been following you since Monday night. Now they know you know they're there, I doubt you're going to see them again.'

'Driving in the dark hills will certainly have alerted them that they're missing a headlamp.' Emma turned to look over her shoulder for the dozenth time as they turned from Franklin up the steep hill of Ivarene. 'If they're smart. They may not be.'

Zal spent the night, and presumably had breakfast with Kitty at some point early the following morning; Emma half-woke to the sound of their voices, dimly in the pre-sunrise darkness of downstairs. She only had time to wonder whether that was Kitty just coming in, before falling asleep again. *Oh, good, I don't have to bring her a clean frock at the studio . . .*

Kitty, she knew, would be filming the notorious (and apparently obligatory) bath-tub scene (Frank Pugh had insisted on its inclusion in the *Hot Potato* scenario) that day ('And Larry better not ask for more than two takes! I don't want to come out of there looking like a prune!'), on a closed set. So her day was free.

When she came down at seven it was to find two breakfast plates and two coffee cups neatly washed in the dish-rack, and a note in Zal's block print that said, 'Dogs fed', notwithstanding the famished insistence of Chang Ming and Black Jasmine to the contrary.

Emma thought about the events of last night as she washed, got dressed, and brushed the dogs. 'They know you know they're there,' Zal had said.

She sat for a time over her second cup of tea, turning in her mind the fact that whoever these people were, they'd known since Monday night where she lived, during which time she'd slept in the house alone twice – and obliquely wondering how the virtuous Miriam ended up in a runaway canoe in the first place. After a time she went to the telephone in the hall, dialed first the Sixth Division police station down on Cahuenga Boulevard, and then the number Nomie Carlyle had given her the previous night.

The man who answered said that Miss Carlyle would be in probably around two, and gave the address, on Third Street. And yes, he'd leave a message for her.

Thanking him, Emma rang off, then went into the living room and collected the most recent issues of *Photo Play, Screen Stories,* and *Motion Picture News* – all of which carried pictures of herself being kissed by Harry Garfield on the sidewalk outside the Café Montmartre. These she stowed in her satchel. In the *Screen Stories* photo, over her shoulder she could see the girl in yellow silk, holding hands at the back of the crowd with the unfortunate young stockbroker who would be dead the following evening.

What had Peggy said? A bootlegger Marina Carver was seeing went crazy over her . . .

She shook her head, conscientiously walked the dogs, then set off down the hill to catch the streetcar for Hollywood Boulevard.

The Hollywood division of the LAPD shared quarters on Cahuenga Boulevard with the local fire station. A few months previously – when one of Kitty's early ex-husbands had turned up dead – Emma had formed a good opinion of Detective Avram Meyer, though she remained mindful of Zal's strictures about how far any of the city's police force could be trusted. *Auram lex sequitur*, the Roman poet Propertius had said (*And he really* was *around at the same time as Julius Caesar!*). 'Gold bends the law.'

So this isn't exactly a new problem.

Still, she reasoned, even if whoever was following her was paying off the police, by this time the police, however corrupt, would have gotten the message that she knew about that part of the scheme, anyway – whatever the scheme was.

If there is *a scheme.*

Did this kind of thing go on at Oxford and I just not know it?

Emma gave her name to the sergeant at the desk, then took her seat on a bench at one side of the room. On a small table beside the bench, several newspapers lay folded. Picking up the top one and turning it over, Emma perused the latest speculations: that someone had seen Clive April meeting a mysterious woman in black at Chasen's drugstore Friday evening. That Clive April's wife had been infected with 'a shameful disease' by Ernst Zapolya. That a young man who resembled Zapolya's former chauffeur had been seen lurking around the Ravenstark set Saturday morning . . .

Nothing about Marina Carver's mysteriously absent mother, I notice . . .

'Mrs Blackstone.' Detective Meyer came out into the station watch room, and half-bowed her into an office easily the size of the pantry cupboard in the Shangs' cottage, a stocky, stubby, balding man whose neat Van Dyke beard was carefully dyed black, complete with symmetrical flashes of white at the corners of his mouth, such as the villains of two-reeler melodramas customarily sported. His dark eyes held a fleeting hint of a smile. 'I hope all is well at Foremost Productions?'

'It is, yes, thank you.' She took the chair he held for her. 'But there's something curious going on, and rather than wait about wondering if the situation is actually dangerous or not, I thought I'd save us both time and speak to you.'

His head tilted slightly. 'Three-quarters of the time, strange situations turn out to be nothing, ma'am. In this town, in your position, you're wise to check.' He sat behind his desk, piled high with papers, yet scrupulously neat. She wondered if, like the directors at Enterprise, he had to share a secretary with every other detective in the building.

Or is he the only one?

Surely not, with all the money there is in Hollywood . . .

'I'm being followed,' she said. Wincing a little, she brought out the screen magazines and opened them on the desk. *Diamonds or not, I definitely will never marry that man . . .*

'I've been asked by the studio publicity department to be seen at the local nightspots with Mr Harry Garfield—'

She glanced at him, a little self-consciously, wondering how much he knew about Harry Garfield and why the studio publicity department would ask such a thing of him. But he only nodded.

'You're far from the only one, ma'am. That's probably not much consolation.'

'It actually is,' she admitted. 'The thing is, I've been followed in circumstances that I should think would be of little interest to a photo-play magazine. Last night after dinner with my *actual* gentleman friend, for instance.' And she related the events of the drive into the hills. 'Last Saturday, my employer and I – Miss Camille de la Rose' – he nodded again – 'went to Enterprise Studios to keep an appointment with the director Mr Zapolya, because he said he had something important to tell her . . .'

The dark eyes narrowed sharply.

'Unfortunately, he had to be on the set that morning – Miss de la Rose was late keeping the appointment, and we didn't have the chance to speak to him. And that was the day he was killed.'

For a moment his little rosebud mouth parted as if to speak, then closed again.

'I know he was supposed to have been shot by one of the contract players in the picture,' she went on carefully, and again, she saw the movement of thoughts at the back of those bright, squirrel-black eyes. 'But it was only after Monday that this following started. So I don't know what to think.'

'And he didn't say what this . . . important *something* was?'

She shook her head. 'He did say – he spoke to me on the telephone early that morning, trying to reach Miss de la Rose – that it wasn't "some Hollywood intrigue".' It was on the tip of her tongue to add his words about lives being at stake, but the recollection of everything she had heard about the Los Angeles police – how much they charged per crate to let illegal whiskey be unloaded and trucked to nightclubs all over town, not to speak of the going rate to let brothels and Chinatown opium dens remain in operation – caused her to let out her breath unused.

Auro venalia jura . . .

'You believe him?'

'It wasn't my business,' she returned. 'I know he and Miss de la Rose were . . . were intimate at one time.' *The man would know that if he read even a tenth of the fan magazines . . .*

Again the sense that he was about to say one thing, then changed his mind and asked instead, 'You were on the set that day, weren't you? Could you tell me about that?'

She refrained from commenting that it was about time someone from the police got around to interviewing witnesses. Possibly the case was being handled by other detectives than he. A little carefully, she described her arrival, with Kitty, in the deep portico of the Ravenstark cathedral, the slim black figure of Nomie Carlyle lying unconscious before the door amid the debris of broken scaffolding and plaster dust, her hands scratched and bloodied from trying to pry open the door. 'I tried to open the door myself and couldn't budge it. One of the explosions had jammed it shut.'

'You didn't see anything that looked like tracks? From that door to Zapolya's body?'

Again she shook her head. 'The explosion that jammed the door – it was the one that wrecked the right-hand corner of the façade, the one away from the palace – cracked a hole just beyond the cathedral door and threw debris over the floor of the set. Mr Zapolya's body, and Miss Carlyle's dress, were covered with plaster dust. Had there been tracks – and even had I been calm enough to look for them, after seeing poor Mr Zapolya's body – they'd have been covered over. And in any case, prior to the start of filming, I believe the pavement of the set would have been swept.'

And did the seven thousand dollars he had in his pocket have anything to do with any of this, or not?

Well, obviously not, if the killer didn't take it . . .

Unless of course the killer knew that the money would come to her later by law.

She couldn't decide how to ask about it without mentioning that Kitty had helped herself to the envelope . . .

'You're probably right.' Meyer smoothed his villainous little mustaches. 'Never hurts to ask. Thank you, Mrs Blackstone.'

He rose from his desk, came around with the polite fiction of helping a perfectly capable young woman rise from her chair. 'I think you're right,' he went on, as he stepped with her to the office door. 'I'd say there's a seventy-five percent chance that someone following you is only some gossip columnist trying to get a story about Harry Garfield's love life . . . but not following you at ten thirty at night up into the wilds of Griffith Park. You didn't know Zapolya, did you? Or hear any scuttlebutt around the studios about somebody who'd want him dead? Other than his wife,' he added, a little grimly.

Somebody . . . so important that he couldn't breathe a word about who it was, Peggy Donovan had said.

And her mind went back to the page three photograph of the young stockbroker in the saddle shoes, lying in his blood.

Conscious of the intent look in those dark eyes, Emma said, 'No. I understand he – well, as the Americans say, he "got about". I gather,' she added, with the deliberate starchiness of one who would never hear rumors that might lead gangsters to think that she should be silenced, 'that "getting about" is the done thing here in Hollywood. No one I've spoken to seems to think very much about it.'

Meyer's teeth flashed white in the dark of his beard. 'It's the done thing, all right, ma'am.'

And maybe that 'someone so important' has his own reasons for pushing the blame on to Miss Carlyle . . .

'And I take it all you've seen of this car is that it's got a dead headlight? Which you know they're going to fix, now they've been out where it's dark enough they realize how come you spotted them.'

'That's all.' She half-shut her eyes, trying to call back the shape that had passed the bottom of the track in last night's darkness. 'It's a saloon rather than an open car, black, I think. Medium-sized – not noticeably long or bulky or particularly small. And it sounded well-maintained.'

'Well, good for you, Mrs Blackstone.' The detective paused, his hand on the knob of his office door. 'Would you do this for me, ma'am? Like I said, it's probably just one of the fan magazines. But if anything else happens that feels . . . *off-kilter* – hinky – would you let me know? And keep an eye out around you. Especially at night.'

They stood for a moment, and looking down into his eyes – he was Zal's height, three or four inches shorter than her gawky five-foot-ten – Emma saw again the dark glint that spoke of other thoughts, other things against which he was matching what she'd told him.

'Hollywood's a weird town,' he said at length. 'You've got men and women both coming in by the thousands, thinking they want to get into pictures and thinking that pictures are like what they see, sitting in the dark alone with nothing but what DeMille or Sennett or Chaplin wants to show them. Thinking it's all real. *They're* the ones who come.'

Orphans and strangers . . .

'The ones who know what the world is really like stay home. But the ones who come, and it's not like they think it should be . . . Sometimes it does something to them. Not all of them,' he added, and opened the door for her.

'But let me know. And maybe watch out that you don't be by yourself out walking around at night.'

TWELVE

t had been Emma's original intent to visit the Los Angeles public library – in quest of information about non-Pythagorean pre-Christian pacifists, among other things (*Zalmoxis of Dacia, perhaps?*) – between her visits to the Sixth Division station and Miss Carlyle's room on Third Street. But the address her fellow Foremost scenarist Sam Wyatt gave for the library – the upper floor of a downtown department store, as it turned out – was no longer current. The library apparently changed addresses like an East End immigrant family dodging the rent collector. 'They're building a permanent facility over where the old Normal School used to be,' provided the store's sleek-haired manager. 'I gather the library collection moves whenever it gets too big for whatever space they've rented for it – I understand at one point it was over a saloon. No, I'm afraid I have no idea where they are now . . .'

No wonder nobody in Hollywood can tell the difference be tween AD and BC.

However, the May Company Department Store had an excellent café attached to it, so Emma was at least able to have a pleasant lunch before taking the streetcar a few blocks up Broadway to Third Street, and so to the stately but slightly dilapidated homes of the formerly stylish neighborhood called Bunker Hill.

Bunker Hill itself rose, steep and surprising, in the midst of the city that had slowly crept around its feet. Handsome clapboard houses and a few genuine mansions of the seventies dotted its weedy slopes, and – *of all things*! – a narrow-gauge funicular railway ascended along Third Street, flanked by a stairway reminiscent of the slopes of Montmartre Hill in Paris. The address Emma had been given was a shabby dowager of a residence opposite the hill's eastern slope, complete with bow windows, ornamental turrets, and scrollwork gingerbread

that badly needed paint. A mended toy bear and a scattering
of alphabet blocks strewed the porch, and a card tacked above
the doorbell listed ten names, with instructions of how many
rings to summon each inhabitant. 'Carlyle' rated eight.

To judge by the length of time between her eight buzzes
and the final sight, through the door's mended oval window,
of Nomie Carlyle coming down the front hall steps, 'eight'
was a long way up.

'Randy told me you'd phoned,' said the girl, opening the
door. 'Would you like some coffee? Ma Jimpson usually leaves
a pot on the stove – if it's too strong I can water it down.'
She stepped aside and led Emma into the parlor, a vestige of
finer days. The plush on its furniture was threadbare and the
drapes faded colorless, save where folds of purple had been
protected from the sun so long that they stood out like stripes
of paint in the dusty velvet. The carpet had clearly been neither
cleaned nor beaten in decades.

No toys here, Emma noticed, and wondered if the dark
monolith of the upright piano was in tune. East of the house,
she had seen, the neighborhood deteriorated precipitously,
where railroad tracks and the labyrinthine dirt lanes of the
'Mexican District' bordered the river.

'Thank you, no, I've just had tea at the May Company,' she
said.

Overhead a woman's voice grated, 'Don't you fucking lie
to me you fucking pencil-dick!' A man shouted something
indistinguishable; the woman yelled back, 'On my bed! On
my fucking sheets!'

'But I needed to speak with you,' Emma went on, with the
eerie sensation of hearing her governess admonish her, *If it
isn't your business you simply ignore it . . .* 'I take it there's
no filming today?'

Nomie rolled her eyes. 'Everything's held up for a week,
until they re-build the whole ballroom set in Stage One.
Meantime that crazy German's doing close-ups from what's
already been shot. Hands reaching for wine glasses on a table
– forty-four takes! Thirty-seven takes of Nan Brickard dripping
gravy down her chin as she eats!'

Through the doorway back to the hall voices came dimly,

'A dollar for a hand job and two for a French . . .' and feet going up the stairs. A pause, and the same voice yelled down, 'Any calls for me, Randy?'

'Today he's got Bruce and Dee – Miss Darrow – going through a scene in the palace,' Nomie went on, resolutely ignoring the escalating din upstairs. 'He did about a zillion takes, 'cause he didn't like the way Dee turns around when Bruce comes into the room. Then he sits down and writes two more scenes. It's like he's making it up as he goes along: maybe it'll look good this way. Maybe it'll look good that way.'

Her voice dropped into an exaggerated version of the director's German accent. 'Let us try it mit der sunlight falling on Bruce's face. Should Bruce be carrying a cat? Should Dee be carrying a cat? Somebody go find a cat. Oops, it's the wrong color of cat. Let's try it in shadow. Jeezus!'

She shook her golden head. 'It's like working with Chaplin. How hard can it be to walk into a room and say, "What are you doing here?" I'm supposed to go in with Dee tomorrow and re-shoot the scene where I tell her I won't desert her, and I bet that's gonna take twelve hours, for something Ernst—'

Her voice stuck for a moment on the name. Emma thought the girl looked drained. *Well, who wouldn't be, under the circumstances?*

On a side table, yesterday evening's *Herald* lay, with the page three headline: A MOTHER'S REVENGE? And a picture of a grim-looking middle-aged woman captioned: *Margaret Colby, Mother of Clive April's Bride.* She tried to recall some of the whispered gossip at Pickfair.

Yet there was more in Nomie's face than simple physical weariness, or the frustration of dealing with a dictatorial Austrian. The strain of waiting for the filming to conclude – of being trapped, waiting for some proof, any proof, to surface before the police closed in – was visible in those lovely brown eyes. There was an emptiness, a deadness that could have been despair. As if she asked herself, Where do I go now? Where *can* I go?

With a little sigh, Nomie concluded, 'He's nuts.'

Emma recalled the director berating the palace guard about

how they should turn. On the way back from Pickfair to the studio Monday night, Harry had said, 'Well, Von's never actually killed anybody, but when they were filming out in Death Valley last summer, about a third of his crew had to be trucked back to LA with heatstroke. I heard the outfit's cook died, and Jean Hersholt spent a week in the hospital . . .'

The couple upstairs, having quieted for a time (*To re-fill their glasses?*), began to shout once more. Emma felt the cold weight in her stomach that she'd known as a paid companion in the house of Mrs Pendergast, remembering when her employer would start on one of her 'headache' days, beginning consumption of 'medicine' when she woke at ten in the morning. Emma had known, by the sing-song note in her voice, what the rest of the day and on into the night would bring, sometimes until two or three in the morning: constant summons, by ringing her bedside bell or thumping on the ceiling with her cane. The harsh, jagged ranting ('Don't you turn away from *me*, girl!').

The knowledge that there was no place else for her to go.

And where, she wondered, would this girl go? This pretty child who for all her sordid reputation was barely eighteen? A man in the hallway yelled, 'Any calls for me, Randy?' and then came into the parlor, unshaven and with clothing that smelled of both liquor and urine from across the room. He took the *Herald* from the side table, slumped into a chair, burped and began rustling through the pages, pausing frequently to fish a brown glass bottle from his pocket and drink. The angle of the bottle indicated there weren't many swallows left. 'Goddam fucken Democrats,' he grumbled, and lowered the paper to glare at Nomie. 'How the fuck they expect Congress to make America safe for real Americans if they keep fuckin' things up whinin' about immigration an' how the government should run everythin'? You tell me *that*, girlie!'

He jabbed a vindictive finger at the two women, then retreated immediately into the *Herald* again.

'When was the last time you saw Mr Zapolya,' Emma asked after a moment, 'before Saturday? To . . .' How does one phrase such a question about illicit lovers? 'To speak to privately, I mean.'

'Saturday night. We wrapped up filming early, and . . . and Marina wasn't on the lot. We went back to his office.'

Despite herself, Emma saw again the necklace of pearls under the desk. Of course, Marina would be at the Zapolya residence on Vermont Avenue.

'Did he ever seem . . . nervous? Frightened?' But he wouldn't, she reflected. Not the lion-proud man who had stood like a king on the balcony. Not in front of a woman he was trying to impress. Nomie shook her head. 'Or speak of this "mystery woman" he was seeing? I only ask,' she went on, as the girl looked baffled, 'because Monday night, someone followed me from Pickfair back down to the studio. I thought it was a reporter from one of the fan magazines, because I was with Howie – Harry Garfield. But the same person – or at least someone driving the same car – followed me last night. And I can only think it has to have something to do with whatever Mr Zapolya was going to tell Kitty – and you.'

Nomie's velvety eyes widened, 'Oh, gosh!' she whispered. 'I haven't – it's sort of hard to tell, you know. If someone's following me, or hanging around, I mean. There's always people on the lot. I know a lot of the extras, but in a big show like *Crowned Heart* there's hundreds of them, and everybody's in costume . . .' She shook her head again. 'It's just hard to tell.'

Somewhere in the house a child began to scream, a frantic note of hunger or pain. The quarrelsome couple simply raised their voices to compensate.

'People come and go all the time. They get called for a better job the next day, and the casting director has to round up somebody else, or Ernst would suddenly decide he needed more people . . . Or somebody'll get hurt, and have to drop out.' Her voice faltered, though whether from the baby's screams or the memory of the little group huddled beside the commissary tent, roughly bandaged and waiting for the next truck to carry them back to the studio gate, it was hard to tell.

'And here,' Nomie went on rather grimly, 'there's always people I don't know hanging around in the street. We're not that far from Skid Row, and Sonoratown's right across the

street, practically. There's always drunks, or guys selling
tamales off carts—'

'You said it, girlie,' yelled the smelly man abruptly.
'God-damned fucken Mexicans an' their goddamn tamale
carts, blockin' up the sidewalk, an' does the government do
anythin' about 'em? Or about the goddamn Chinks? And will
you for Chrissake shut that kid up!' he added in a louder roar,
jabbing his finger towards the back of the house.

Nomie said, with the patience of too many months of repeti-
tion, 'Lucy isn't my child, Mr Brinker. I've told you before,
she's Amy Platoff's—'

'Amy Platoff's a whore!' Mr Brinker exploded. 'And even
if the brat ain't yours, you go shut her up anyway before I
drown her! Women got no right to let some brat go disturbin'
a man's rest.'

Nomie rose, took Emma by the elbow, and guided her to the
parlor door. It was clear there would be no more conversation
in the room that afternoon. 'I'm sorry,' she whispered.

'It's all right.'

The girl shook her head. 'He's Ma Jimpson's brother,
see.' The tightening of her lips made Emma wonder if relation
to the landlady entailed any sort of arrangement with female
boarders in arrears of rent. 'Anyway . . .' Nomie straightened
her shoulders and made an effort to relax. 'Why would anybody
be watching *me*? Or you, or Kitty?'

'I don't know.' Emma shook her head. 'But I felt that you
needed to be warned.'

Beside them, the telephone on the hall table jangled. An
unshaven man in a singlet and dungarees emerged from the
doorway beside it – the obliging 'Randy' presumably – limping
heavily on a crutch and two artificial legs. Mr Brinker burst
out of the parlor door and snatched the instrument from him.
'That'll be Goldwyn . . .' and yelled into it, 'Brinker here—'

Nomie opened the front door. 'Thank you,' she said again.
'Thank you for telling me.'

'If you do see anyone –' Emma lifted her voice over
Brinker's shouts at his caller to stay off the goddam line –
'anyone who turns up again and again, for no reason, or
anything . . . odd . . . that happens, would you let me know.'

The young actress' eyes widened in alarm, but she nodded. 'I will. And *thank you*, more than I can say, for getting old Jesperson to hire that crazy Hun. We're a week behind schedule already and now he's having the Isle of Love sets re-built out on San Clemente Island. *Thank you!* By the time shooting is done, they've – they've *got* to find the real killer . . .'

And when they do, thought Emma, as she walked along Hill Street toward the trolley stop, what then? *Orphans and strangers . . .* And this girl, she sensed, was both, struggling valiantly to keep from sliding into deeper poverty. At one point, she recalled, Nomie had spoken to Kitty about a sister. Was that sister still in the picture? Or was that desperate young girl utterly alone?

It was clear to her at least that Nomie was right about people coming and going in this neighborhood. Looking about her, Emma saw how impossible it would be for the girl to tell if she were being watched and followed. Trucks set up with racks of vegetable crates drew men and women alike from the shabby neighborhoods on the other side of Hill Street. Smaller barrows, as Nomie had said, vended tamales and lemon ices under faded green umbrellas. Men – and women – loitered near the trolley stop, smoking or chatting in Spanish, the men in shirtsleeves rolled up their arms, something Emma was still getting used to seeing out in public, though Americans seemed to think nothing of it. *How could you tell if the same person is there every day, or every time you come out your door?*

And why?

Her mind returned to that seven thousand dollars. To the fear in Zapolya's voice, and the page three photo of the young Romeo in the saddle shoes, dead on the bloody sidewalk.

It was clear to her at least that Nomie herself was no threat to anyone.

So who was *Zapolya afraid of?*

Why Kitty? Why Nomie?

And what's Miss Burdon going to say when I explain to her that she'll need a dugout canoe and it won't go nearly as fast as a Red Indian vessel – and where in Roman Britain would you find a river capable of sweeping Miriam away to her peril?

The Ouse? The Cam?

I suppose if there were a flood – in which case we'll need a rainstorm . . .

How much do rainstorms cost?

Ascending the steep hill of Ivarene Street – the soft gray overcast of the morning having burned off into mellow sweet sunshine – Emma was conscious again of the difference between this neighborhood and the one she had left behind her. These hills on the northern edge of Hollywood – like Mount Olympus and the canyons to the west – were what Bunker Hill had been back in the seventies, an enclave of quiet wealth, albeit more eccentric architecture. And Emma had to smile, thinking of what Jim would have had to say about the ersatz castles and twenty-five-room fairytale 'cottages' with ten bathrooms. Few motorcars passed her as she climbed. The stylish Spanish colonial villas below Kitty's on the hillside were widely spaced and set in well-tended gardens. A loitering stranger would be noticed.

But Kitty's pseudo-Moorish fantasy was almost the last house on the street. There was another mansion half-built in what struck Emma as a hashish-vision of Tudor nightmare, and a sprawling stone mansion further up the hill that housed one of the 'spiritual colonies' in which California evidently abounded: white-robed ladies who danced by moonlight and had installed a marble outdoor shower-bath at the bottom of their garden. Further along Beechwood Drive, a still-more-exclusive enclave of luxury homes were still in the planning stages: the advertising sign, HOLLYWOODLAND, on the slopes of the so-called Mount Lee, was plastered with light-bulbs and could be seen for miles at night.

But the lots immediately to the north and south of Kitty's were vacant, as was the whole of the hillside opposite. Sagebrush, manzanita, and other forms of odd, spiky, gray-green foliage shawled the landscape, overgrowing what had once been tracks cut by optimistic real-estate agents. Emma was well aware that anyone could be hiding on the hillslope, watching the house . . .

Why?

It all came back to that.

The dogs scurried to her when she unlocked the front door, tails tucked, licking their noses anxiously, restless as she squatted to stroke their round, silky heads. *What is it?* she wondered, as she stepped across the threshold. *There's something amiss . . .*

Mindful of her duties, Emma set down her satchel, opened every window in the front room and the dining room – she was generally used to the lingering smell of Kitty's cigarettes, but it seemed to saturate the air today – and gathered up leashes. Behind the garage – the rear half of which was the gardener's cottage – and far up the hillslope, she could see Mr Shang patiently cutting back the surrounding greasewood and chamisa, and felt a twinge of relief.

Why relief? Am I that afraid that masked Venetian bravos are going to sneak up under cover of darkness?

They could have done it any night in the past week . . .

And she smiled, remembering Zal's arms around her last night. The strength of those sturdy shoulders, and the faint chemical sweetness of raw film that clung to his hair.

And how many takes did it require, for Kitty to register the proper degree of moral decay as she lolled in Cincinnati Wilder's bath-tub, among floating orchids, drinking champagne? *Do they periodically refresh the hot water, or is poor Kitty going to be blue and shivering by the time they get to take thirty-five? Do orchids* (those had been Mr Pugh's idea) *get water-logged and sink? And if so, what is their budget for replacements?*

Mrs Shang, hanging shirts and blue cotton trousers on the clothesline (and smoking like a chimney – *maybe that's her cigarettes I smelled in the house . . .*), nodded a greeting and gestured towards the house. 'Coyotes,' she said. '*Xiao-xing quan.*' She smiled at the dogs, fished for English words, then gave a startlingly accurate imitation of the Pekineses barking, complete with hunched shoulders and staring eyes.

Emma laughed. *Hence their spooked restlessness . . .*

But it was only an hour later, after making tea and telephoning Madge Burdon about the cost of rainstorms ('She'll phone you back as soon as she's done filming,' Vinnie at the switchboard assured her), that Emma went upstairs to her room to find notes about Neo-Platonism . . .

And glimpsed through the half-open bathroom door a cigarette end on the edge of the sink.

Her heart seemed to shrink behind her breastbone for a moment, and she had the jarred sensation of having stepped off a curb and found it much higher than she'd thought.

What?

Kitty never – not *ever* – left cigarette ends lying anywhere in the house. She was almost as fanatic about it as Mrs Shang was: it was one of the reasons Emma was able to bear living in a house with two smokers. (*Well, one and a half, since Mrs Shang sleeps down in the cottage . . . Well, two and a half, counting Dominga the cleaning woman . . .*)

Emma stepped into the tiled extravaganza of the bathroom. Stood looking down at the stub on the black marble sink.

It was Turkish, with a little gold emblem of a stylized jackal head – Anubis, Egyptian god of graves – stamped near the smoker's end. Her father's friend Professor Playfair of Baliol had smoked them.

Kitty smoked American Chesterfields. The Shangs puffed on Camels, when they weren't lighting up hand-rolled twists of paper like the Poverty Row cowboys did. Emma wasn't certain about Dominga, but she knew the cheerful little Mexican wouldn't be spending her money on a gold-stamped Murad – and she would no more have left a cigarette end on the edge of the sink than she'd have emptied the kitchen garbage pail in the middle of the living room.

Though she knew it was only a cigarette end – and she knew also that spooked as they were now, the dogs would never have tolerated the continued presence of an intruder in the house – Emma backed from the bathroom, as if that shred of evidence was in itself a danger. She searched her own room, prey to a sort of anxious double-vision. *Did the handkerchiefs in the drawer look* exactly *like that when I dressed this morning? Were my shirts in the wardrobe hanging* just *that way?* There was no smell of tobacco in her room. *Of course, that's why he left his cigarette in the bathroom.* And there was no way to tell whether she actually smelled the left-over whiff of smoke from the searcher's clothes, or whether it was her imagination.

In her heart, she knew her room had been searched.

Kitty's room almost certainly, though it was impossible to tell whether the gorgeous litter of silk pillows, discarded kimonos, astrology magazines and gramophone records – not to speak of the bejeweled chaos of her dressing table – had been disturbed or not.

He's gone, she told herself again, as she descended the stair to the living room. *He's not here. The Shangs are right down in the yard and the dogs will give the alarm. No wonder they were barking earlier, as Mrs Shang said!*

She telephoned the Sixth Division station, and of course Detective Meyer wasn't in.

And Zal's filming . . .

And what would I say to him?

I really should just go back to work and deal with how Miriam happens to be in a runaway dugout during the worst storm the British Isles has ever known . . .

Or at least search the telephone directory to see if the University of Southern California permits mere screen-writers to paw through their library.

But she only sat in the living room, the dogs around her feet, as darkness settled on the hills, staring straight before her until the scrunch of tires in the driveway, the clamorous delight of the Pekes, and the clatter of diamanté heels on the back steps announced Kitty's return.

THIRTEEN

Detective Meyer came the following morning, with a man from the Burglary Squad who fingerprinted his way through the house and found only smudges – not greatly to Emma's surprise. 'If they did search the house, they were very careful about it,' she sighed, when the fingerprint officer was packing up his kit. 'I can't imagine they'd take pains about that, and forget to wear gloves.'

'You'd be surprised the mistakes crooks make, if they get rattled.' Meyer took a final sip of the coffee Emma had made for them – it was barely eight thirty – and folded up his notebook. 'Like remembering not to take a smoke into a bedroom where the smell might linger, and then forgetting to snag the butt off the sink when he – or she – went downstairs. But he knew he had to act fast. The pooches would have been barking up a storm, and if it went on it was only a matter of time before the gardener came up to see what was going on.'

He stooped to ruffle Chang Ming's fur: the red-gold dog had recognized him at sight as a beloved and long-lost benefactor and had followed him faithfully from room to room. Black Jasmine, more businesslike than his sturdier pal, had accompanied the fingerprint specialist, observing the process alertly with his single eye and occasionally letting out a gruff little quack.

'You tellin' me I missed a spot, buster?' asked the man, with a straight face.

Buttercreme had retreated to the farthest recesses under Kitty's bed. Emma wondered if she'd come out when it was time to join Kitty at the studio, or if she'd have to nudge her out with a broom.

'And nothing's missing?' Meyer asked for the second time, looking down at the glittering pavement of Kitty's jewelry, which Emma had spread out on the kitchen table. One of her first self-directed tasks, upon coming to live in the house seven months previously, had been to inventory the collection, which included some startling pieces: Tiffany cigarette holders ringed with tiny emeralds, earrings of diamond-and-amber flowers that dangled to her shoulders. Another two boxes held the costume pieces – necklaces of pearls concocted by Foremost's prop department, aigrets the size of sunflowers to be pinned to her hats.

All pieces were present. Even Harry Garfield's diamond bracelet was still in its velvet case in a drawer of her own nightstand, something no thief could have failed to find.

'Whatever they're lookin' for,' he went on, when Emma shook her head, 'it ain't dough.'

'That should make me feel better,' she replied slowly. 'But it doesn't. Worse, I think.'

He growled a little in his throat, but didn't answer immediately. Possibly, she guessed, he didn't want to unsettle her further by expressing the same opinion.

'It may be that having tossed the place, they'll figure they were wrong about Zapolya handing you something before he was shot.' He said it as if that were a comfort. 'I doubt they'll be back, but keep an eye out, and let me know if Miss de la Rose sees anything. Or Miss Carlyle.' He hesitated, glanced toward the front door, through which the fingerprint officer had disappeared. 'And if you would, Mrs Blackstone – I'd appreciate it if you didn't leave a message at the station with either Miss Carlyle's name in it, or Miss de la Rose's. Zapolya's murder isn't my case, and information that comes in about Miss Carlyle might be detrimental to that investigation. Or to this one.'

'Oh.' Emma paused in the act of wrapping an opal moon in tissue paper, to return to its box. 'Of course not.'

'You said you went downtown to speak with her yesterday. She isn't being followed, is she?'

'She didn't think so.' Emma hoped she sounded innocent. Her brother Miles had always told her she was the worst liar in the world. *Do you mean, has she noticed someone from the police watching her?* The vision of rival lurkers scrupulously avoiding one another outside that shabby mansion on Hill Street made her struggle not to smile. *The police and . . .*

And whoever it was who broke into the house yesterday.
Whoever it was who killed Ernst Zapolya.
Whoever it is who thinks that we – Kitty, and myself, and
possibly Nomie as well – know something, or have something,
or heard or saw something . . .
    . . . And what?
'I think if someone had searched her room, she would have
mentioned it.'
    'You warn her about being tailed?'
    Emma nodded, and returned her attention to wrapping up
jewelry. *If the police are watching her they won't appreciate*
that . . . 'Miss de la Rose's picture is going on location next
week, into the mountains,' she said. 'We'll be there for probably a week. All this –' she gestured to the royal ransom
strewed across the red-patterned breakfast enamel – 'is going
to the bank, needless to say. I've given Miss Carlyle the
telephone number of the lodge where the company will be
staying, the Seven Summits in Big Bear Lake.'
    'Good girl.' He donned his hat, presumably for the purpose
of tipping it to her. 'Better safe than sorry.'
    And thus matters stood, until the fire at Big Bear.

When Emma – with dogs in tow – arrived at Foremost that
morning, it was to be greeted by Larry Palmer, with a request
that Scenes 740 to 769 (Nick Thaxter's murder and Marsh
Sloane's accusation of Kitty for the crime) be re-written to
accommodate Marsh murdering Kitty's maid as well ('We
gotta have a little more punch in here, Duchess . . .').
    'Cincinnati Wilder doesn't have a maid.'
    'Oh, write her in earlier. It'll just be a couple scenes.'
    And readjusting a dozen others to account for her presence
. . . and completely changing all scenes (including the bath-
tub sequence) establishing Miss Wilder's living situation and
economic standing . . .
    She asked the director about the cost and logistics of rain-
storms. ('Shit, that's a swell idea! Wonder if we can work a
rainstorm into *Kentucky Derby Katie*?' Which was, apparently,
Harry Garfield's next vehicle. 'You do and you're a dead man,'
warned Zal, bringing Emma a cup of tea.) Filming resumed.

But at seven – when Kitty had confronted Margaret MacKenzie for the twenty-third time over the disastrous results foreseen for a marriage between herself and Harry, and Larry had declared himself satisfied ('If I had to do that argument one more time I really *would* have murdered somebody,' declared Kitty, fortifying herself from her gin flask) – and Emma crossed to Stage One to ask Madge about rainstorms, the director met her halfway up the studio street. 'I tried to get hold of you yesterday, Duchess – we're gonna ditch the canoe. Miriam gets kidnapped, see, by the Druids, and they're gonna sacrifice her to Odin.'

Odin was a Norse god, not a British one, Emma knew better than to say.

Isn't there a branch of the University of California somewhere here in town?

'That's our big climax, see! My sister was telling me, the Druids used to sacrifice people – they'd stuff them into these big wicker images and light them on fire.'

Oh, Darlene Golden's going to love *doing that . . .*

'Of course.' *Someone in Hollywood has actually* read *Caesar's Commentaries*?

And when she returned to Stage Two, it was to be informed that a fortunate cancellation at the Seven Summits Lodge would permit Palmer's company to start shooting in Big Bear on Monday, rather than the following Thursday. Frank Pugh had immediately closed with this offer, which gave him an excuse to accompany Kitty to the mountain resort rather than remain home with the hostile Mrs Pugh (and her lawyer). Emma wondered if her stealthy watchers would follow them into the wilds of San Bernardino County, and if she'd be able to recognize them if they did. (*Presumably they've fixed their headlight . . .*)

'You can put your date with Harry up to tomorrow, instead of Wednesday, can't you, Duchess?' said Pugh, as Ned Devine and his minions from the prop department loaded Kitty's gramophone, folding chairs, cushions, picnic basket, and wicker dog boxes into the Packard outside her dressing room in the slow-gathering California twilight. 'We've got good response from the fans about Harry's romance with a "beautiful war widow", so I'd like to have a couple more pieces next week in *Screen Stories*. I've already been on the horn to Fortunato's,' he added, naming the newest nightclub on Hollywood Boulevard and beaming with fatuous joy as Kitty emerged from her dressing room. 'They've got a table for the two of you at eight.'

For the next three days, between packing, making arrangements with the Shangs for extra care with watching the house, further attempts to find the Los Angeles library (*Did the Druids* actually *burn sacrifices in wicker cages? Surely wicker burns too quickly to make a very effective prison* . . .), and a clandestine meeting or two with Zal ('Hey, there won't be reporters in Big Bear and shooting ends when the sun goes down . . .'), Emma had very little opportunity either to seek out the university or to determine whether she was still being followed or not. Driving back from the Fortunato's on Wednesday night with Harry, she saw no evidence of a single headlight behind them.

Roger Clint, as promised, had indeed bought her a corsage of orchids for the occasion.

As she climbed the steps to the front porch at ten – mindful of the need to be on the train to San Bernardino in the morning – she crossed paths with Kitty, on her way down to meet 'Benito' ('He's the most *gorgeous* extra at National . . . Frank brought me home early because we need to catch that train . . .').

Hollywood . . .

To Emma's intense relief, Kitty actually returned to the house thirty minutes before they had to leave for La Grande Station ('It won't take me ten minutes to freshen up my makeup, dearest . . .'). Thanks to Kitty's reckless abandon behind the wheel of the Packard, they actually reached the extravagant pink pseudo-mosque of the Santa Fe station a full four minutes before the train departed for San Bernardino, and Zal was waiting for them by the entrance with Ned Devine and three porters: two to bear the suitcases, gramophone, picnic hamper, and dog baskets at speed through the station's tiled archways and one to tactfully thrust aside the reporters who surrounded the little caravan like sharks inspecting a leaky lifeboat.

BLACK HAT FOUND IN KILLER'S HIDING-PLACE
bellowed a news-stand headline under a picture of the
Ravenstark set. 'Speculation is rife that Zapolya's killer may
have slipped on to the set unobserved.'

'C'mon, Kitty, you'll miss the train!'

Since this was not the first time Emma had gotten her
sister-in-law on to a train, she knew to keep a firm hold on
Kitty's elbow and repeat to her, 'You can't give them a picture
now, we'll miss the train . . . No, you can't stop and buy a
newspaper . . . No, trains are forbidden by law to be held
up for anyone . . . You can give an interview when we get
back . . .'

Flash-powder coruscated.

'Oh, but, darling, they'll hold the train for *us*. Everybody
always looks so terrible when they're just running like
this . . .'

'Mr Fishbein will make sure none of those pictures get
printed.'

Once safely on the step of the first-class car, Kitty turned
back, Black Jasmine tucked firmly under one arm (and Zal
and Emma poised behind her to grab her as the train jolted
into motion), tossed her witch-black hair, smiled the smile that
shredded a thousand hearts, and waved.

Emma wondered if their pursuers had missed the train.

Or, possibly, if they'd been wrecked in traffic trying to
follow Kitty at Ben-Hur velocity through downtown.

Big Bear Lake lay in the midst of the San Bernardino
Mountains, two hours (including three tire punctures) via a
narrow, twisted, and rather sketchily paved road: a thriving
little town strung out along the edge of exquisitely blue water,
that reflected the surrounding mountains like a tourmaline
mirror a thousand miles deep. Emma, whose previous experiences with 'location shooting' had involved the ruins of a
desert ghost town and the arid mountainsides above Reno,
Nevada, stepped from the studio car feeling that she'd arrived
in a world wrought of silence and crystal.

She'd seen adverts proclaiming: This is America!

But she hadn't really believed them.

She said, softly, 'Oh.'

Zal slipped his arm through hers. 'A lot of the film people come up here when they have the chance,' he said.

'I can see why.'

The Seven Summits Lodge stood a mile and a half outside Big Bear proper. A long wooden structure – the lodge itself – faced untouched miles of pine forest to the northeast, the sparkling lake to the southwest, raised on a wooded hill and bordered on both sides by terraces strung with green-and-white striped awnings. In the groves that surrounded it, Emma could see a score or more spruce little cabins, doors painted green, graveled pathways tidy. Squirrels flashed up the trunks of those impossibly tall trees and chittered, flagging their tails and calling the intruders rude names. Crows glided among the dappled shadows, or sat on high boughs and cawed prophecies of doom. Doc Larousse's lighting men paced around with their meters and talked about what time they had to get out to the set tomorrow, while the prop men unloaded the trucks that had driven out from Los Angeles that morning: sections of fence-railing, discreet tubs of tomato and cucumber plants suitable for simulating a rustic kitchen garden, the component pieces of the humble cabin in which Cincinnati Wilder had been born and raised.

(*So how does she afford a maid . . .?*)

(Stipendium peccati, *I suppose . . .*)

'Alvy Turner and I'll be roughing out camera set-ups all afternoon,' said Zal, as he walked Emma to the cabin assigned to herself and Kitty, carrying Buttercreme's wicker box. Emma had uncrated and leashed Chang Ming and Black Jasmine, the bolder males frantic to explore every clump of laurel and claim ownership of every tree (*And get themselves eaten by coyotes or bears in the process . . .*), tangling their leashes and barking furiously at lizards, squirrels and birds. 'But there's a couple of good diners in town, if you want the walk and don't want to eat at the lodge.'

Emma glanced back, to see Frank Pugh – relaxed and at ease almost for the first time since she'd met him – strolling up towards the lodge with Kitty, pointing something out to her, his head bent down to hers. Harry Garfield ambled in another direction, toward one of the cabins from whose door his friend Roger Clint emerged, lean and sandy and smiling, and said something that made Harry laugh.

'I'd like that,' she said.

For four days, the Seven Summits Lodge was transformed into a miniature studio in itself, with the forest, the lake, and the ersatz Wilder cabin (allegedly tucked away in the mountains of Tennessee) instead of a shooting stage. By day Emma walked the dogs, and watched the endless takes and re-takes, rehearsals and close-ups and walk-throughs as Kitty wept bitterly and repeatedly in 'featured player' Hazel Tully's arms, hid in the barn when the police came looking for her (the barn had also been transported up from Los Angeles in pieces), and contemplated either suicide or matrimony with bit-player Jake Nangle out of sheer despair. ('Let's see a little more pain in your eyes, Kitty, when you shove him away . . .').

She also – at the folding makeup table just outside the shot line where Kitty's base camp (gramophone, rack of kimonos, picnic basket, pillows, and bin of astrology magazines) had been set up – returned to the problem of Miriam and her lovers. This issue was exacerbated by Frank Pugh's request that *The Gryphon Prince* be re-set in pre-war Paris ('Nobody knows who Julius Caesar was anyway') and re-titled *Peril Under Paris*. Seth Ramsay was now a wealthy playboy who realizes that the suave and sophisticated major who's been making love to his beloved is actually a German spy . . .

The evenings she spent with Zal.

'It's different up here,' she said.

'I'm glad you like it.'

They'd swiped a blanket from the dormitory cabin Zal shared with the other two cameramen and their assistants, spread it on the sloping ground above the lake. It was too early in the year for mosquitoes, and though the western shapes of Butler Peak and Hana Rocks were yet outlined black against the dusky rose of the downed sun, cold was beginning to set in.

'It's quiet.' Emma rested her head on the firm comfort of Zal's shoulder. 'We usually went to the seashore in summers when I was a child – my mother's health was a little fragile – but one summer when she was quite ill and couldn't go at all, my father's cousin Stuart rented a cottage in the Highlands, and my brother and I stayed with him for a week. The silence was like this. The sky was like this.'

The feeling was like this. The feeling of being absolutely safe, and utterly at rest.

Hollywood was astonishing – like being caught inside a kaleidoscope. California – this place, or the coast highway where it ran along the sea – was beautiful in a way that she had never experienced in the green sweet stillness that was England. But she didn't feel safe here.

Zal took in his breath to say something, but let the silence stay instead. Without his glasses his face looked different, younger, in the moonlight, every eyelash casting a small shadow on his cheek. When he spoke, it was as if he'd turned aside from a question that it was too soon to ask. 'How old were you?'

'About ten.' Emma smiled. 'My brother – Miles – was fourteen, and convinced we could find the ruins of a Roman fort in the hills under Beinn Fhionnlaidh. It was one of his summers for thinking he'd like to be an archaeologist like Papa after all. Most of the time he wanted to invent better electrical circuitry – Papa abominated electricity. We'd walk across the moors to the River Cannich, with the hills rising up all around us . . . It was like being on another world.'

The rose in the sky was fading. Stars had come out, and the pure baroque pearl of the gibbous moon. Jupiter, Zal had pointed out to her, one evening in the dark at the top of Kitty's drive, when he'd brought her home late. Orion just setting, the long, dusty rainbow of the Milky Way. It was a time for talking.

'I don't see how Kitty can . . . can play at grief,' she said, turning her head a little on his arm. 'I don't see how Miss Carver can perform those . . . those *histrionics* one day, and then go on to the set the next as if nothing had happened.'

'They're actresses,' replied Zal. 'I don't know how you could, either. But some actors can step back from things – even awful things, like killing somebody – in a way other people can't.'

'*Killing* somebody?'

'Howie was in the 91st Infantry at the Argonne,' said Zal. 'That's where he met Roger. The two of them have probably killed more men between them than are in the crew up here. Like Kitty says about a couple of her husbands, that water's not only gone under the bridge, it's miles out to sea by now.'

How long does it take, she wondered, *for water to get miles out to sea, glittering faintly in the moonlight?*

After a time she said, 'Sometimes I feel as if I'd . . . as if I'd fallen down and broken my arm. Something that just happened, through no fault of my own. Sometimes it hurts. Sometimes I can't use it. But I know it will heal.' She reached back, a little awkwardly, to take his hand. Square and strong on his thick wrist, with short fingers and a little dusting of red hair on the back.

Nothing like Jim's hand.

'It's all right,' said Zal. 'I've got a couple of broken bones myself.'

'Did you ever get out to the countryside as a child?'

'I didn't know there *was* such a thing as countryside when I was a kid. I don't think I got above 57th Street until I was fourteen. First time I ever got lost in the woods was in Central Park.'

'So who taught you about the stars? And how to shoot pictures?'

And they told stories, and laughed, until the night grew too cold to linger.

When Emma slept, she dreamed of Scotland, and of Miles, hip-deep in heather on the slopes of Beinn Fhionnlaidh, arms thrown out and laughing. Full of schemes about how to improve motorcars with better electricity, or how to use an electrical coil to detect Roman ruins even through earth and rocks. Fair hair, lighter than her own smoky mouse-brown, riffled by those cold Highland airs that smelled like nothing else on earth. 'We're coming into a world that nobody has ever seen before, Em! Anything is possible!'

Oh, Miles, she thought, remembering even in her sleep the thing that had been shipped home from Flanders in 1918, eyeless and voiceless and giving no sign that he knew her or anyone around him or where he was.

He turned to her now – still fourteen, still happy, still Miles – frowning suddenly, as the smell of burning poured down on them, acrid in the moorland wind. 'Em, wake up!' he said.

Somewhere, the dogs were barking.

She woke, coughing, in darkness flame-lit and filled with smoke.

FOURTEEN

C hang Ming grabbed a corner of the blanket and tried to pull it off the bed. Black Jasmine ran back and forth. *Where's Buttercreme?*

Emma sat up, looked across at Kitty's bed . . .

Empty.

Flame flickered through the nearly-impenetrable smoke along the wall past the foot of her bed, just beneath the cabin's window. A falling fragment of curtain landed on the foot of the bed, the blanket catching . . . Panic seized her. She rolled out of bed, stumbled over something – *slippers? Buttercreme?* Staggered blindly towards where she thought the door would be, blundered into the wall. The dogs were barking. No door . . . Smoke and blackness, burning her eyes, choking her, disorienting. She knocked into some piece of furniture – *chair or table?* The chairs and the room's little table – *right or left of the door?* She wasn't familiar enough with the room to be sure . . .

The heat swamped her thoughts. Impossible to breathe, impossible to think . . .

Her hand swept the wall in the darkness, closed on the door handle. Coughing, sobbing, she yanked it open, stumbled out and nearly fell into Zal's arms on the two plank steps outside. Somewhere in the inky dark behind Zal Kitty screamed, 'Chang! Jazz!' and wiping her eyes, Emma saw her, wrapped in an enormous bathrobe, kneeling as the three Pekes (*Three . . . Oh, thank God . . .!*) scrambled to get into her arms. Black Jasmine turned back, to brace his tiny feet and bark at the flames.

Emma clung to Zal's shoulders as he half carried her down the steps, away from the burning cabin, the pouring smoke. Everyone around them swirled back away with them. The flames inside illuminated almost nothing, but Emma had the impression of dozens of people, all of them shouting things like, 'Is she OK?' and 'What the hell—?'

And, in the leaping firelight at the other side of the grove, she was aware of both Alvy Turner and Chip Thaw – Zal's fellow cameramen – hastily setting up their cameras to get a good shot of the burning cabin. Now that she knew that Kitty and the dogs were safe, she didn't know whether to go over and slap them or laugh till she cried, and settled for coughing half a universe of smoke from her throat.

'Are you all right?' gasped Zal. 'Are you all right?'

Emma nodded, and went into another paroxysm of coughing. Lights went up in one of the barracks-like dormitory cabins that the crew shared. The whole mob around them shuffled and surged up its steps. Somebody draped a blanket around her shoulders. She sank down on one of the half-dozen beds in the long room, and a dozen flasks clinked and jostled in front of her face. The smell of liquor stung her burning nostrils.

'What happened?'

'Goddam wiring in the lamps,' said somebody.

And from just outside the door, 'Shit!'

Red light silhouetted Harry in the barracks doorway, rumpled, barefoot, and furry-chested in a pair of white-and-blue-striped pajama trousers. 'The tree by the cabin's caught—'

More noise, men rushing about outside. Suddenly sick, Emma leaned her head down on her hands. Somebody put a cold, wet wash-cloth on the back of her neck. 'Where's the goddam doctor?' demanded Zal.

'Coulda been a cigarette . . .?' surmised another voice.

'Shut up, you goon, she doesn't smoke.'

'They got a pump,' said somebody else, and for a time the noises blurred, the Pekes' barking cutting through the din that suddenly seemed cloudy and far-off. The smell of smoke trebled and quadrupled. Liquor burned her mouth. Somebody asked, 'They get that all on film?'

And if somebody asks me to write a burning-cabin scene into Hot Potato *I really will scream . . .*

'How you feeling now, Duchess?'

Emma opened her eyes and discovered she was now lying on one of the dormitory cots. Most of the people had somehow disappeared (*I didn't really faint, did I?*) and Roger Clint, rumpled and barelegged in cowboy boots and a white-and-blue-striped pajama jacket, brought her – of all things – a cup of tea from the barrack's little hot plate.

'Can you sit up?' Zal's arm slid around her shoulders, and she nodded, and coughed again. Her lungs felt like she'd inhaled sandpaper.

Darkness outside, without flame. The air smelled as if someone had emptied a bin of wet ashes over the entire world. On the other side of the long room, Chip Thaw and Alvy Turner were trying to discreetly stash the magazines of film they'd shot of the blaze. Like actors, Emma supposed, stepping back from the implications of what they'd just done.

Hollywood . . .

Kitty, adorably disheveled, perched on the next bed and cradled Buttercreme in the folds of the frogged velvet robe she still wore, obviously cut for someone of (for instance) Frank Pugh's ample dimensions. Chang Ming pressed to her hip, licking her wrist as if to comfort her; Black Jasmine tugged at the leash that someone had used to attach him to the bed's foot, quacking impatiently at not being permitted to go out and supervise the fire crew.

The tea was like the elixir of life.

Emma became aware that she was in her nightgown, and tugged the blanket closer around her shoulders. 'I was asleep.'

'Coulda been the wiring on the lamp,' repeated Harry, as Frank Pugh – fully if somewhat hastily dressed – loomed suddenly in the doorway. 'Was it still on when you fell asleep, Duchess?'

'Coulda been the hot plate,' surmised Pugh.

'No.' Emma shook her head. 'I made sure both were off. One of my uncles started a fire from a cheap lamp that way. My mother would never have the house wired, for just that reason.'

'You can't trust those things,' grumbled the producer. 'We'll be able to tell in the morning. Just glad neither of you –' he bent a significant eye on Kitty, who nodded earnestly, as if she'd been innocently asleep in her own bed – 'were hurt. I'll be bunking in here for the rest of the night,' he added. 'You

ladies can sleep in my cabin. Thank God we got most of the
filming done.'

He glanced at the two cameramen and gave a heavy nod of
approval, then turned his head sharply at voices outside. In
the light that fell through the doorway Emma recognized the
pajama-clad manager of the Seven Summits, and several men
from the stable and grounds staff, soot-smudged and damp
from fire-fighting efforts.

When Pugh went out – Harry and Roger had slipped
discreetly away behind his back – Zal handed Emma back her
tea, said, 'Doesn't look like the fire took much of a hold before
they got it squelched. Frank tried to slip the manager four
hundred dollars to let the cabin burn to the ground for a better
shot, but I guess he could get more from an insurance claim.
So your scenario and notes may even have survived, though
they'll be pretty water-damaged. I'll go over there in the
morning . . . I'm afraid you're gonna have to get a new squawk-
box, Kit—'

Emma caught his arm as he would have risen. 'Zal, I . . .
Can you get someone to-to watch outside Mr Pugh's cabin
until morning? Please.' She was aware that she was shivering
despite the blanket. 'That fire wasn't an accident. I know it.
I don't see how it can have been.'

'Electrical wiring—' began Zal.

'I not only made sure the lamp, and the hot plate, were off,
I unplugged them,' she insisted. 'I have every night we've
been up here. That fire started – I think – right under the
window. Right beside my bed. There was no lamp on that
side, and the whole end of the cabin where the hot plate was,
was dark. I'll swear that window was either forced open, or
broken. Is it? Do you know?'

'I can go look. But with the fire crew running around like
the Keystone Kops, trying to put out the trees that caught on
that side, that won't really tell us anything.'

'No.' Emma subsided into the blanket's scratchy folds, and
coughed again. The inside of her throat felt scorched, her eyes
smarted and her chest ached. While everyone had been milling
around and asking questions in the barrack, Emma had heard
all three Pekes sneeze and cough repeatedly. 'But when we

get back to Hollywood, if it can be arranged, I think I should like to have a better look around Mr Zapolya's office. Just to see what might be there.'

The window in the cabin shared by Emma and Kitty had been broken from the outside. Glass shards littered the floor just beneath it, and strewed the foot of her bed. But that, she knew, could easily have been done by the fire crew. 'We'll have to wait for the insurance company report for evidence about the cause,' said Pugh.

There had actually been relatively little damage, although, as Zal had predicted, Emma's notes and the pages of the re-written scenario for *Peril Under Paris* were water-spotted and stank almost unbearably of smoke. Only a few pages were missing, though they'd been scattered at large all over the room. Presumably, reflected Emma, when she'd blundered into the table in panic and darkness.

Less explicably, her suitcase, and Kitty's, had been found open on Kitty's unburned bed, their contents likewise strewed over the whole unburned side of the room.

For three nights after that she dreamed of fire, to wake with pounding heart, thinking she smelled smoke. Remembering not being able to find the door. Clinging to Zal's shoulders as he stroked her hair, whispered comfort to her in the darkness.

Lou Jesperson – when telephoned upon the company's return to Hollywood on Monday – said that he would read over the police report but didn't see any need for Mrs Blackstone or anyone else to have access to Ernst Zapolya's files. The police, he hinted, had a pretty fair idea who'd done the murder and why, and it didn't have anything to do with Emma or Kitty. 'Or any of that crap they been printing in the papers.' MYSTERIOUS VAGRANT LURKING OUTSIDE ENTER-PRISE, screamed the *Tribune*. A MOTHER'S VENGEANCE! shrieked the *Record*, referring to Betsy April's mother, who had in fact gone to Minnesota to take care of *her* mother, who was gravely ill – rather than to Marina Carver's.

'Putz.' Kitty dropped the phone's earpiece back into its cradle. They were in Kitty's dressing room at Foremost, while lights and cameras were being re-set for the final reconciliation between Cincinnati Wilder and Buddy's widowed and grief-stricken mother ('You bet she's grief-stricken,' Kitty had harumphed over the scenario, 'if Buddy inherited Daddy's millions and she's got to kiss up to Cincinnati to pay the bills.'). 'I wonder if Peggy can sneak us on to the lot again? You do it, honey,' she added, passing the phone to Emma and turning back to her makeup mirror. 'They know my voice at the switchboard.'

But Peggy Donovan, said the Enterprise operator, was not on the lot that day. No, she did not expect her to be there tomorrow either. No, she did not know when Miss Donovan could be reached. She would be delighted to take a message . . .

'Nertz.' Kitty sipped her coffee – not spiked with anything, for once, since it was eight in the morning. Half a commissary donut lay on a plate on a corner of the makeup table, a half-smoked cigarette balanced precariously on the opposite side of the plate's rim. 'Fatima La Encantada says Leos like me will encounter obstacles from the small-minded this week, and this proves it.' She extended a manicured finger to tap the May issue of *The Wisdom of the Stars* that lay beside the little sugar-and-tobacco still life, and cogitated. 'Let's see if she's home.'

She dialed.

'Won't she be asleep?'

'Darling, she'll just be taking off her makeup for bed—'

The phone was evidently still ringing in Peggy's ersatz castle on Wedgewood Place when someone tapped on the French door of the dressing room, called out, 'They've got the lights set up, Miss de la Rose.'

'Thank you, darling!' She handed the phone to Emma, took a final swig of coffee, and set forth.

Five rings later a woman's voice, with the soft accents of the American South, asked, 'Who is this calling, please?'

Maid, thought Emma.

She introduced herself as Camille de la Rose's secretary, and received the information that Miss Donovan was away on location. 'Well, fooey,' said Kitty, when Emma delivered this news to her, two hours later while the lights were being re-set for the close-ups. (The formidable Margaret MacKenzie was surprisingly good at bursting into tears, and Kitty, for a wonder, had crossed the room and clasped her in her arms, if not entirely convincingly, at least to Larry Palmer's satisfaction on the fifth try). Larry, Zal, and Chip Thaw were in conference about the lights around the stand-ins for Harry and the two actresses, while Harry and his 'mother' played pinochle with the musicians.

Kitty cogitated some more.

'Didn't Miss Carlyle say they were going to . . . was it San Clemente Island? Is that far?'

'It's an all-day trip. But you'll love it,' added Kitty, with her dazzling smile. 'We can drive down to Newport tomorrow morning – they'll just be shooting all the B-story stuff with Ken and Darlene here tomorrow and Wednesday. I can phone and arrange a boat, and we can talk to Peggy about getting on to the lot, and be back in Newport for dinner. Then we can go to Enterprise Thursday, and be back here for the pick-up shots Friday . . . Does that sound like a good idea?'

It sounded like a very long day – Emma recalled seeing Newport (*presumably Newport Beach?* Unless there were *two* Newports, which was perfectly possible . . .) on a map, about fifty miles south of Hollywood. But the memory of the mountain air and the mountain quiet – at least for most of the expedition – lingered, and the thought of going to a little beach town was a pleasant one. Sea wind, and memories of Brighton. And crossing at least a fragment of the Pacific . . . 'Is there anything on the island?'

'Oh, gosh, no. Not even trees. It's all barren hills and seagulls and goats. Even the bootleggers won't put in there, because it's so far out, over fifty miles. They all go to Catalina, where at least there's hotels and speakeasies and things. Would my tiny treasures like to get on a big boat and go across the sea?' She leaned from her folding chair to ruffle Black Jasmine's fur.

'But Ernst had a big set built out there for the Isle of Love in *Crowned Heart* – a palace and gondolas and a grove of fake trees – and Peggy told me Von spent another ninety thousand dollars having the set turned into a real palace, not just a false front, so they could shoot indoors, and Jesperson just about had a coronary.' She smiled happily at the thought. 'And he's got about five times as many extras as Ernst was going to use for those scenes—'

'We're ready for you, Miss de la Rose.' Larry Palmer's assistant hastened over to the ring of folding chairs.

Kitty checked the mirror once more, turned to Emma, batted her eyelashes and gave her the look of soulful, loving sympathy which she'd be doing at least a dozen times for the camera for the remainder of the day. 'Of course I love you, you nasty old trout – you only tried to have me sent to the chair for croaking your husband . . .'

Then: 'Oh, and you know what? Von – Mr von Stroheim – and Ernst were friends, so maybe we can ask him who'd want to kill Ernst. I bet the police haven't.'

Then she resumed her expression of pity and love, and sashayed into the Livingstone parlor where her adoring bridegroom and his weeping mother were putting up their cards. The elegant Mrs Livingstone touched a silver curl into place and declared in her ripe Scots voice, 'Let's get this bloody panto in the bag and go get a drink.'

FIFTEEN

Leaving directly after an early breakfast – dogs in tow, along with a picnic basket, portable gramophone (a gift from Mr Pugh. 'Darling, it's *four hours* out to San Clemente Island! Of course we need it!'), parasols, pillows, and a satchel filled with fashion magazines and flasks of gin – Emma and Kitty, with Harry and Roger Clint along as bodyguards, drove south, first through rolling hills cloaked in vineyards and orange groves, then along the sea. Harry was still of the opinion that the fire had been the result of a badly-wired lamp or hotplate, but Roger – leathery and laconic in workman's jeans and cowboy boots – said, 'Won't hurt to go.'

Black Jasmine in her lap, Buttercreme enshrined like a favored concubine in her wicker palanquin and Chang Ming panting happily between the two men in the back seat, Emma breathed the swoony sweetness of miles of orange blossoms and closed her eyes against the caress of the wind.

England, for all its lush green beauty, had nothing like this.

'Besides,' said Kitty yesterday – when Zal had suggested the scheme, between close-ups, medium close-ups, and discussions with Larry about whether Margaret should press her hand to her heart, or should Kitty gasp and cover her lips or clasp her hands to her bosom? – 'we'll need somebody to carry the gramophone.'

Then they reached the sea, and drove for miles beside a stinking dark forest of oil-derricks, like Dante's City of Dis in glaring daylight, between the road and the narrow strip of beach.

So far as Emma could tell – and she found herself looking back frequently – nobody followed them. The road before them and behind was largely empty, save when they drove through the little beach towns: Seal Beach, Sunset Beach,

Huntington Beach. Strings of shops and clapboard houses, and the grimy, inland streets of cottages for the men who worked in the oil fields.

'What are they doing out there?' asked Emma at one point, when the Packard blew a tire just south of Huntington Beach and the men deployed jack, spanners, and lug wrench at the side of the road. Shading her eyes, Emma could look down between the derricks and see the sands: gay beach umbrellas, children plying shovels, small gray birds racing down in the wake of the retreating waves to pick for sand crabs, then dashing frantically back to dry land as the next wave washed in again, as if terrified they'd get their feet wet. Men, dripping swimsuits plastered to muscled bodies, sat far out from shore on long, narrow, round-nosed planks, watching the incoming swell. The waves were running high, and when a particularly strong one approached, the watchers would paddle their planks furiously towards the shore until the rising green wall overtook them, at which point they would spring to their feet on the planks and ride them, standing, balancing like circus riders as they rushed toward the beach with the speed of a freight train.

'Surfin'.' Roger came to stand at her side while Harry tightened lug nuts.

'They do it in Hawaii,' Kitty amplified, joining them, enchanting in a sailor suit and pearls. 'The natives there invented it, and a lot of men do it, here along the beach.'

'I wonder they don't get killed!'

'Like ridin' a fast horse, m'am.' Clint offered her a hand-rolled cigarette, then when both she and Kitty declined, lit it up for himself. 'Safer'n it looks, 'f you know what you're doin'.' Half a grin touched his face. 'Lotta fun, too.'

Emma couldn't keep herself from thinking – as she thought about so many things here in California – *Jim would love to see this. Jim would* try *it . . .*

Miles would try it. The idiot . . .

And despite her love for Zal, a part of her asked – the part that had been asking for the past six years – *Why aren't they here?*

She watched Roger and Harry replace the tools in the

Packard's boot, joking like brothers as they climbed into the front seat ('You girls rest back there . . .'). Sometimes it felt like she'd seen her husband, her brother, her parents, only the day before yesterday. Sometimes it felt like part of some other lifetime. Zal was right, she thought. Actors were different. It wasn't really sadness that she felt, but the thought of them remained.

'There's pretty much nothing on the island,' Harry had warned, when the brown whaleback shape of San Clemente Island finally came into view. 'Couple of ranchers run sheep and goats. Other than that . . .' He shrugged.

When the fifty-foot *Hospidar* came around the rock headland at the southern tip of the island – Kitty had asked its owner-pilot to at least give them a glimpse of the *Crowned Heart* set before putting in at the studio's temporary wharf – Emma exclaimed, 'Good heavens!' and the pilot grinned at her reaction through a black tangle of beard. 'It's an actual palace!'

It was, in fact, she realized, an actual palace: specifically, the Royal Marine Pavilion at Brighton, with heavy graftings from Neuschwanstein and the cathedral of St Basil the Blessed. Groves of trees surrounded it – the only trees she'd seen on the island – and garland-festooned gondolas paddled like water-bugs around a decorative boathouse and quay.

'It actually is a palace *now*,' Kitty agreed, shading her eyes against the afternoon sparkle of the sea. 'Ernst had them build a shell for the long shots, with nothing in it but framing and camera platforms, like the cathedral at Enterprise. He planned to shoot the main action at the studio, where he could control the lighting. But I guess Von insisted there should be real rooms inside, with furniture and everything, so they could shoot interiors and you'd see the cove and the trees and the gondolas through the windows, and people walking up from the terraces. And Willa Jesperson backs him up. She sort of had to, because the last time anybody told Von he couldn't have a set built on location the way he wanted, he just went ahead and built it anyway and had the studio billed for it. Lou Jesperson is about tearing his hair out. It'll look great on film.'

'You think that's something?' Harry considered the gaudy set across the water, as Captain Kapolk's crew – a teenaged boy and girl as sunburned and Slavic-looking as the pilot himself – scrambled to put the craft about toward the larger, temporary studio wharf. 'Get a look at Chaplin's back lot these days. He's doing a film set in Alaska, so it's all flour and salt. They better finish before November when it rains, or they're gonna end up with the world's biggest matzoh on their hands.'

A little tent-city surrounded the wharf, hidden behind the 'Balance Rock' headland and out of any possible camera angle from the palace. They found Peggy Donovan playing pinochle and drinking gin with stout Teddy and two female extras in the wardrobe tent; it was two in the afternoon and most of the male extras were out playing baseball behind the commissary tent, a game which appeared to have been going on for days.

'The whole gang's been sittin' on our cans since Thursday,' complained Peggy, handing off her cards to Harry and picking up a couple of bottles of Coca-Cola as she led her guests to the rear of the tent. 'The man's re-written Stephan coming down on to the terrace six times and filmed about twelve versions of each try. At least he made sure that everybody who was in the boat-sinking scene could actually swim, and Bruce talked him out of using real knives in that knife-throwing scene . . .'

Her eyes got big, however, when Emma related the events in Big Bear. 'Tried to *kill* you?'

'I don't know if it was me they were trying to kill,' said Emma, 'or Kitty. But whoever this is – whatever is behind this – we need to find them. And I have the impression the police aren't really interested in who the real killer is—'

'Oh, goshers, no.' Peggy dumped judicious cap-fulls from her flask into each bottle of pop. 'The last thing Jesperson wants is the cops maybe finding out that Marina really *did* bump off Ernst – or risking the papers opening up that whole question again, even if she didn't.'

'Which I personally don't think she did,' put in Kitty

unexpectedly. 'I mean, she might have taken a potshot at Ernst while she was drunk at a party—'

Peggy sniffed. 'Like that was nothing?'

'No, of course it was something, honey, and she had no business shooting at you that time – I mean, she'd *invited* you . . .'

'I thought that was Desiree she shot at?' broke in Emma, and Kitty waved the query aside.

'That was another time . . . But why go after Emma and me to shut us up? Anything Ernst would have told me, she could probably find out, and what would it be anyway?'

'Could it have been about money?' Emma hoped her tone was sufficiently casual.

Peggy considered the matter. 'I don't think so.' She fished in her dirndl pocket for her cigarette case. 'Marina makes shitloads more than Ernst ever did, and she's not a miser – she blows it as soon as she gets it. Or gives it to her crazy mother. And Ernst gives you a lecture if you even *mention* money – *gave* you a lecture,' she corrected herself. 'He was always in Dutch with Jesperson because he never knew what things cost, like Chaplin and Pickford do.'

She sipped her drink, made a face, and added more of whatever was in the flask. Emma had observed bowls of peanuts on the trestle table with the guardsmen's caps and the bins of silk flowers. 'I think you have to be cold sober to kill for money, unless it's in something like a crap game, on the spur of the moment.'

To Emma's request for further details about the mysterious 'other woman', Peggy, upon consideration, had little to add. 'He was sort of drunk when he told me about her. And it was real late. This was back in March when we started filming, and Ronnie had been flubbing his lines and we couldn't get the conspiracy scene right and the lights were giving us all kinds of shit. Ernst was wound up like a watch spring so we went back to his office for a couple of drinks and one thing led to another, so it was about two in the morning by the time I was leaving. He bundled me up in a coat and hat to walk me to my car and I said, Lou wouldn't care if word got around.'

Her eyes narrowed, gazing through the tent opening at
the baseball players, who were trying to drive a half-dozen
goats away from second base. 'He said it wasn't Lou, but
a woman he was seeing who was jealous. I said, "Nomie
Carlyle doesn't have a jealous bone in her body," and he
said, "Good God, what could that little coosie do to me?
It isn't the ones who come to you for favors," he said, "it's
the ones who are in love, who feel the great passion, that
are dangerous. Particularly if . . ." And then he stopped
himself, and said, for me not to tell anybody what he'd
said because this woman, whoever she is, is someone
he absolutely couldn't afford to be connected with. "It
would be the end of me," he said. It's the only time he
mentioned her.'

Kitty sniffed. 'He always did expect girls to be sticking
their heads in the oven because they loved him so much.'

'Maybe.' Peggy lit a cigarette – a plain American gasper,
Emma noted – and picked a fragment of tobacco off her lip.
'Except the next day, he took me aside first thing I walked on
the lot, and made me promise again that I'd never repeat a
word of what he'd said. He said again, "It would be the end
of me.".'

'He never mentioned that it might be – well – a bootlegger's
girlfriend, did he?'

'Oh, you mean like that poor sap Mark Todhunter, who got
knocked off the week before last for smooching Pinky
Poubelle?' Peggy contemplated. 'Coulda been. Ernst went to
some pretty scroogy dives sometimes.'

'Is he the kind who'd keep love letters in his office?' asked
Emma. 'I don't suppose he'd have anything at his home. Not
if Miss Carver could look through his things while he was at
the studio.'

'I dunno. If he was smart he wouldn't.'

'If he was smart,' said Kitty, 'he wouldn't get himself
mixed up with some gangster's squeeze who was spoony
on him. But Ernst wasn't really smart, you know. Not about
women, that's for sure. Marina's nuts,' she went on. 'And
a lot of times she thinks she was in love with Ernst. But
she was divorcing him, which is a lot smarter than killing

somebody and cheaper, too – especially if the four-flusher was screwing Nomie Carlyle and six other extras and some bruno's moll as well. It's not like she'd have to pay a detective to learn about it. And that *still* wouldn't explain anybody trying to kill Emma and me.'

'Is there a chance,' asked Emma, 'that you could get us on to the lot again, to have a look at his office? Is there a way you could get a key?'

'I could get you on the lot,' said Peggy thoughtfully. 'I mean, I could go out to the back lot by the gate where they bring in the horses and the hay and all that, after it's locked up for the evening, and unlock it for you – the key's just in the tack room. They've put Von into Ernst's office, but Mike Nye shares the building with him, and I can probably talk Mike into giving me his key. Jesperson went through the desk, and took Ernst's camera and film rolls – just in case he'd taken any snapshots of anything he wasn't supposed to. And I sure hope he didn't find the ones of *me*. But there's still drawers and boxes full of shit in there. It's mostly accounts and invoices from the pictures he made. He had to keep that.'

'Having waked up with my room in flames,' said Emma quietly, 'and found evidence that someone has been searching the house, I think I'm willing to take the time to look. It can't be any worse than searching through 1887 archaeological field notes for the location of non-communal burials in the Apennines. He never gave any other hint about anything . . . odd?' She recalled just how long it had taken her to find reference to the grave of that middle-aged woman who had been buried with a sword, a dagger, and a helmet (for what reason her father had never been able to ascertain). 'Anything that didn't seem to fit?'

'Beats me. I didn't know him that well, you know,' Peggy added. 'We only screwed when we were making a picture together – well, after I got feature roles, anyway. Except when I was an extra in *Atlantis*, but I don't think he remembered me.' She shivered at some memory, and for an instant she looked older, and grim.

Emma opened her mouth to wonder that any of those

hopefuls would lie with the man who hired sharpshooters to fire live ammunition over their heads because it looked better on film.

And closed it again, as somebody shouted something outside the commissary tent, and Peggy added, 'Shit,' and looked at her watch. 'By the time he gets the reflectors set and walks us through every single person's part, the light'll be going. Can you come back to the dressing-tent with me and hook me up, Duchess?' She was shedding her kimono as she walked through the wardrobe tent to the baked landscape outside, Emma and Kitty at her heels.

'Remember to take off your watch,' Kitty said.

The two young women found Erich von Stroheim thirty minutes later in the orchard that lay below the palace walls. Stiff-leaved dwarf oak trees reared from immense pots, the white carnations wired to their branches wilting already. Emma wondered whose task it would be to replace them before filming commenced. The pots themselves were semi-camouflaged with honeysuckle and jasmine, from which the afternoon sun coaxed dizzying perfume. At the edge of the grove closest to the palace, groundsmen moved the trees around as cameramen set up scrims and filters, under the smiling gaze of a black enameled mermaid, sitting with outstretched arms on a globe of the world above the palace door. All of this, the director watched with a critical eye.

'A woman?' he said, when Kitty introduced Emma and broached the subject of a mysterious *amour* and the fear Emma was certain she had heard in Zapolya's voice. 'Ernst wouldn't put himself in danger for Helen of Troy and Cleopatra rolled into one. The man was a satyr but not a fool.'

His voice was firm and pleasant and his accent less than Nomie's caricature had made of it. Like many film actors, he was small and seemed a little underweight in his riding breeches and neat tweed jacket. Close up, his cropped head – shaven at the sides, like the Polish Cossacks – and the monocle he affected gave him a military look, were it not for the wicked brightness, like an evil elf, of his sharp-featured face. He smoked Russian cigarettes, nearly twice as long as American, and gave the impression of a Teutonic nobleman about to summon his lackeys to have a peasant thrashed.

'He never mentioned to you a woman whom it was dangerous to . . . to visit?'

'He did,' agreed von Stroheim. 'But I can't see him continuing such a liaison once he realized the danger. There are men who take pleasure in making love with a loaded gun on the nightstand. Ernst wasn't one of those. For him, women were a pleasure, an indulgence – like too much ice cream . . .' He cocked a dark, reproving eye at Kitty, who stuck out her tongue at him. 'But not an obsession. Myself, I think it far likelier that what frightened him – that what he was trying to conceal – was his political views.'

'Political?' said Emma, startled.

'He was a member of the Communist Party,' said the director. 'Not like Max Eastman and his pet socialists, but the blood-red Bolshevist side of the movement: men who regard Lenin's smallest farts as holy doctrine. For some years now, the Russians have been trying to establish connections in the studios, with the intention of making films to showcase their view of how society should be organized.'

He exhaled a thin track of smoke. 'They sent that fellow Plotkin here with a delegation a few years ago, supposedly to see how American films were made but actually to learn whatever they could about how to build cameras, lighting, editing equipment – and to raise money. They see – as Americans are only beginning to see – how powerful is the effect of a story, upon someone sitting in the dark for two hours, absorbing whatever the director of the piece chooses to tell them. There is nothing like it.'

'Honestly!' Kitty made a gesture like a woman shooing flies. 'Next you're going to tell me that Charlie Chaplin is responsible for a wave of disorderly butt-kickings spreading across the United States.'

Von Stroheim grinned, the sinister aristocrat vanishing,

monocle notwithstanding. 'Time to invest in pies, I suppose
. . . No. But think about how long women's frocks were before
the war, before every woman in film – except those portrayed
as silly and old-fashioned – started wearing hemlines three-
quarters of the way up their calves. That's ten years – not
really very long. Or the way women drive cars now, or smoke
cigarettes in public, something they see women doing in films
all the time.'

'*I* was certainly smoking ten years ago . . .'

'When you were ten?' He raised an eyebrow, and Kitty
drew herself up to her full five-foot height.

'I started early.'

He clicked his booted heels and bowed deep acquiescence,
then turned back to Emma. 'I think they're imbeciles – well,
you'd have to be an imbecile to believe that humankind is
actually going to stop being greedy and selfish and willing to
accept only what they need, so that others may have all that
they need. But I can name you a dozen men in the studios
who support the Wobblies and Sinclair.'

'Oh, God, yes,' agreed Kitty. 'Dirk Silver is *always*
passing out copies of *Pravda* and *The Daily Worker* to the
camera crews and extras, when he thinks nobody's going
to report him to Frank. Chang, *no!*' she added, yanking the
leash as Chang Ming – clearly under the impression that
the trees around them were genuine – attempted to treat
the nearest one as such. The little dog looked at her
reproachfully.

'But Ernst didn't believe any of that anymore for *years*,'
she went on. 'He told me so . . . and told Peggy, too.'

'And this was on the same occasion that he told you he
loved you?' Von Stroheim raised one brow again. 'And Miss
Donovan too, of course.'

She made a face at him again. 'Ernst *never* told me he
loved me. Well, except that time we were screwing on his
desk in his office and he was kind of drunk. Oh, and that
time in the prop room. I don't think he *ever* said that to
Peggy.'

'Perhaps he became an advocate of unvarnished truth once

the Bureau of Investigation began deporting Communists.' Von Stroheim bowed again. 'Particularly Communists from places like Russia and Poland. But the fact remains that since Lenin's death in January, there has been a split within the Communist Party itself – indeed, before Lenin died. There are those who advocate keeping elements of European and American ways of doing things, like trade unions and private farms: Trotsky, and Zinoviev – and those who claim autonomy to Soviet daughter-states like Georgia and the Ukraine. Josef Stalin – who has been helping to run the country during Lenin's illness – is working to consolidate his power, and there are a number of followers of Trotsky and others who have decided it might be a good idea to get places in the delegations that the Moscow Art Theater is sending to places like Hollywood and New York.'

'I sure would.' Kitty performed a theatrical shudder. 'But why would he want help from *me*? Nobody in their right mind would.'

'And he said nothing to you? Not on the day of his death, but earlier.'

'Not so much as the filling in an ant's back tooth. And why would anybody be trying to kill me and Emma, over something that Ernst wanted to tell us? And the cops just want to go along with Jesperson and sweep the whole thing under the rug – it's enough to make you think Jesperson's got something to hide.'

'I would not be surprised to learn that he did.'

'Do you have,' asked Emma, 'Mr Zapolya's files still in your office on the Enterprise lot? His personal files, I mean. And might there be a chance that we can see them?'

'You are welcome to them, of course, madame.'

At this point Black Jasmine barked gruffly, and the director turned his head as a sizeable army of peasants – led by a dirndl-clad Peggy Donovan clutching a petition for Peace and Justice in her hands – appeared on the edge of the orchard.

'If you ladies will excuse me.' Von Stroheim clicked his heels and bowed again, then reached down to scratch all three

Pekes on the napes. When he moved to pat Buttercreme, the shy little dog approached him, then scurried a few feet away, then turned back, looking flirtatiously over her shoulder at him – advanced and retreated, as if doing a little fan dance with her tail.

The director grinned again: 'A Hollywood coquette, that one. Myself –' he straightened up – 'I think that if Ernst was indeed involved with a woman who was a danger to him – or whose husband or lover was – he would keep no mention of it, unless it were in his checkbook, in the record of expensive little gifts from Arpels's or Tiffany.'

'Not even that,' sniffed Kitty. 'The pearls he gave *me* were straight out of the prop department.'

'And any communication he had with the Communist Party,' the Austrian went on, 'he would keep hidden likewise, not for some script-girl or assistant director to stumble upon when seeking for notes concerning the Storming of Ravenstark or the Grand Entry of King Hubert to the Isle of Love. I will let you know,' he finished, bowing again over Emma's hand, then Kitty's 'when I return to town, and you will be welcome to whatever you can find. But I suspect that it will not be a great deal.'

And he turned, to marshal the some two hundred royal guardsmen, who had appeared hard on the heels of the peasants (*If the war's still going on why aren't they at the Front?* wondered Emma), while his cameramen skirmished on the edges of the crowd and glanced nervously at the slowly sinking sun.

'Well, nertz.' Kitty kicked at a stone as the two young women returned along the trackway toward the production camp. 'And at this rate he's going to be chasing his tail out here for another two weeks, and God knows who's going to try to murder us in the meantime. I wonder if Lou Jesperson really *is* up to something? Or if he'd try to murder me just to put *Hot Potato* behind schedule, and then blame it on the Communists or Ernst's gangster snuggle-bunny or poor Nomie for that matter? I wonder if Dirk Silver would know anything about the Reds?'

'If he did,' reasoned Emma, reining in Black Jasmine when the tiny dog attempted to pursue a jackrabbit twice his own size into the scrub, 'I doubt he would admit it. I wonder how one would get in touch with the Bureau of Investigation?'

SIXTEEN

As events transpired, a search for representatives of the Bureau of Investigation turned out not to be necessary.

The following day Emma was at the kitchen table, patiently trying to transpose Miriam the beautiful Briton slave-girl into Marianne the beautiful country girl, newly arrived in Paris (*Searching for a long-lost brother? Fleeing from a broken heart . . .?*) and under the sway of the arrogant and commanding (*arrogant and commanding what? General? Diplomat? Old-line aristocrat?*) Jules Poilu, when all three dogs began to bark, and someone knocked at the door.

Drat it . . .

One of the men was tall and thin and bespectacled, rather resembling a poorly-made marionette. The other was short, stocky, and blue around his fleshy jowls. Both wore suits – one blue and one brown – so anonymous they could have come from the Foremost wardrobe department for use in a spy film. *The Secret of Agent X . . .*

They almost visibly skulked.

'Miss Camille de la Rose?' asked the short man.

'I'm sorry,' said Emma. 'And your name is . . .?'

'Or Mrs Chava Flint?'

The use of Kitty's actual legal name took Emma aback. To her knowledge, only Frank Pugh, Conrad Fishbein, Zal, and the Foremost lawyer Al Spiegelmann knew the name under which Kitty had been born, much less that of her most recent husband.

'I'm Mrs Blackstone,' she said firmly.

'John Peth.' The man held up his wallet to display a buff card bearing his photograph and the legend: *United States Bureau of Investigation*. 'Bureau of Investigation. Mrs Emma Blackstone?'

She said, 'Please do come in. I was just going to telephone you.'

Chang Ming dashed up as the two agents crossed the threshold and flung himself ecstatically on his back to have his tummy rubbed. Both men looked down at him as if they'd never seen a dog before. Buttercreme ran and hid behind the liquor cabinet.

'May I offer you some lemonade or Coca-Cola?' Emma gestured them to the sleek chrome-and-black leather couch. 'Are you here about the murder of Mr Zapolya on the third? Or the attempt on my own life and that of Miss de la Rose last week?'

The two men traded a glance that they tried hard not to look startled. 'The Bureau was not aware of any attempt on yourself and Miss de la Rose,' said the taller agent disapprovingly. 'Perhaps you would care to give us an account of it after we've discussed Mr Zapolya's death.'

'I would love to,' said Emma. 'Please do excuse me for a moment . . .'

She descended the four steps to the kitchen, fetched ice and soda-pop, arranging the tray neatly as her nanna had taught her to do in the long-ago predictable peace of Oxford (*How can that have been only ten years ago?*).

As she re-entered the living-room Kitty said, 'Darling, *Coke*? That's very sweet of you, but would you boys like a real drink?'

Clothed in a kimono of burgundy silk embroidered with peacocks, her hair in fetching disarray but every square millimeter of her makeup camera-perfect, Kitty descended the stairs, stooped gracefully to lift Black Jasmine in her arms. It was past noon – Emma wondered whether she had already been making up when she'd heard the voices downstairs, or whether the sound of them had rolled her out of bed and galvanized her into this rapid cosmetic perfection. The task usually took her hours.

'The Eighteenth Amendment to the United States Constitution expressly forbids the manufacture, sale, or transportation of intoxicating liquors,' reported the taller agent.

'Oh, that's perfectly all right.' Kitty widened her kohl-dark eyes at him. 'According to the label it was manufactured in Canada, and I didn't buy or transport it. I found it on my doorstep. It was my birthday. There was a bunch of the most *beautiful* yellow orchids with it.'

Emma set the tray on the coffee table before their guests.

Agent Peth said, 'Neither Agent Shardborn nor I drinks, Miss de la Rose.'

'Oh, I'm *so* sorry,' she sympathized. 'But I do, so would you be a darling, Emma, and fix me a highball? Thank you! Fix yourself something, too, sweetheart, if you'd care to.' It was, as Emma had noted previously, only a few minutes before noon.

Kitty produced her cigarettes and fitted one to her amber holder. Both agents, with the air of men performing an unfamiliar task in which they have been rigorously rehearsed, produced lighters and struck flame for her, and she gave them a heart-stopping smile of gratitude. 'Guess you want to hear all about what happened on the third?'

'Thank you,' said Agent Peth, 'yes.' Agent Shardborn took a notebook from his pocket; Agent Peth drew up the covered chinoiserie bowl on the coffee table which contained the assortment of candy to which Frank Pugh was deeply addicted.

Emma related her part of the story first: that Kitty had had an early call at the studio (*Let's not get into the issue of where her starting-point was that morning . . .*); that she, Emma, had answered Mr Zapolya's call, and had relayed the information to Miss de la Rose when she herself had arrived at the studio an hour and a half later.

'And he said that it was urgent that he speak to Miss de la Rose that morning?' Agent Peth unwrapped a tootsie-roll, carefully folded the paper, and stowed it neatly in his jacket pocket.

'He emphasized it several times,' agreed Emma. 'He said, "This is not some Hollywood intrigue", that it was a matter upon which lives depended. Perhaps, he said, the future of this country.'

The two agents traded another glance.

'He asked us to tell no one of the meeting—'

'Well, *that* went without saying,' put in Kitty, with another wide-eyed glance. 'His wife's the most jealous heifer in Hollywood.'

While her guest, with the deliberation of a maiden aunt, unwrapped and consumed five more tootsie-rolls, Kitty went on to describe their late arrival at Enterprise, their attempt to catch the director after the explosive chaos of the Storming of Ravenstark by the American Expeditionary Force, and their coming upon Zapolya's body, with a distraught actress lying unconscious amid the debris nearby.

'That would be Miss Naomi Crumm?'

'Nomie Carlyle is her working name. Ernst had asked her to meet him, but I don't know if it had anything to do with his meeting *me* or not. I mean, *I* was supposed to see him at eight about the future of this country, but *she* was only going to meet him after the filming was done – since his wife was on the lot that day. She said she saw a woman in a black dress come out of the set while the shooting was going on, and head away from her. She tried to follow her, when she saw Ernst was dead, but an explosion had jammed the doorway shut. That's probably all in the police report, isn't it?'

'It is, miss. We understand that Miss Crumm – Miss Carlyle – is out of town filming and should be back tomorrow.'

'Not with von Stroheim directing, she won't.' Kitty took a long draw on her cigarette. 'You'll be lucky to see her before Saturday. They're out on San Clemente Island in the Channel – I hope you don't get seasick easily.'

Both agents appeared alarmed at the thought, but Agent Peth went on bravely, 'Thank you, Miss de la Rose.' He popped yet another tootsie-roll into his tight-lipped little mouth, and folded up and bestowed the waxed paper in his pocket yet again. 'You were well acquainted with Mr Zapolya?'

'Not really.' She frowned a little. 'I mean, we'd screwed a couple of times when I was an extra on . . .' She hesitated infinitesimally, as if calculating the date of the production in question against her purported current age. 'That is, we had a little fling last year when he was doing *Caribbean Bride*, and we've met socially ever since . . .'

Emma recalled the pearl necklace under Zapolya's desk and said nothing.

'Did he ever mention belonging to a group called the Workers' Liaison? Or a man named Plotkin, or members of his delegation?'

Kitty shook her head.

'Francisco Castillo? I don't know what name he'd be going by in the States. Dmitri Druganin? Or Mats Brochnow?'

'Didn't Brochnow used to write scenarios for Monarch?'

'He did, miss.' Agent Peth consulted a notebook of his own. 'During and immediately after the war, a number of German and Russian socialists sought work in motion pictures, and more recently, the Soviet government in Russia has begun to nationalize and organize a film industry in Russia itself, for propaganda purposes. They've been trying to gain influence with the studios in this country, and a number of Communist actors and directors are active in Hollywood.'

'Do you mean Communist, or socialist?' asked Emma, and Peth gave her a fishy stare.

'They're the same thing, m'am.'

Emma opened her mouth to point out that the formation of labor unions did not inevitably lead to the nationalization of industry, and closed it. Argument, she understood – as with Madge Burdon and the first-century tiger population of the British Isles – would get them nowhere.

'Many of these friends and supporters of the Soviet regime have offered jobs, financial assistance, and support to outright Communist agents,' Peth continued. 'For some years now the Bureau has been searching for a Mexican agent named Francisco Castillo, who was active in the uprising against General Obregón and disappeared across the border into Texas. Recently we've been given reason to believe he's in Los Angeles. We know Castillo was interested in the use of films for revolutionary propaganda, and that he worked with Ernst Zapolya when Zapolya was at Azteca Films in Mexico City during the war. Does any of this sound familiar, Miss de la Rose?'

Another tootsie-roll.

'I knew he'd worked at Azteca.' Kitty considered the matter, and Emma reflected that for all her appearance of empty-headed frivolity, her sister-in-law had some surprising areas of knowledge, rising like islands from a sea of persiflage and gin. 'Mostly what it meant was that he got invited to Romy Novarro's parties, and he'd get just *armies* of Mexican extras from Pedro Carmona, and he'd laugh when the horse-wranglers from Chatsworth Livery would make jokes about Lou Jesperson in Spanish. But like I said,' she finished, widening her dark eyes, 'other than sleeping with him I didn't really know him that well.'

She shrugged. 'And after he married Marina Carver last year, he steered clear of me, which was just fine with me. Well, except for that time at Frank's birthday party. But if *I* was married to Marina Carver, I'd be careful about who I took into my office to see my etchings.'

'What makes you think this Castillo would have gotten in touch with Mr Zapolya?' asked Emma, and again received the blank wariness of Peth's dark glance.

'These are only routine enquiries, m'am.'

'I only ask,' she went on, 'because an attempt was made to murder Miss de la Rose and myself last Friday night in Big Bear. Have *you* been following us? Either of us?'

The brown eyes shifted sidelong again to meet the blue. Agent Shardborn said, 'It's standard procedure to ascertain who we're dealing with, before we make contact, m'am.'

I suppose that means 'Yes' . . .

'Did you search this house?'

Again the sidelong look exchanged.

'It is standard procedure . . .' began Agent Shardborn.

'I only ask,' repeated Emma, 'because I did notice that on Tuesday – the day after we returned from Big Bear – when I refilled that candy dish, there were almost no tootsie-rolls left in it: tootsie-rolls being Mr Pugh's favorite candy. And you did know what was in the dish before you opened it, because you drew it to you the moment you sat down.'

Agent Shardborn gave Agent Peth a stare of deep disappointment.

'And you left a cigarette end on the upstairs bathroom sink. A Turkish Murad.'

Both men frowned. Almost in unison, Agent Shardborn produced a packet of Camels; Agent Peth, a pack of Lucky Strikes. Shardborn added earnestly, 'Neither of us would ever smoke a cigarette tossing a house, m'am. The smell stays in the curtains.' He replaced the cigarettes in an inner pocket, picked up his notebook again, and thumbed back half a dozen pages. 'When did you find this cigarette butt?'

And he held out the notebook. His printing was tiny and painfully neat, like the work of a neurotic ant, but Emma could read at the top of the page Kitty's address, followed by the date, May 15, 4:47 p.m.

On the fifteenth of May, she had been lying on a blanket with Zal beside Big Bear Lake, speaking of a broken arm when in fact she meant a broken heart.

'Und this you believe?' Dirk Silver – known at Berlin's UFA studios as Dieter Schwebler before his rather hasty exodus from the German capital – transferred his startling blue gaze from Zal to Emma to Kitty, took a drag on his cigarette (a gold-tipped brown Sobranie), then set it down and began mopping cold cream on to his face.

'Was Mr Zapolya indeed a Communist?' asked Emma.

Zal translated, but by the way the star's eyes snapped she guessed he understood *Zapolya* and *Communist*, and answered almost before the words were out of the cameraman's mouth.

'*Pah! Ein Magermilchkommunist, ohne Verstand und ohne Eier!*'

Kitty poured drinks for herself and Dirk from her flask, and Dirk – in the process of removing a thick maquillage of Motion Picture Yellow, powder, rouge, and kohl – embarked on a long harangue, periodically jabbing at his guests with one manicured finger.

'First,' explained Zal, when the German paused for breath (and a drink), 'you ladies are idiots for believing a word that scabrous lackey of capitalism told you, but he adds that it's just like women.'

'He's got a lot of nerve,' retorted Kitty. 'If he swallows half the horsefeathers the Russians say about how wonderful things are in Russia—!'

'Be that as it may,' said Zal quickly, seeing Silver's head snap around at the scorn in Kitty's tone. 'He says Ernst was no true Communist, just a cowardly backsliding Trotskyite who would sell out the Revolution for bus fare and wouldn't walk across the street to keep a working man from being murdered by government pigs.'

'*Der Mann hat Blut an seinen Händen.*' Anger darkened the handsome face. '*Drei Schauspieler hat er getötet, ermordet – drei! – nur um des Spektakels willen. Ein faules und gefühlloses Schwein!*'

'Killed . . .' translated Emma painstakingly. 'Murdered . . .'

'I'm afraid he's right about that, Em,' said Zal quietly. 'He means the extras who were killed filming the downfall of Atlantis – and at least two others that I know about, on earlier films who were crippled by explosions. Jesperson just bought 'em off . . . cheap. About two hundred dollars apiece.'

'*Was kümmert ihn der Arbeiter? Er würde die Revolution verraten, Zinoviev den Hintern küssen und Stalin den Hunden verkaufen!*'

'You see,' said Zal, as Kitty poured another drink for Silver and, outside the French doors of the dressing room, Madge Burdon shouted goodnight to the departing camera crews – the palace of Versailles having closed down for the night – 'since Lenin croaked in January, I guess the whole Communist Party is split over who's going to step in now and run the show. Trotsky's got the Red Army behind him, and Stalin was originally teamed up with Zinoviev. But now I've heard they've started fighting among themselves as well.'

Silver turned in his chair, muscular and powerful in his undershirt and the gleaming satin breeches and silk stockings of a French aristocrat of the *ancien régime*, and recommenced his lecture with a torrent of words in which Emma caught 'Castillo, Mexico' and '*halbherziges sozialistisches Weichei*'.

'I guess Castillo's a socialist in favor of land reform in

Mexico,' translated Zal at last. 'Which makes him a *Weichei* – a soft-boiled egg – as far as Stalinists are concerned.'

'*Er will das System reparieren. Wenn Sie das System reparieren, haben Sie immer noch dasselbe verrottete System!*' declared Silver passionately. '*Sie müssen das System zerstören!*'

Zal asked him, 'Is Castillo here in LA?' Emma knew enough German to follow the question, and Silver flung up his hands in disgust, with another spate of commentary.

'Let me guess,' said Emma. 'He doesn't know and he doesn't care.'

'Actually he says that he hopes Castillo has sunk to the bottom of the La Brea Tar Pits and good riddance to a dish-licking capitalist lackey who'll set back the cause of true Communism in Mexico, but he actually doesn't know if he's in town or not.' He turned to listen to another tirade. 'OK . . . sounds like Castillo's supporters have been trying to put together a deal with the Zapatistas and President Obregón for land reform, and about damn time if you ask me. I'm guessing Castillo went to Zapolya for help getting back into Mexico. The prop department can come up with some pretty convincing travel papers.'

A query as to whether Zapolya had ever mentioned Castillo – or connections among the socialist groups in Los Angeles – elicited only obvious scorn and further references to soft-boiled eggs and a word that Emma thought meant either 'eyes' or 'eggs' but apparently didn't.

'I still don't see what any of this has to do with *me*,' protested Kitty, after they'd walked Silver (now cleansed of makeup and natty in street clothes) back to his new and shiny car, parked behind Wardrobe, and seen him drive away into the cool mists of the California night. With the conclusion of Seth Ramsay's duel with Dirk earlier that evening (the evil Dirk, in the character of the sinister Comte de Noailles-Roquelaure, had cheated), the studio was now quiet, the last of Herr Volmort's makeup crew just making their way to the gates to catch the final streetcars down Sunset Boulevard. The lights all shut off in the stages. Silence lay among the medieval villages and New York streets of the back lot.

In seven hours, reflected Emma, the extras would start lining up outside the door of Belle Delaney's little office. In eight, Zal would be back with his eye to the lens of his camera, adjusting the settings while Kitty's poor stand-in Ruby Saks posed beneath the glare of the lights on Stage Two and Kitty herself prepared for a spectacular double wedding with Harry, Ken Elmore, and Emily Violet.

'It may have nothing to do with you,' pointed out Zal, hoisting Buttercreme's wicker carry box into the back of the Packard. 'I'm guessing Francisco Castillo is holed up in one of the barrios east of the river, or out in the San Gabriel Valley . . . I know there's at least one camp of socialists still hiding out from the Revolution in the Cahuenga Hills only a couple miles from your place on Ivarene.'

'And the Bureau of Investigation thinks another socialist like Zapolya would tell *Kitty* where he's hidden?'

'He'd have to be out of his *mind.*' Kitty climbed into the driver's seat in a great fluff of marabou and fringe. 'Everything I know about Mexican revolutionaries you could write on a French postcard and still have room for one of Nick Thaxter's jokes. And that still doesn't explain why somebody would follow Emma all over town. Or try to kill *me.*'

Zal shook his head, helped Emma into the car, and handed her Black Jasmine and Chang Ming. 'Don't look at me. But the last thing Stalin wants is for a moderate socialist to go back to Mexico and calm things down between angry workers and the new president there. Like Dirk says, you fix the system, and you've still got the same rotten system. The point is to destroy the system.'

'By shooting the director of *Crowned Heart*?'

Zal shrugged. 'Maybe Stalin just doesn't like Ruritanian romances.'

He gave Emma a quick kiss, climbed into his own Bearcat, and followed the Packard out the studio gates. But as the Bearcat turned right into the thin midnight traffic of the Boulevard, heading for the oil derricks and barley fields and, eventually, the absurd little beach town of Venice, and the Packard turned (hair-raisingly) left, Emma thought she saw a car pull away from the curb half a block away.

Either it isn't the same car, or they've fixed their headlight. Or I'm imagining things.

No one followed them up Ivarene. But it took her a long time to fall asleep that night. And she dreamed about the smell of smoke.

SEVENTEEN

The following afternoon – Thursday, the twenty-second of May – as Emma crossed back from Stage Two where Kitty and Harry, Ken Elmore and Emily Violet were doing so-called 'pick-up shots', close-ups, or bits of business to amplify scenes already filmed, when she entered Kitty's dressing room she saw the slight dimming of the light from the French door behind her, and turned to see that Seth Ramsay had followed her in.

'Hey, Duchess.' He gave her a smoldering smile – but his eyes did not smile at all. 'You been avoiding me or something?'

He was clad, as Dirk Silver had been yesterday, in half a costume – an undershirt that showed off the muscles of his powerful arms, skin-tight doeskin breeches, and knee-boots. *The stuff that dreams are made of,* reflected Emma, *if one happens to be a fourteen-year-old girl . . .*

He came towards her and she thought, *If I slap him Zal's going to hear of it and take up for me . . . Pugh would get rid of a cameraman sooner than a box-office star . . .*

She stood her ground as he reached to take her in his arms, then said, 'No, in fact, I've been meaning to find you. I was looking at last week's dailies from *The Thornless Rose—*'

As she suspected he would, he stopped. There might be actors who would prioritize rape over hearing about their own dailies, but Seth Ramsay wasn't one of them.

'I don't wish to be critical, but you're an artist – and a very fine one – so I knew you would appreciate knowing . . . Are you aware of how badly you slouch when you walk? It's very easily corrected,' she went on, as Ramsay, dismayed, tried to pull himself straighter without being obvious about it. 'But it is *very* distracting. And I do think you need to pay more attention to your gestures, particularly in the fencing scene. Your wrist-motion is all wrong. My brother fenced for his regiment, you know, and . . . Again, I'm sorry' – Ramsay was staring at her as if she'd pulled a gun on him – 'but I know that as an artist you'd want to know about something that . . . well, that *obvious*. Because your footwork is too narrow, and too small.' She scooped up her notes for *Peril Under Paris*, beamed upon him, and slipped past him out the door.

She continued her re-writing work for the day in Kitty's 'base camp' in Stage Two, trying to shut from her mind Larry's patient coaching ('Let's try it leaning more to the left, Kit, and maybe lean back a little more away from Harry's arm . . . C'mon, Ken, this is the love of your life telling you she understands, that she's yours – this is what you've been hungering for the past seven reels . . .!'). But anger made it difficult to focus her mind, a situation not improved when an hour later Madge Burdon entered ('Damn, what the hell's got into Seth? He was practically tripping over his own feet and walking like he's got a stick up his ass . . .') with further revisions required for *Peril Under Paris*.

'Now Pugh's saying every-goddam-body in Hollywood is doing horseback chases, and can we come up with something that DeMille and Griffith haven't done? I'm sorry to pile this on you, Duchess, but . . .'

'No,' said Emma, 'that will be quite all right. In fact,' she went on, after a moment's consideration, 'what about a chase through the sewers of Paris? Poilu and his henchmen pursuing in a boat, poor Gaston swimming, floundering, trying to find and rescue Marianne with the waters rising in flood all around him—'

It it's good enough for Victor Hugo and Gaston Leroux . . .

'Wow!' The director's eyes flared with delight as she visualized the scene. 'It's pouring rain outside . . . the river's coming up . . .'

'And rats,' amplified Emma, picturing soaked and muddy rodents creeping over the fastidious Seth Ramsay's maize-gold curls. 'Swarms of them . . . He stumbles into one of their lairs, and the walls are carpeted with the vermin—'

'*Yes*!' Hands clasped to her bosom, Madge Burdon groaned

the word like a bride discovering the meaning of the universe on her wedding night. 'Wow! That's *amazing*!'

'No, wait!' cried Emma, carried away on the wings of her own inspiration. 'The evil Poilu *traps* Gaston, and ties him up in the Chamber of Rats—'

She thought Madge was going to take her in her arms and kiss her, à la Seth and Harry . . . *and pretty much everybody else in Hollywood . . .*

The director settled for snatching off her tweed cap and hurling it to the floor. 'Frank'll shit!' she crowed. 'He'll love it! He'll roll around on the floor!'

Everybody in the Livingstone parlor – Larry and both cameramen and the stand-ins included – had ceased even attempting to amplify the love lives of the principals with tender close-ups and were craning their necks to overhear.

'And the water's flooding in . . .' enthused Madge.

'Can you film underwater? The filthy, garbage-filled water closes over his head as he struggles with his bonds—'

'Shit, yes! Keaton's out shooting underwater even as we speak – Williamson was doing it back before the war! Man, *rats swimming underwater*!'

'And blood clouding up in the water when the knife slips and he cuts his hand . . .'

Unwilling to take the time to pick up her cap and fling it down again, Madge hugged herself in artistic rapture. 'I owe you lunch!' she swore. 'Fucken hell, I owe you a night out at the Coconut Grove! DeMille'll croak with envy! Von'll burst a blood vessel! Von was telling me last night *Crowned Heart* needed something different, something nobody's done before! I owe you a weekend in San Diego at the Del!'

'Mr von Stroheim is back from San Clemente Island?' asked Emma, as Madge snatched up her cap and prepared to depart, like a steamroller in mating season.

'Oh, yeah.' The director paused in her tracks. 'He's drivin' 'em nuts over at Enterprise today, gettin' ready to re-build the town square set for *Heart* so he can blow it up again. Next week they're gonna start more construction on the San Clemente set – he says there aren't enough trees and the gardens look like his coachman's grandma's potato patch back in Vienna, and the gondolas all look like rowboats and the whole thing's gotta be re-shot. Jesperson's ready to cut his own throat.'

She grinned at the prospect, then strode away down the length of the stage through the Livingstone family bedroom and poor Cincinnati's humble shack in the woods of Kentucky, practically bouncing up and down at the prospect of rats swimming franticly in the blood-clouded (and filth-laden) waters that closed over Seth Ramsay's head. *With luck*, reflected Emma, *for at least twenty-seven takes.*

'What the hell was that all about?' Zal came over to the base camp as Larry demonstrated the effects of hopeless passion for Ken Elmore and Emily Violet, one more time.

Emma smiled. 'Vengeance,' she said, and handed him a cup of coffee.

'Like the Italians say,' agreed Zal, 'it tastes best cold.'

As the denouement of Cincinnati Wilder's romantic entanglement appeared likely to stretch into the evening, Emma packed up her satchel, and took the streetcar along Sunset Boulevard and up Hyperion Avenue to the Enterprise lot in Edendale. The guard at the gate found her name on a list and admitted her; she threaded her way among bustling stagehands and electricians – passing again a company of soldiers, these much cleaner and in dress uniforms (*Is the Broadway Bluebird to be shown idolized by the troops?*) – and then down between the shabby gray bungalows, to what had been Ernst Zapolya's office.

No one answered her knock at the door, but it wasn't locked. As she stepped into the tiny outer office – more cluttered than ever with flags, megaphones, boxes of files, and cans of film – a Teutonic voice from the open inner doorway asked, 'Did he not have the papers?'

And then, as Mr von Stroheim appeared in the door and stopped, surprised, at the sight of her: 'Madame Blackstone!' He executed his usual smart military bow.

'Please forgive me for interrupting you during your work—'

'Work?' He gestured impatiently around at the office.

'Nothing can be done of "work" until that money-grubbing hack has had his say about it – and until Mrs Jesperson has yet again to explain to the man that if you pay for a Poverty Row pie-throwing contest that's exactly what your film is going to look like . . . And of course, since we *are* back, the Great Man has disappeared with his little red-haired poopsie and won't be seen until Monday morning.

'Please excuse me for speaking of such things,' he added, bowing again, and the anger went out of his voice. 'But I am . . . I am out-done with this constant carping and picking. What can I do for you, Mrs Blackstone? I am at your service.'

He brought up a chair for her beside his desk, offered her a cigarette ('No, thank you . . .') and a drink (ginger ale: he had a dozen bottles in his office) and listened to her account of her conversation with Agents Shardborn and Peth, and Dirk Silver's subsequent revelations. 'So you see,' she concluded, 'the matter is growing serious. The police seem to be simply following the studio lead – that it's poor Nomie Carlyle – in order to keep anyone from asking questions about Miss Carver; and I suspect that none of the studios would welcome a widening of the investigation to include Communists who may or may not exist. There are enough stars and producers who are socialists, or socialist sympathizers – everyone from Dirk Silver up to Mr Chaplin – that unless there's some real proof, all it would do is open the floodgates to more newspaper stories and more letters to the editor – something nobody needs right now.'

'But the police want someone,' remarked the director quietly, 'to close it all down. People want it to be like a film. You have the answer in seven reels, and you can go home to your dinner.'

'Yes.'

'Sometimes it's very hard not to hate humankind.' Von Stroheim tapped the ash from his long cigarette. 'So you have come to look through Ernst's files here?' He gestured toward the stack of three wooden bankers' boxes in a corner beside the office door.

'I have, yes. I didn't know if Miss Carver had taken them, or sorted through them . . .'

'I doubt she's even given them a thought.' The brown eyes narrowed. 'Ernst told me that his wife would search his study while he was out of the house, go through the drawers of his dressers and even the shoeboxes in his cupboards, looking for love letters from other women. He would set little traps for her, tiny slips of wood where they would fall out of a drawer if it were opened, fragments of paper lightly gummed to the edges of his handkerchief boxes, that sort of thing. And anything that might have been here, that hyena Sellars will have carried away.'

He gestured toward the wall opposite the desk, where the framed photos of women had hung. Nothing remained of them but a shabby constellation of nails driven into the plaster, and a couple of dangling wires. 'And of course the photographs of the women he lay with.'

She said, 'Oh!' She was disconcerted, and cynicism sparkled in von Stroheim's eyes, like a brand-new razorblade.

'I am already planning to use something of the kind in the next scenario that I write – if ever I'm permitted to produce my own work again,' he added, bitterly. 'He was no Ansel Adams, I'll say that for him. Would you like me to have those files sent to your home? Though I doubt there is much in them. Only records from the films he made. You share quarters with Miss de la Rose, I believe?'

'I do, yes,' she said. 'Thank you. Thank you very much.'

'I shall arrange it.' He followed the sudden quick turn of her head, as her attention was caught by the small bronze dish on one corner of the desk: the dish which contained a strand of pearls. Each pearl, separated by a tiny diamond.

'Excuse me,' she said, seeing that she'd been caught staring. 'I'm so sorry—'

'Is it yours?'

'No, I . . . Where did you come by it?'

The puckish lips curved as he studied her face. 'It was in the desk drawer,' he said, and his gesture welcomed her to examine it more closely. 'Go ahead. It's prop-department trash. You could probably get a better one out of a box of Cracker Jacks.'

Emma picked it up, fingered the smooth curve of a pearl.

'Do you know how to tell if they're fake? Rub them against each other, or on your teeth – the real ones feel a bit gritty. I shall have to use that, too,' he added, still watching her hesitancy at making this unhygienic test. 'That's good – it's how my hero will tell if the girl who's proclaiming her innocence to him is as innocent as she pretends. That she doesn't know – or that she *does* – how to test a pearl he gives her. I'm sure if you gave this necklace to Miss Pickford she would be charmed and grateful –' with wicked accuracy he mimed the star's well-known expression of girlish surprise – 'and have the thing in her mouth the minute you're out of the room.'

Emma giggled. 'I shall use it if you don't, sir. I've been trying to establish how the heroine of my scenario – which started out in first-century Britain and is now in Paris before the war – knows her way through the sewers, once she escapes the villain's clutches. I doubt it's something most Parisian girls know, let alone an innocent from the country.'

'If she's an innocent from the country, what's she doing in Paris?' he asked, interested.

'Looking for her sweetheart.'

'Whom she doesn't trust enough, that he will come back to her? She was not able to reach him by letter? She doesn't have a cousin or an aunt she can write to and ask, What's happened to Prince Charming?'

And, when Emma hesitated, he went on, 'The whole of your story lies in your characters' pasts, you know. Every character – every extra, as it were – from the hero to the gardener's crippled daughter. You must ask yourself – you must *know* . . . Who is this girl? Who are these people? Who is the man who kidnaps her, once she gets to Paris? Why take the trouble? Why is this girl in Paris and not still at home with her parents? Are they dead? Is she truly seeking this bone-headed young man? How many young ladies do you know who come to Hollywood because the young man they love has gone there, and hasn't written? They say, "Pouf! So much for *you*, Chummy, I'll just marry Fred or Tony or Aloysius instead." Do this girl the compliment of giving her a better reason than that.'

Emma said slowly, 'You're quite right, sir. It would be much more interesting.'

'And more real,' said the director. 'What is real is always more interesting. How did she come to be here? Does she have anyone to go home to? Why not?'

And for a moment Emma saw the glance Nomie Carlyle shot across the parlor at the half-drunk Mr Brinker. Smelled again the pissy whiff of the carpet where sun hit it through dirty window-glass.

'Is she seeking vengeance? Vengeance for what he did to her? Or for a wrong done to someone she loves? Vengeance perhaps on behalf of the dead? Paris is an evil place,' he continued softly. 'And a frightening one, to little farm girls. Who is playing this little lost sylph, by the way? Miss Golden? I suppose she will demand that the answer be a simple one.'

She sighed. 'I suspect you're right, sir.'

'And if you filmed the reason behind her quest – any reason beyond a tender kiss beneath the honeysuckle vines – they would cut it out anyway, these producers. They would much rather think that these young ladies are as they see them in bathing costumes on Venice Beach: pretty and simple and obliging.'

He scooped the necklace from its bronze dish, held it out to her. 'Would you like it? It's not badly made. On film it looks like the real thing. I've found at least six little trophies like this, here in this office: hair combs, earrings, a pair of those white cotton gloves that women wear on special occasions, when they wish to dress up. A very nice pin of artificial flowers that I think I recognized someone wearing in a Sennett film. Under the cupboards, or dropped behind chairs . . . No wonder his secretary spent very little time in this building.'

The telephone rang on his desk. He picked it up, listened, then said, 'So don't tell him. Simply put the billing through. He'll not return until Monday.'

And then: 'Tcha! You know his wife will put it through in the end, so why make trouble?' Hanging up, he turned to Emma, rose from his seat, and bowed once more. 'They are fools,' he said. 'They know as well as I do, that it is Mrs

Jesperson who signs the checks . . . I fear I must deal with this.' He offered her his hand, to help her rise. 'And I fear that beyond turning over to you my predecessor's files I have not been of much help.'

'On the contrary . . .' Emma slipped the pearl necklace into her handbag (*Drat it, I forgot and left the diamond bracelet back at the house again . . .*) 'You have been of the greatest help, sir. While you were tidying up the office for your own use, did you ever find cigarette ends among the *disjecta membra* under the cupboards or behind the chairs?'

'A few,' he said. 'And a great deal of ash. The woman who sweeps these offices has a dozen to do every evening. I do not wonder at it, that her job is carelessly done.'

'Did you ever find the end of a Turkish Murad?' She recalled the man's meticulous eye for detail.

He looked a bit startled, then said, 'I did. And I thought it odd, as I knew that like myself, Ernst smoked De Reszkes.' His pale, sparse brows drew together. 'Odder still,' he added, 'that I found it a few days *after* I had moved my things into the office; that is, after the good Mrs Micklesohn had swept and cleaned. It was there on the windowsill –' he pointed – 'a place where I am fairly certain I would have seen it. I thought it an expensive brand, for a woman whom I am sure Mr Jesperson pays less than the extras who get shot at and soaked and fall off roofs to make a nice show on the screen.'

EIGHTEEN

'When it's convenient,' said Emma quietly into the telephone, 'there are a few things which I found in Mr Zapolya's office, that I would like to return.' The silence on the other end of the wire was so long that for a moment she wondered if the exchange had disconnected them. But at last the voice on the other end said, 'Would it be convenient, to bring them out this evening?'

'That would work very well. Thank you.'

'Darling, *of course* I tested them!' Kitty switched the Packard's headlamps from low to high as the hills behind them shut out the glitter of Los Angeles, and the cool darkness of the twilight deepened toward actual night. 'I tested them when he gave them to me. But I knew they were trash, because Ernst never gave away actual jewelry, you know. He'd just have the prop department make copies of things he'd seen, in Tiffany's or Arpels's or on people he saw at parties. Connie Talmadge was ready to *murder* him over a pair of emerald earrings she wore to DeMille's holiday party three years ago, that turned up six months later in a scene in *Six Dudes and a Dame* . . . Mr Griffith had had them designed especially for her, and the real ones cost *fifteen hundred* dollars!'

She frowned at the lights that flickered through the trees to either side of Huntington Drive, as they approached the stylish little resort town of Pasadena. The big car flashed past the glowing box of a trolley, ambling its way down the middle of the street, women going home from shopping downtown, men returning from work.

'No wonder she was furious,' Kitty went on in a quieter voice. 'How utterly *mortifying*! But does that mean she and Ernst—?'

'I don't know what it means,' returned Emma quietly. At her feet, Buttercreme snored gently in her carrier. Black

Jasmine and Chang Ming bumped and pushed at each other in her lap, and Emma headed off the smaller dog's tenth attempt to crawl over into Kitty's lap to take over the wheel. 'It's what I hope to find out.'

'Well . . .' Kitty craned her neck to see the lettering on the street signs, half-hidden among the foliage. 'At least I'll get to keep the fakes.'

A maid answered the door of the jewel-like Renaissance town palace that stood in the quiet midst of Italian gardens on Rosemont Avenue. Emma could not keep herself from glancing at the door handle as she stepped through and yes, it did appear to be made of solid gold. While smaller than Pickfair or Frank Pugh's pharaohnic mansion in Beverly Hills, Palazzo Jespersonio showed the same marks of wealth: Regency furniture exquisitely kept; an Aubusson carpet; a cabinet of first editions on one wall of the living room with its frescoed walls and carven ceiling. ('Not that either she or Lou has ever read more than a scenario,' Zal had said.)

No effort had been made to turn the transplanted antique into a museum, however. There were well-made upholstered modern chairs before the marble fireplace, beaded lamps with pierced bronze shades and several small, beautiful marbles and bronzes that drew Emma up from her chair once the maid had gone. Most were reproductions – very good ones – but one, given pride of place in a niche above the mantel, was obviously an original.

Roman, guessed Emma. Second century. A gladiator, sitting on the sidelines . . . waiting for his fight? Or just come out of it, too exhausted even to be glad, yet, that he was still alive? His head was bowed over his clasped hands, his face hidden but every knuckle and sinew and finger beautifully executed where they wrapped around the hilt of his sword, propped before him. An artist's hands.

She heard the door open and shut behind her and looked around as Willa Jesperson came into the room. Impulsively, she nodded toward the statue, asked, 'Does he have a name?' and the wintery tension in the other woman's face unfroze a little, with the touch of a smile.

'My cousin called him Vulcan.' Emma recalled the flat vowels of the woman's mid-South accent. 'She made up a whole series of stories about his adventures, when we were little girls, and I was afraid of the dark.'

She crossed the room to Emma, held out her hand to shake, and when Emma returned to her chair, took the one opposite her, on the other side of a low table before that clean-swept hearth. 'You're Mr von Stroheim's friend, aren't you? The one who spoke to me about hiring him.'

'I am, yes.' Emma brought the necklace from her handbag, the genuine necklace. She'd had to mark the fake with a scrap of ribbon, so close had the superficial resemblance been. 'This is the real one,' she said. 'Miss de la Rose had been given a copy, made up probably by the prop department at Enterprise. She thought that's what she was wearing the other night at Pickfair. No wonder you were angry.'

In a tone of rigid control, Mrs Jesperson said, 'Thank you,' and picked it up.

'I'm sorry to have to ask you this,' Emma continued, with an effort, 'but the circumstances surrounding Mr Zapolya's death – and some of the things that have happened to me and to Miss de la Rose since then – make it imperative that we learn more about what actually took place. All the police want to do is hush the matter up and arrest the obvious suspect.'

A sharp, slight movement of the other woman's head, sharply stopped.

'So far, I've found nothing else in his files or effects that have mentioned your name.' Emma took a deep breath. 'But I do need to know. Were you his mistress?'

Willa Jesperson looked on the point of snapping, *How dare you*?

But she only turned her face away. Her fingers closed tight around the slim rope of pearls. After a long moment, a tear coursed from each shut eye.

Emma repeated, 'I'm sorry.'

The other woman inhaled, exhaled. Silence. 'The ones who are in love, who feel the great passion,' Zapolya had said.

'It was perfectly all right with everyone in this town,' she said at last in a steady, cool voice, 'if my husband satisfied himself with every pretty chippy who came along wanting to be in the movies. For a woman it's different. My father settled his money on us such that in the event of divorce, the funds would be returned to the Shaney Family Trust. Neither of us would receive more than a pittance. My husband has siphoned a good deal of money into the studio. If there's a court battle . . . I have no idea what would happen. Neither does he.'

She let her breath out in another tightly controlled sigh.

'Ernst never thought about money. Never talked about it. I loved that in him. You have no idea what a relief that was, Mrs Blackstone. To be able to see things in terms of the world beyond investments and power and getting people to come to movies. To Ernst, the films he made were stories. Passion and grief, beauty and joy. It was how he lived his life.'

Passion and grief and joy and explosions that would look good on the screen . . . No matter what the cost.

'Did he ever speak of being followed?'

Another sigh. More relaxed, this one. 'By the Bureau of Investigation? They searched his office, more than once, he said. They opened his mail. He was a socialist, you know. The unforgiveable sin.'

'Was he a communist?'

'No.' The woman waved impatiently. 'Not any more. He broke with them when Lenin fell ill and that bank robber Stalin started taking over power. All the communist leaders started fighting each other over power like a bunch of club women quarreling about who's going to be queen at the Veiled Prophet Ball. It's only money, under another name.'

She winced. As the daughter of the wealthiest man in St Louis, Emma guessed, Willa Shaney Jesperson had undoubtedly had her fill of the internecine viciousness of society club women.

'His wife had detectives follow him,' Mrs Jesperson went on after a moment. 'Sometimes she wanted to better the terms of her divorce – her mother put her up to that. Sometimes she wanted to find something that could be leveraged into making him love her. Making him be hers alone. I think he was more afraid of her than he was of the Bureau of Investigation. Her, and that jealous harpy mother of hers.'

And yet, reflected Emma, Zapolya had said, 'It would be the end of me', had she learned of his casual liaisons. Marina Carver evidently wasn't the only one who craved possession.

'Eunice Eggwall – Miss Carver's mother – hated Ernst,' she went on. 'Hated him for making Miss Carver choose between them. Hated him because Miss Carver chose him.'

Emma recalled the news photos of The Angel Next Door lying in a faint across her husband's coffin (in two different poses), swearing that she had heard him whisper her name through embalmed lips.

'She'll do things, and then convince herself either that she had no choice, or that they never actually happened, like that *circus* at his funeral. If she had learned that he and I . . . that he found in *me* what *she* could not give him . . . I would not have put it past her to use that knowledge to blackmail me. To get her better roles, or more close-ups. To force me into pushing my husband to insist that she be in Ernst's films, like that little blonde tart who threw herself at him for months before he gave up and took her in his arms.'

At the tired poison in her voice Emma winced inwardly, with pity. How long would it have been, she wondered, before Zapolya put her aside?

'And is that why you searched our house?'

Mrs Jesperson looked away, and this time Emma could see the hot pink that stained her cheekbones. 'I am sorry about that,' she whispered. 'When I heard Ernst had asked Miss de la Rose to meet him, on the day of his death, I thought – I feared – that he had given her something, I don't know what . . . Something he wanted to hide from his wife. Or maybe from me,' she added bitterly. 'I was positive of it, when I saw the detectives she had hired, coming away from your house . . .'

'Detectives . . .?' It was Emma's turn to be startled.

'Oh, yes.' The other woman looked surprised. 'I knew you usually go with Miss de la Rose to the studio during the day, to look after those nasty dogs of hers. I knew she'd be shooting that ridiculous bath-tub scene, and that it would probably take them all day to do it. But I was careful to park out of sight, in one of the empty lots down the hill, and walk up. While I was still some distance away I saw a car on the road above the house. Three people came out of the house – two men and a woman – and locked the door behind them. They climbed up to the car and drove away. I had what was supposed to be a skeleton key – my chauffeur had gotten it from his bootlegger, he said – but when I got up to the porch I saw that the windows on either side of the door were open at the top – not latched. So I got in that way.'

She paused, turning the necklace in her fingers. 'And then those horrid dogs started barking again. And I realized that if thieves had already been through the place, they must have been barking for quite some time – enough to bring the gardener, surely. So I simply ran up the stairs, had a quick look under her pillow and around her bedroom, and got out of there. I didn't even know what I was looking for – we were very careful, not to put our names to anything we wrote. But I still have every scrap. Every piece of paper his hand touched.

'We were . . .' She turned her face away again, the hard-held calm of it breaking for a moment, and put a quick hand to her lips.

Emma thought again of Peggy, blithely fornicating on the director's desk because 'one thing led to another'.

'If my love tells me she is made of truth,' Shakespeare had written, 'I will believe her, though I know she lies . . .'

'Lou doesn't want to hear that Marina might have killed him,' Willa Jesperson went on after a time. 'I guess you know that. Marina's pictures bring in hundreds of thousands of dollars apiece, and I don't know how much he spends, getting the fan magazines to write about how kind she is, and how sensitive: The Angel Next Door. If you could have read the . . . the *balderdash* they printed when they got married! And before that, the stories around her divorce from Clive April – which wrecked his career, you know. Yes, the man drinks, but he had no trouble getting roles before the divorce. Now I think the most he can manage is playing Romy Novarro's chauffeur in some film over at Metro.'

'Do you think she killed him?'

The narrow lips pressed tighter. 'I think she was capable of it,' she said at last. 'Either she or that mother of hers, if her mother had reason to fear that Miss Carver would change her mind and call off the divorce.'

'The three people that came out of the house that day,' said Emma. 'I know you were too far off to see much, but what did they look like? Two men and a woman . . .?'

'One man was taller than the other – thinner, too. They both wore hats, and suits – not workman's clothes, I mean. The woman was as tall as the shorter man, and slim; she wore a plain dark frock, blue or brown, like the men's suits. The car was a black saloon model. I couldn't see the license plate.'

'Could the woman have been Miss Carver?'

Mrs Jesperson grimaced at the name, and quickly touched her eyes. 'I don't think she was. One would have to check at the studio to be sure. She was slim and brown-haired, light brown like yours. But . . . I would know Marina Carver anywhere. In the dark, in the distance, in my dreams . . . I would see her. I know how she walks, how she moves, the smell of her perfume. I will see her, I think, for a long time.'

She reached for the cigarette box on the table. Blue-and-gold lacquer work, and obviously made for her, for in place of her initials, the cartouche on its lid bore the tiny gold silhouette of the resting gladiator, who had defended two little girls from fear of darkness. As if suddenly recalled to her duties as hostess, she nudged it across to Emma, asked, 'Cigarette?' and opened it. Her fingers shook a little, at the memory of the man she had loved.

Gold-tipped brown Sobranies, like Dirk Silver smoked. Handmade and expensive.

'Thank you,' said Emma, 'no.'

'That doesn't mean she doesn't smoke Murads, too,' observed Kitty, as they navigated the long drive to the street again. 'Or that she wasn't lying about just taking a little peek under my pillow. I bet she tossed the whole house and there weren't *even* detectives . . . And what about, "This isn't some cheap

Hollywood intrigue"? It sure sounds like a cheap Hollywood intrigue to *me* – if Ernst was telling the truth.'

Beyond the hills and the trees, stars prickled an ocean of indigo sky. The dry sweetness of chaparral and dust breathed over the car. Emma thought again of English nights in May, found herself – as she sometimes still did – listening for the bells of Oxford, surely just out of sight beyond the hills and the trees?

It had been a very, very long day.

Chang Ming, as if sensing her weariness, anxiously licked her wrist. *You OK?*

'Anyway,' persisted Kitty, 'why would Ernst have called *me*, if he had secret love letters from Willa Jesperson – I bet as tight-laced as she is, she's a volcano in bed! – or Stalin's secret plans to invade Mexico, for that matter? That's what doesn't make sense about any of this. Why would the Katzenjammer Kids from the BOI try to roast us in a burning cabin? Why would somebody be following us all over Southern California – is there anybody back there, by the way?'

Emma leaned around to look back over her shoulder. In the darkness, one pair of headlamps looked much like another, in the dark of Huntington Drive. 'Did you see anyone pull out on to Rosemont after us as we left?'

'Sweetheart,' sighed Kitty, 'after spending twelve hours setting a wineglass down on a table and looking soulfully over my shoulder at Harry – and I *swear* to you that's all I did, all day! – I wouldn't have noticed if Ben-Hur had pulled out behind us in a chariot! Oh, and marrying Harry . . . over and over . . . with the same two tears trickling down my cheeks each time, and again for the close-ups . . . Can I *really* sleep in tomorrow? Really and truly? Do you hear that, my darling Jazz-ums?' She took one hand from the wheel and her entire attention from the road to caress Black Jasmine, still eagerly attempting to climb into her lap.

Kitty continued to blither happily – moving from Larry Palmer's shortcomings as a director to what Mary Blanque in Wardrobe had told her about Marsh Sloane – of all people! – and Bitsie Weber in Accounting, to the prospect of the studio's adorable child star Little Susy Sweetchild in a feature film ('If that happens Madge is going to murder Little Susy's mother before the first reel is in the can . . .'), while Emma watched the stars, and the hills . . . and, more and more often, the road behind them.

There was something here, she knew, that didn't fit.

Something they didn't know yet.

'Who are these people?' von Stroheim had asked. 'Every character, from the hero to the gardener's crippled daughter . . .'

Who is Kitty, for that matter . . .? She turned her head on the soft leather of the Packard's upholstery, studied that jewel-like profile in the reflected headlamps, the peacock eyes fluttering in the bandeau that bound her storm cloud hair. Camille de la Rose . . . Kitty Flint . . . Chava Blechstein . . .

What was it in *her* connection with Ernst Zapolya's past, that made him trust her . . . with either secret love letters from a woman who could ruin him professionally or with Josef Stalin's plans to conquer Mexico?

'. . . and it said that a man named Farnum, who used to be Marina's chauffeur, committed suicide the very day *after* the murder . . .'

The lights of Los Angeles away to their left. The garish white glare of the sign that proclaimed: HOLLYWOODLAND. The dark of the hills behind them, then the thickening traffic along Sunset Boulevard. The memories of waking suddenly in a room full of smoke, the glare of the flames and Chang Ming's barking . . .

'. . . and did you read the latest, about Marina going down to the Hollywood Cemetery and trying to drink poison on Ernst's grave? A gardener wrenched the bottle out of her hand . . . Darling, it was all over the *Times*! But there was a photo of it, and I recognized Buck Heeley, one of the extras from Enterprise as the gardener, and anyway what would a photographer have been doing at the Hollywood Cemetery at one o'clock on a Wednesday morning . . .?'

Three boxes of papers ought to tell us something, Emma reflected. She smiled a little, recalling her father's return from Arretium in 1912 with six crates of pottery shards and notes.

'They don't put the important things all in the same place, you know,' he'd said. It had taken them months to go through even the first crate. *I suppose two and three-quarters of those boxes are just going to be cost requisitions and payouts from every film Mr Zapolya ever directed . . .*

Yet thinking about those crates of notes, the explanations that her father's scholastic colleagues had devised for anomalies in pottery styles and the placement of graves, brought one of his favorite sayings to mind: *Pluralitas non est ponenda sine necessitate.* The medieval scientist William of Occam had said it. 'Explanations should not be multiplied unnecessarily'.

The *lex parsimoniae,* her father had called it. *What is the simplest explanation?*

'. . . said that he overheard Ernst yelling into the phone just the night before, "I dare you to do your worst! You don't frighten me!" But I don't think Ernst ever used coke . . . Shit!'

The car lurched, and Emma instinctively whipped her head around, scanning for headlights in the darkness behind them. They'd left Sunset Boulevard and begun the climb up Ivarene into the hills. In the silence, the explosion was shattering, terrifying . . .

Kitty followed her initial comment with another even less ladylike, wrestling the Packard's wheel as the big car slewed back and forth and Emma clutched both male Pekes to her and set a foot firmly on top of Buttercreme's carrier.

Blowout . . .

The car bumped its front wheel into the ditch and stopped. Emma looked swiftly around them. Dark hills under a cloak of camisa and chaparral; the thick grove of eucalyptus that told her they'd just passed Ivar Avenue. Stars in far-off velvet, and not a light to be seen.

Nobody following us . . .

Nobody with their lights on, anyway.

Her heart was pounding.

'Well, balls.' Kitty set the hand brake. 'Are my little celestial creamcakes all right? Was my little Jazz-ums scared?' She turned in her seat, caressed first Black Jasmine, then

Chang Ming. 'Darling, can you make sure Buttercreme is OK?' It took some effort to shove her door open, for the car was tilted sharply to starboard. The reflection of the headlamps showed the ditch wasn't deep, the right front wheel only a few inches down into it. 'I bet I can just back up . . . Do you know how to change a tire, sweetheart? Shit,' she repeated, and squirmed her way out of the seat. 'I *knew* we should have brought Harry or Roger along.' She teetered on her high heels, and cursed again. 'Damn it, I can't find a thing in the trunk . . . There's a flashlight under the seat. We aren't being followed or anything, are we?'

'I don't think so, no.' With gingerly care Emma opened her door, ascertained how much ground there was before the drop-off into the ditch, and wondered if Kitty scrabbling around in the darkness of the back seat would or could somehow unbalance the car and make the whole situation worse. Chang Ming and Black Jasmine, of course, leaped out the moment the door was open, and Emma hooked her arm through the loops on their leashes, maneuvered Buttercreme's carrier out and worked her way carefully back along the chassis, Kitty cursing matter-of-factly as she groped beneath the driver's seat . . .

'There!'

Yellow light sprang into being. 'I should have a . . . What the hell?'

Kitty sat back on her heels and Emma, still edging towards the back, stopped and looked over her shoulder. 'What is it?'

'Fuck if I know.'

Kitty held the flashlight back a little, to show the thin sheaf of photographs in her other hand. 'These were under the seat.'

Emma angled her head around, trying to determine what she was looking at.

The wooden framing of a roof, like that in the attic of her friend Anne Littleton's grandmother's Elizabethan cottage at Deeping Hatch? No – the wooden framing of a filmset, like the maze of two-by-fours and canvas that backed the cathedral set and the palace square of Ravenstark. Another photograph showed a rough plank floor, with a couple of support beams at the edge of frame, chalked numbers showing their placement.

Another, the same section of floor, with one of the planks taken up. 'What's that underneath?' asked Emma.

Kitty held the flashlight closer, and shook her head. 'Fuck if I know,' she said again. 'It's a package or something . . .'

She shifted to the next photo – another view of framing. And then another.

'What the . . .?'

A doorway, that Emma knew she'd seen before, ornate pilasters and a black enamel mermaid above it sitting on a globe, her arms outspread.

Then the same doorway from a distance . . .

'It's the palace on the Isle of Love,' said both girls, recognizing the place at the same moment.

Emma said, 'He put these here. In your car, outside his office, when he couldn't give them to you – the day he was killed.'

'Well,' said Kitty. 'Damn.'

NINETEEN

Which was exactly what Zal said, when he arrived at a few minutes short of ten, in response to Emma's telephone call.

'Look.' Emma spread out the photographs on the kitchen table. 'They're a sequence. A map. Like a series of shots within a scene. Here's the establishing shot of the palace. Then the north side of the palace beside the garden, showing the door; then a medium close-up of the door itself. I think this one has to be next, because you can see the doorframe at the side of the shot, and through it the orchard outside. See the camera platform here? Now that platform is in this one, a view down the length of the set – you see the line of uprights? That stair you see at the side is in this one—'

'So you don't mix it up with the other ten stairs you've got in a set that big,' commented Zal. 'That canvas there must be the back-side of a room within the set—'

'Peggy tells me Von's had about four other rooms built into the set,' warned Kitty. She had changed her clothes the moment they'd returned to the house, though in the process of changing the tire had managed not to get a speck of dirt on her olive silk frock. By the look of it, she had completely renewed her makeup as well. 'Like, a ballroom and a boudoir and a library with French windows . . . So it won't look like this anymore. And they're going to start work on more next week.'

'Yeah,' agreed the cameraman. 'But I bet we can still find the place if we go tomorrow. This one must be the view from the top of the stair – if that's the handrail. You can see a camera platform . . .'

'That will be the same platform in this other view,' said Emma. 'There's the two uprights that are in this medium close-up of the floor—'

'And there's the floor with the plank taken up.' Zal folded

his arms, studied the sequence. 'That's our close-up. Like that crane shot of Belshazzar's feast Griffith did in *Intolerance*, with the camera starting out a hundred feet up, on the whole giant assembly and then closing in and down, until you're practically in Seena Owen's lap.

'And whatever is in that package,' finished Zal, 'is what Ernst wanted you to have.'

'And if it's a bag of cocaine,' said Emma, recalling the seven thousand dollars that had been in the dead director's pocket, 'I am going to be very, very cross.'

Kitty shook her head. 'He didn't do coke.'

'That's not what the Reverend Bushrod Pettinger said in his letter to the *Times*.'

'The Reverend Bushrod Pettinger is a numbskull. He said I slept with . . .'

'Coke is one of those things, that if the cops don't have an answer for a murder, that's what they'll point to.' Zal picked up the last photograph, to more closely look at the dark packet half-hidden in the space between the floor joists. 'Bootlegging or smuggling drugs. Bet me, if their case against Nomie falls through, that's what they'll say was behind this.'

'If Ernst wanted coke,' protested Kitty, 'all he'd have to do is catch Taffy McDonald or Nankie Spink or one of the other regular dealers around the studio. Knowing Jesperson, he could probably just get it from the studio infirmary.'

'Would he have been smuggling it in to sell?' Emma glanced across at Zal. 'I gather one can make a great deal of money that way.'

'And one can get a great deal of shot by the boys who make it their regular business,' he replied. 'Including three or four running their show from City Hall. It's not a game for amateurs, Em.'

'Hence his need for someone else to do the pick-up?'

'*Kitty?*'

'I could too smuggle dope if I wanted to!' Kitty bristled at the implication. '*And* elude gangsters!'

'Sure you could.' Zal grinned. 'Absolutely. I only meant' – he retrieved his position – 'that if you're going to do something that dangerous, there's plenty of chauffeurs and gardeners and guys who work in the prop department you could pay to do it.'

Kitty glowered at him suspiciously, but only said, 'So what time do we leave in the morning?'

'I still don't understand,' reflected Kitty, some twelve hours later as the Packard sped through the ranches and citrus groves of Orange County, 'why Ernst wanted to mix *me* up in all this? It's not that I couldn't do it – if he *was* smuggling cocaine,' she added, with a sidelong glare at Zal. 'But you're right that he could have found anybody to pick something up from the Isle of Love set.'

'Would he have smuggled cocaine if he needed money?' Zal, Emma noticed, kept his eye on the rear-vision mirror as he spoke – as she herself, in the back seat, had found herself almost constantly aware of the road behind them. 'For his divorce from Marina Carver, for instance? I can see how somebody could bring in a boat to the set and hide the stuff – it's a great idea, if you don't want to get in trouble with the regular bootleggers who just bring the stuff in to San Pedro.'

Hollywood, reflected Emma resignedly. *No mention of getting in trouble with the police . . .*

Not Jake Ricelli's woman. Jake Ricelli's business. Or anyway somebody's *business . . .*

For the thousandth time, she wondered what she was doing in this place.

'Oh, yes.' Kitty shook back the fronds of her hair that had escaped from her chaotic chignon, watching the road before her through tinted sun-goggles. 'Ernst was kind of a fanatic about things that he wanted. Like getting a scene the way he pictured it, with people running in screaming panic and bullets flying . . . he didn't see anything wrong in it, if it made a good picture. And Willa Jesperson always backed him up. I guess we know why, now. He always said, the extras knew what they were getting into.'

Zal made a growling noise in his throat.

'He was like that about a lot of things,' she went on more somberly. 'I never really minded being seized and kissed in my dressing room, but I know back four or five years ago, it scared poor Stella Hightower – she's over at Famous Players now – pretty badly. Especially when he wouldn't let her go.'

The soft gray overcast had begun to burn off. Since the weekend was beginning, it had taken Kitty several hours of telephoning to find a motorized charter boat and pilot available to take them out to San Clemente Island, and it was well past noon when they reached Ballard's Boats in Newport Beach – only to discover the little whitewashed office on the harbor front shuttered up and locked. 'Ain't been in all day,' said the woman who ran the fish market next door. And, at Kitty's indignant protest: 'Oh, Marv answers the phone from his house. I'm purely sorry you been inconvenienced, miss. Anybody in town'll tell you, Marv'll promise the moon and take a down payment, then he'll go out for a pack of cigarettes and stop by the local speakeasy to say hi to his friends and that'll be the last you see of him. But tell you the truth, miss –' she leaned confidentially across the tin counter, and nodded towards the open side of the market that overlooked the office and wharf next door – 'you're probably better off. Myself, I wouldn't go across the harbor in that scow of Marv's.'

Following her gaze, Emma noted the peeling paint and rusty railings on the *Princess Josephine* and meditated upon the workings of Providence.

She was to return to that meditation – and resolve to pay more attention to the guidance of Providence in the future – in good earnest somewhat later in the day. 'What men expected never came to pass,' her ancient colleague Euripides had pointed out over the bloody remains of his protagonist. 'And what they did not expect, the gods brought about . . .'

Mrs Sharp at the fish market directed them to a Mr Sardo on Balboa Island across the harbor, whose three motor launches turned out to be all rented out for fishing parties that day. Mrs Sardo obligingly telephoned three other establishments (two of which Kitty had already telephoned that morning before leaving Hollywood), and finally located a Mr Cimino, who could take them across in the *Marlin* that afternoon. 'And I come pick you back up tomorrow, anytime you say,' he promised, when they reached his small boatyard at a quarter to two. Then he studied them, Kitty cheerfully nautical in her sailor pants and striped jersey (and pearls), Emma in her usual sensible tweeds. 'You folks not camping?'

'There's just something we need to get from the filmset on Pyramid Cove,' said Zal, and looked from the kiosk that served as an office down the length of the pier. 'You can't wait?'

Mr Cimino, rotund and graying, thought about it, and glanced at the sky. The boat at the end of the pier, Emma saw, was a thirty-foot yacht, sails neatly furled and ready to go and not an engine in sight. She remembered the four hours it had taken to reach San Clemente Island the previous Tuesday. Even going straight to the palace set and coming straight back to the temporary wharf, she guessed it would be dark before they reached Newport again.

'Two hundred and fifty dollars,' said Kitty. 'Cash.'

The man's eyes narrowed. 'I don't want to get into no trouble . . .'

Emma assumed he did not mean trouble with the ever-obliging police. *Not much compared to what Odysseus went through to hitch a ride back to Ithaca. Still . . .*

'Three hundred.'

The sun was three-quarters of the way to the horizon when the *Marlin* put in at the little wharf on the other side of the headland. The palace wharf – with its ornamental boathouse and fleet of gilded gondolas – was far too short, and its waters too shallow, for even a thirty-footer. 'I know this cove,' had said Mr Cimino, as he'd gathered in the sheets to put his diminutive craft about. 'Those little toy boats the movie folks got, they draw like two feet of water. The engines they got in 'em wouldn't run a motorbike. They're just for show, you know. You get 'em out in the real ocean, they'll flip right over.'

The whole palace, Emma reflected, as they foot-trekked around the headland and followed the path towards the set, looked very much 'just for show' in the late-afternoon still-ness, tawdry and already a little shabby. 'No wonder Mr von Stroheim wants to re-build it,' she remarked. 'I can see what he means about it looking like his coachman's grandma's potato patch back in Vienna.'

'Not that his family back in Vienna ever *had* a coachman,' commented Zal. 'I think his dad was a hat maker. But he has a good eye for what looks real, and he's seen the old nobility of Austria close-up. He wants a set to be a real construction, not that bunch of flats and two-by-fours they have on the back lot. The audience knows it, too,' he added. 'They can tell, when there's no room behind a window – or when your Imperial Guard are wearing uniforms they borrowed from the Venice High School marching band. That might have worked five years ago over at Keystone, but audiences learn fast.'

'Who are these people?' the director had asked. Emma smiled a little to herself. People as well as buildings needed to be real.

'I thought "von" meant you were noble,' said Kitty.

'No, "von" means that in the United States, anybody can stick three letters into their name if they want to,' corrected Zal. 'Like Howie Mellnick calling himself Harry Garfield, or Theodosia Goodman getting billed as Theda Bara. Three years ago Von nearly bankrupted Universal having that replica of Monte Carlo built up north in Monterey,' he went on, as they climbed the last of the path towards the gimcrack palace in its artificial orchard. 'It's amazing on film. The final film was something like thirty reels – over six hours. The studio chopped it to pieces. That looks like the door we want.'

He stopped, and held up the second of the sequence of photographs: a beautiful portal wrought in papier mâché and now – Emma realized as they approached it – replaced by an identical frame in actual bronze, the mermaid above it smiling her enigmatic smile. She wondered how many future Enterprise films would feature that mermaid, now that they had it in their prop warehouse.

And how much it had cost . . .

'This isn't in the photographs,' she objected, when Kitty had broken the window next to the door ('Who's going to know, darling?') and reached through to unlatch it. Instead of the maze of scaffolding extending back to the camera platform, the three friends found themselves in a beautiful Louis XV parlor, gorgeous with pink brocade chairs, gilt boiserie, and a mediocre copy of the Mona Lisa in an elaborate frame propped against the wall near the pillared and pedimented fake marble fireplace.

Fifteen feet above them, the sea breeze rippled in the muslin nailed in place of a ceiling, filling the room with a sort of wan twilight, like Stage Three back at Foremost Productions, where they shot Little Susy Sweetchild's sentimental two-reelers and the Larry and Jerry comedies.

A moment later she said, 'Oh, I see,' took the photo from Zal's hand, and paced the width of the room. There was a door to her right, beyond the fireplace. She opened it, and compared it with the image in her hand. To her left, instead of the pictured scaffolding, the wall of the parlor continued back, presumably enclosing another room – there were two doors in that wall. But from here she could see the stair that ascended to the camera platform, as well as the walls of three or four more room sets, breaking up the forest of scaffolding, stairways, catwalks, and camera platforms that surrounded them.

She glanced at her watch, thankful that Zal had thought to bring an electric torch and that, mindful of the chill of ocean winds, she had placed two neatly rolled-up cardigans – one for herself and one for Kitty – in the bulky satchel she carried. It had been a nuisance that afternoon in Newport, but, as her father had invariably said when packing for an expedition, *In omnibus negotiis . . . adhibenda est praeparatio diligens.*

Better safe than sorry.

It would be nearly dark before they returned to the *Marlin*.

'Dammit,' said Zal, 'is this the right platform?'

Emma examined the supporting beams. 'No. The numbers here are wrong . . .'

The correct platform stood three-quarters hidden behind a room set, sight of it further obscured by frameworks holding up what Emma assumed (the walls of the set hid everything but the chains and electrical wiring) to be chandeliers. The set

was beginning to acquire a creepy air as the muslin-filtered
light faded, and as they crossed to the correct stairway, Emma
found herself glancing behind her again and again . . .

Movement in the shadows?

A coyote, slipping away around a corner.

Was that the creak of a stair? The squeak of door hinges?

No wonder poor little Nomie couldn't be sure of anything
she saw behind the cathedral set. A dim-lit maze such as this
one was sufficiently disorienting, even without the added
distractions of explosions a few yards away and wondering if
those stray bullets were going to come tearing through the
plaster.

'That's it.' Zal had to angle the photograph, to catch the
weakening daylight from above. The western end of the platform had been built up, to better overlook the room below – a
ballroom, Emma saw, with a floor of shiny linoleum patterned
to look like wood, and a poor copy of Rigaud's portrait of
Louis XIV propped against the wall. From what she'd learned
so far about Mr von Stroheim, the director had probably
commissioned a couple of originals in oil and would re-shoot
the scene . . .

Emma produced a screwdriver from her satchel and Zal
knelt, to pry open the trap door. The trap itself was barely
visible, given the scuffed and dirty condition of the platform's
boards. Only careful study of the final photograph – and
counting boards over from the uprights – let them find the
correct crack.

The trap came up stiffly. There was a sort of conduit underneath, for electrical wiring. And, tucked into a corner, exactly
as shown in the photograph, was a small packet wrapped in
brown paper, about the dimensions of a quarto-sized book.

This Kitty seized and ripped like a child on Christmas
morning, while Zal fished the torch from Emma's satchel and
shone its beam down on to the prize.

'Oh!' said Kitty, in slightly puzzled delight. 'It's Emilio
Esparto.' She held up a red-backed passport booklet and opened
it. The photograph showed a handsome dark-haired man in
his thirties, staring straight into the camera with large, intent
dark eyes. 'He and I worked as extras on *Love's Conquest* for

Paramount, and I fell just *passionately* in love with him. He's the reason I probably didn't get killed,' she added. 'I was working for Ernst on *The Fall of Atlantis*, only I played hooky and went over to Paramount that day to be with Emilio, and that was the day they filmed the earthquake and flood . . .' Her dark eyes clouded with distress. 'I only heard about it that night, when I got home.'

She shook her head quickly, putting the memory aside, and thumbed through the passport booklet. 'Only he had a mustache then . . . And . . . Oh!'

Emma took the other papers from the packet. A California driving license. A savings-account book at the Bank of Italy containing twelve dollars and forty-nine cents. Two letters in Spanish signed (as far as Emma could make out) 'Your adoring wife, Maria'. A paycheck stub from an oil company in Huntington Beach, much grimed and folded. All of them in the name of Luis Vasquez . . .

Which was also the name on the passport.

'But that *is* Emilio,' Kitty protested, her thumb on the printed name. 'I'd know him *anywhere*.'

Zal, holding the electric torch above the packet, reached down past Emma's shoulder and brought out a bus ticket from Los Angeles to Hermosillo, Mexico, and a small leather bag that jingled heavily with coin.

In a quiet voice, he said, 'That's Francisco Castillo.'

TWENTY

Kitty objected, 'But . . .'

'He fled the Revolution in 1918.' Zal wedged the flashlight under one arm, to unravel the knots on the bag. Emma, kneeling at his side, took it from him, dumped a few of the coins it contained into her palm.

They were Mexican pesos.

'And that's why Mr Zapolya called you.' Emma slewed herself around on her heels, to look at her sister-in-law. 'Because you know him by sight. He must be in one of the "barrios", as you said, Zal, or camped up with the socialists in the canyons. Mr Zapolya was trying to get him back into Mexico, wasn't he?'

'Looks like.' The flashlight gleam slithered across the lenses of Zal's glasses as he studied that stiff face, the unsmiling mouth. 'He had a little beard back then – you can see where this picture's been re-touched. Ernst probably did that himself. He couldn't risk taking it in to the prop department – probably didn't want to risk trying to fake the stamp by taking a whole new shot. The rest of the passport, and the bank book and pay stub and the other stuff, could be faked up by the prop department – they do that all the time, when they're shooting a spy movie.'

'It's why they were following us.' Emma gathered the papers, re-wrapped them slowly. 'They – whoever *they* are, I assume members of some Stalinist group, as Dirk said – were hoping we'd lead them to him. That's why they searched the house. And . . . You remember how little damage was actually done to the cabin at Big Bear? How the suitcases were open and scattered the way they were? On the unburned side of the room?'

'Like Sherlock Holmes chucking a smoke bomb into whats-her-name's parlor in one of the stories,' agreed Zal. 'And I'll tell you something else. I had a look at the footage Chip and

Alvy shot of that fire. They finally developed it yesterday.
And around the side of the cabin, you can see three people
coming around the corner and running away, where there's
nobody from the fire-fighting crew coming in yet. Two men
and a woman. My guess is they threw in something like a
Coke bottle full of gasoline, just to stampede you ladies out
of there so they could toss the place.'

'They sure succeeded—'

As Kitty said the words she turned her head, and her eyes
flared with shock at what she saw beyond Emma's shoulder.
She drew in her breath but Emma didn't even have to look to
know what she saw, in the direction of the platform stair.

In the same second that a gunshot cracked, and a bullet
splintered the upright next to Zal's back, Emma scooped
one of the folded cardigans from her satchel and pitched it
over the edge of the ballroom wall set. She grabbed Zal's
wrist, pointed the flashlight beam back in the direction of
the stair, but only got a glimpse of the man and woman –
dark clothing, pale faces, glinting gun metal – who turned
and plunged down the steps. A second man – fair hair,
stocking cap, were all the details Emma could take in –
hesitated at the top of the steps, gun in hand, not knowing
for an instant whether he should follow his companions
down or stay and . . .

Shoot us?

Risk being overpowered?

She shoved Kitty toward the rail of the platform before
them and Kitty didn't hesitate for one single second. She
slithered under the rail (*How far a drop to the floor if there's
no cross-braces on the scaffolding . . .?*), Emma following
her even as the question appeared and vanished in her mind.
Yes, there were cross-braces, barely visible with the last of
the daylight disappearing. It was like getting out of the
burning cabin – there was absolutely no time for thought and
Emma wasted none. She heard a second shot above her
and felt the platform scaffold sway a little as the flashlight
beam went out.

ZAL . . .!

But a glance showed her Zal scrambling down the

scaffolding above her. The clatter of Stocking Cap's feet on the steps, another gunshot as he fired at skittering movement away in the dimness of the darkening set. Emma learned later Kitty had slid her sunglasses across the floor as hard as she could sling them.

Another shot, and Emma flung herself through the first door in the first wall she could see. *Zal doesn't need me to be caught . . . They'd use me to bring him out of hiding . . .*

Voices cursing somewhere, close. Feet running. Emma yanked open the door on the other side of the room – she had a dim impression of richly carved book cabinets and what were clearly inexpensive plaster copies of the Aphrodite of Knidos and Rodin's 'The Kiss' in niches – then ducked back into the enormous fireplace, curled up tight behind its enclosing proscenium.

Flashlight beams, dimmer and more yellow than Zal's torch, jerked and wobbled as the man and woman ran through the room, straight for the open door and through it and away into the dark. An impression of a man shorter and heavier than Stocking Cap, of a woman in a plain dark frock and stout shoes, bobbed mousy hair cut severely at her jawline. For a split-second Emma weighed the thought taking off her shoes for silence but knew it would take her longer to lace them on again, and the ground outside – which was after all her goal – was rough.

Disoriented – it was nearly complete dark now – she saw another flashlight glare approaching. Not Zal's . . . Cursing herself for wearing a white blouse that day she darted up the steps of a camera platform, froze still as Stocking Cap ran by beneath her. Tried to get her bearings – the platform was a high one, higher than the one on which they'd found the papers. That platform was over to her right, there was a chamber beneath her . . .

Madame X and Agent Y dashed by in another direction.

A voice whispered, 'Em . . .'

A dark shape on the lower camera platform on the other side of the chamber. A glint of round glasses, like insect eyes. He beckoned.

There was a frame hung between the two platforms,

supporting three immense chandeliers. Instinctively Emma looked up, trying to determine the size and strength of the hooks that attached it to the set's high beams. They were overshadowed by the canvas and framing of the palace dome, it was impossible to see. In the sunken box of another one of the room sets, the reflection of flashlight beams on the walls.

We have to get out of here before they do.

Before they figure out that all they have to do is double back to the boat and wait for us.

She took a deep breath, pulled up her skirt, and straddled the beam. *I am not going to be like the heroine of a film and walk across something that's hanging from the ceiling . . .*

If Zal got across it, I should be able to.

His hands were strong and firm, catching hers to help her down at the other end of the beam, where the platform was a good five feet lower. Without a word she followed him down from the platform, into the room set – impressions of a curlicued bed draped in silver lamé and ostrich feathers – to French windows. Only after Zal unlatched them, helped her through, did she breathe, 'Where's Kitty?'

She had never held on to anything tighter than she held on to his hand as they slipped across the strip of moonlight outside, and into the darkness of the sterile, gaudy orchard.

Moments later, Kitty's voice whispered from among the chrysanthemum-bearing trees, 'You OK, darling? Are those the Commies Dirk told us about?'

'I think so, yes. If the Bureau of Investigation wanted us, they wouldn't be shooting—'

'You'd be surprised,' muttered Zal. He pulled them back into the scented dark.

'Well, whoever those fuckers are, they mean business! We've got to get back to the boat—' Kitty made a move towards the pathway, but Zal's hands closed on her arm and Emma's.

'They left somebody at the boat,' he whispered. 'Don't you see? That's our only way off the island. It's the only deep-water pier. All they have to do is follow us down the path and catch us between them.'

'Oh!' gasped Kitty. 'Oh, poor Mr Cimino—'

'If the man had any sense he went over the side and swam

for it. They don't want him. They may have dropped somebody at the pier at Wilson Cove at the other end of the island as well, where the ranchers sometimes have a couple of guys stationed to look after the sheep.'

His grip tightened. Through the gap in the trees Emma saw their three pursuers emerge from the palace – through the window that Kitty had originally broken – and stride down the path toward the harbor. They'd switched off their flashlights, and at this distance she couldn't be sure they carried guns, but guessed that they did. Her friends in the Socialist Club at Oxford flashed through her mind, and their rivals in the smaller and more radical Oxford Communist Reading Group, earnest young men and women given to saying things like, 'Well, of course it will involve a violent revolution' and 'It's a historical imperative, that the old system must be swept away before pure Communism can take root. And yes, some will die . . .'

She wondered if any of them envisaged those grim, dark shapes in the moonlight, or the savage power struggles currently racking the Workingman's Paradise in Moscow. Beyond doubt, had Socialist Club President Alfred Warnock, or little Peter Bradford in his red tie and spectacles, actually entered that violent revolution, Stalin would have had them shot.

If the Germans hadn't shot them already at the Front . . .

She watched the dark figures retreat up the path: squat man, tall man, the woman striding ahead of them with a man's long pace.

'How far is it to land?' She barely breathed the words.

'Fifty-five miles. Thirty-something, if we head north to Catalina.'

'And do we build a raft out of that silly bed in the palace?'

But Zal was already hurrying them out of the shelter of the trees, through the blue moonlight down to the palace's over-decorated wharf and dainty boathouse in its garlands of flowers and banners. He used the screwdriver to split off the hasp on the boathouse door, switched on his flashlight. 'They leave any gas?'

The four little gondolas – seen floating in a picturesque

fashion in the foreground of establishing shots of the palace – had been drawn up out of the water, exhibiting propellers scarcely larger than luncheon plates. The largest of them, on which the plucky Mary Strong (Desiree Darrow) and her loyal maid (Nomie Carlyle) had arrived on the enchanted isle, sported two, affixed to an engine that looked barely capable of powering a sewing machine. Emma brought up a petrol can and Zal checked, and filled, the royal gondola's tank.

'We can hug the coast all the way up the island,' said Zal as he worked. 'After that we head straight north – either of you ladies happen to have a compass on you?'

'I knew I was forgetting something,' joked Emma nervously, which made them all laugh. 'Can you find the North Star?'

'Pretty much, but I'd rather have a compass. There any life vests?' He flashed the beam of light around the gimcrack inner walls. 'Figures. This is Ernst Zapolya we're talking about – and Lou Jesperson.' Bitterness twisted his voice.

'They have a motorboat, don't they?' Emma asked, as she and Kitty pushed the gondola into the water, and Zal strode ahead to unbolt the doors that opened into the cove.

'They have to.' He helped the two young women into the craft – which tipped and wobbled like a floating dish pan – then, as Kitty held his flashlight for him, he cranked the engine hard. 'They could have rented one while we were hunting all around Robin Hood's barn in Newport – you remember that place where we got there fifteen minutes after the last motorboat had gone out? Depending on the size of their engine, they could have made it across to the island in a couple of hours, hung off behind a point of land watching for us, then come in after us and followed us up here.'

Slowly he nudged the accelerator. 'Kill the flashlight, Kit,' he ordered, as they cleared the boathouse doors. 'If these guys are working for Joe Stalin,' he went on quietly, 'they don't want witnesses. When we don't show up at the boat, I'm hoping they go around the other side of the island up to the pier at Wilson's Cove, or hunt us through the hills. Because we can't outrun them in this thing.'

Darkness on the ocean, the wind flowing cold. Ivory moonlight, and stars down to the horizon, like diamonds on a velvet gown. Emma shivered, bitterly regretting the cardigan she had sacrificed back in the palace to distract their attackers; Zal pulled off his own lightweight jacket and handed it to her. 'I'm the captain of this boat and that's an order,' he added, when she shook her head. 'I'm too scared to be cold anyway.'

Kitty produced a flask of gin. They all had a drink. 'Save the rest,' Zal advised. 'In case this thing runs out of gas.'

So clear was the night – so dark the sea – that it was hard to find the seven stars of the Dipper against the background of smaller lights. The moonlight showed them the uneven black bulk of San Clemente Island to their right, and caught now and then on the fringe of white along its shore. 'When we get close enough we should be able to see Catalina,' said Zal. 'It'll be daylight before we get there. There's pretty much nothing left of the old casinos and hotels in Avalon, but we should at least be able to telegraph across to Pugh, and get a boat back to Long Beach.'

Emma pulled her borrowed jacket closer around her, and shivered, less from cold than from the determined cheerfulness in her friend's voice. A wave hit the side of the gondola and the little craft reeled like a drunken chorus girl.

'And what if one of the gods does wreck me out on the wine-dark sea?' Odysseus had asked. 'My heart is inured to suffering and I shall steel it to endure that as well. I have had many bitter experiences in my time, in war and on the wild waves. It only makes one more.'

Easy for you to say, she reflected bitterly, and tried not to think about the depth of the wine-dark sea, or how far thirty miles was, in a shallow-draft boat through increasingly wild waves.

TWENTY-ONE

Zal said, 'Damn it!'

There were buckets under the gondola's seats. If Ernst Zapolya hadn't thought the extras worth the cost of cork life vests, he had at least considered the expense of a sunken gondola.

'Jove turned his counsel against him,' Homer had sung of poor Menelaus, who only wanted to get his wife back, 'and raised the winds til the waves ran great as mountains.' The gondola lurched and yet another wave slopped over the shallow gunnels.

'There is nothing that is worse for breaking a man than the sea, no matter how strong he may be . . .'

Emma reflected bitterly, *Or a woman either, drat you, Odysseus . . . At least bailing will keep us warm.*

This proved to be a myth.

They had cleared the end of the island. The sea grew worse. It was, Zal said, about fifteen miles to Catalina. 'We'll see it on our right . . .' But the horizon lay black and empty, the darkness before them endless as the Mediterranean before Odysseus' little raft. The top-heavy gondola rocked and heaved and took on water like a thirsty camel. Kitty cursed: at Ernst Zapolya, at Lou Jesperson, at Josef Stalin, in both Yiddish and English. Some of the expressions Emma had never heard before, despite being married to a soldier and driving ambulance-loads of them – wounded and exhausted – from the Oxford train station to Bicester Hospital. Zal clung to the tiller, a bespectacled Odysseus in the moonlit darkness, and said less and less.

Nobody knows we're here, Emma thought. *They won't even miss us, maybe not for days.*

At least Mr and Mrs Shang will take care of the dogs.

When at last Zal spoke again he said, 'Shit,' and turning

her head, Emma saw what she had feared since setting forth
from the Isle of Love.

The light of a boat behind them.

There was enough moonlight that they could be seen, she
thought. *If we don't sink first . . .*

Water slopped, freezing, around her ankles, and she couldn't
feel her hands or her shoulders as she dipped and threw, dipped
and threw water over the side.

> Clutching his trident, Poseidon rammed the clouds
>   together,
> Whipped the waves to chaos,
> Hurled gales from every direction,
> Thunderheads shrouding over earth and sea . . .

The light grew nearer.

Kitty whispered, 'Emma, Zallie, I'm sorry. I'm so sorry—'

'You should be. When we get out of this, you owe us dinner
at the Montmartre.'

'Don't be silly, Kitty, none of this is your fault.'

'But it *is*.' Kitty was shivering all over, her long black hair
hanging soaked in her eyes. 'I got you into this. Because
Nomie really . . . I mean, Nomie's sister—'

'Em, take the tiller.' Zal caught her arm, drew her back to
the rear of the foundering craft. 'Look out there.'

Emma looked. Far ahead of them, she saw a pinprick of
yellow against the black of the ocean. Two thin spikes of mast
pierced the star-flooded sky.

Zal caught up the flashlight, stood – ankle-deep in the
sloshing water – and flicked it on and off, on and off. Three
short, three long, three short. Emma recognized the near-
universal code: SOS.

Kitty swore again, like a cry of hope. 'Can they see us?'

'Are you kidding? If it's the coast guard they're keeping an
eye out for rum-runners, and if it's rum-runners they're keeping
an eye out for the coast guard. They'll see us, all right.'

SOS.

SOS.

'Look, they're turning—'

Shots behind them. Emma threw a glance backward, saw the searchlights of their pursuers. The moonlight showed her the low, sleek lines of a small motor launch, white foam boiling around it like petticoat-lace. 'I'm going to dodge,' she warned.

'Good girl!' Zal said. 'Stay down, Kit, and keep bailing.' He caught his balance as Emma swerved the tiller and a bullet tore the low railing beside her hand.

He's a standing target . . .

She could see, clearly now, Stocking Cap and Madame X at the prow of the boat – *Agent Y must be steering . . . Thank Heavens they don't have a rifle . . .*

She swerved to starboard, Zal turning his body so that his signal could still flash out in darkness towards the larger boat that was – yes, definitely – heading their way in a froth of silvery foam.

The water was up to her calves.

'King Zeus crowning the whole wide heaven black/ churning the seas in chaos/ gales blasting/ raging around my head from every quarter . . .'

Two more shots, and a sharp swerve to port.

I'm going to drown and I can't get the Odyssey out of my head . . .

Dr Etheridge at Somerville would be so proud of me . . .

More lights on the bigger vessel; men moving along the railing. Another shot from behind, then the pursuers cut their searchlight, turned tail, and headed east, the moonlight shining on a pale flash of stern, like a fleeing white-tailed bunny exhibiting the name, *Gin Rickey*.

The approaching boat slowed – its own name coyly obscured by a tarpaulin draped over the bow – and searchlights stabbed down at them. The wash as the vessel came near almost finished the gondola; men on the deck flung down a rope ladder, and big, rough hands helped Emma up. The first person she saw, ugly face like a collection of potatoes in the reflected glare of the searchlight, was Jake Ricelli.

'You OK, m'am?' He had a voice like a bucket of gravel rolled down a flight of stairs. 'What the fuck was that all about?'

'Reds,' panted Zal, scrambling up the ladder behind Kitty. 'Red agents. They tried to shoot us back on San Clemente. We were making a pickup of lists of union contacts – Art Shields' – Emma vaguely recognized the name from the newspapers as an organizer on the San Pedro docks – 'said something about Bolshevik agents trying to move into control the unions for their own reasons.'

A number of comments from the men on the deck, some in English, some in Italian – none (Emma gathered) approving. *And thank heavens for all the publicity about Red agents a few years ago, that Kitty spoke of . . .*

'We came across on the *Marlin* out of Newport,' added Kitty helpfully. 'And I'm afraid – I think they shot poor Mr Cimino . . .'

Angry cries of '*Brutto figlio! Cazzo di merda!*' and 'Poor old Mr C? Bastards!'

'Guido, get on the horn to Borgia,' rumbled Ricelli. 'Tell him to phone the Bureau of Investigation—'

'I have their card here.' Emma produced it from her skirt pocket.

'You do? Great, honey!' The gangster beamed with his enormous teeth and handed it to Guido, who Emma vaguely recognized as part of Ricelli's entourage outside the Montmartre.

Maybe the same man who killed that poor young stockbroker . . .?

'Tell him they're probably comin' into Newport, in a motor-cruiser. You get the name, m'am?'

'The *Gin Rickey.*'

'*Grandissimo!* Guido, tell 'em it's murder an' piracy. *Dio cane*, old Mr C wouldn't hurt a fly! *Bastard* fucken Commies!' He turned back to Emma, genuinely distressed.

'Rocko,' he called out to another of the crew, 'get these nice folks downstairs an' get 'em some coffee an' a couple blankets, OK? You guys look froze. We should be in Long Beach in about two hours—' He broke off, staring suddenly at Kitty, who had shaken back her dark hair from her face and was looking around her with interest. 'Say,' he said, 'you ain't . . .?'

She raised her eyes to his, in exactly the fashion (and pose)

that she'd used in every one of her films since 1919. Emma
had seen a dozen actors do this: be perfectly ordinary human
beings one moment, then assume that slight change of stance
and expression – like donning an invisible costume – and
suddenly one found oneself, to one's astonishment, looking at
Rudolf Valentino, or Charlie Chaplin, or Lillian Gish.

Zal held out his hand, said firmly, 'Zalman Rokatansky; I'm
a cameraman at Foremost Productions. This is Miss de la
Rose, and Mrs Blackstone.'

Every man of the crew, rather awkwardly, bowed.

Once the crates of liquor bottles had been re-arranged in
the cabin to provide seating – Mr Ricelli personally opened
some club-owner's very expensive cognac to go with the coffee
– it was an extremely comfortable trip back to land.

Since Kitty's yellow Packard was still parked somewhere in
Newport Beach, Jake Ricelli personally (once he'd handed off
the invoice for 250 cases of Canadian whiskey to Frank
Borgia's men) drove the three companions back to Hollywood:
Zal watchfully alert, Emma wondering slightly how she got
herself into situations like this, and Kitty, between them,
sleeping like a baby. It was sunup when the gangster's big car
maneuvered its way down the drive, gray fog clinging to Los
Angeles but little more than a thin overcast in the hills. 'You
want I should leave Rocko here, just in case them Reds get
up to anything else?' (Rocko had accompanied his boss on
the drive.)

Kitty thanked the men effusively, promised she'd meet
Ricelli for drinks the following week at the Ship Café on
Venice Pier, and signed an autograph for Rocko before they
left. ('*With all my gratitude . . .*')

'Even if they weren't intercepted by the Boys from the
Bureau when they stepped ashore,' said Zal, as the huge black
Ford regained the pavement and disappeared down Ivarene, 'I
doubt our Bolshevist pals are going to come calling at this
point. They knew the gig was up. So if you ladies want to go
to bed, I can come back—'

'Don't be silly.' Kitty yawned, ruffled her hair again, and
led the way back into the house. 'Those awful agents are going

to phone in about an hour and a half . . . Yes, yes, darlings, Mama's home and everything's all right . . .' This to the Pekes, ecstatically circling her ankles and begging to be picked up and patted and, if possible, fed . . . 'And I *have* to put some makeup on before they get here. I look *catastrophic*! Darling, could you just go down to the cottage and let the Shangs know we're back? You go make us some breakfast, Zallie. We might as well save the Katzenjammer Kids the drive down to Venice to look for you . . .'

She scooped up Black Jasmine and Buttercreme and retreated upstairs to her boudoir, Chang Ming scrambling up adoringly after her. Emma and Zal regarded one another for a moment, bemused and speechless, then fell into each others' arms and burst out laughing.

It was very good to be alive.

By the time Emma returned from the cottage, Zal was asleep on the couch, his glasses on the floor beside him. He didn't even stir when Agent Peth telephoned. Emma made herself some strong tea, tiptoed quietly upstairs – Kitty was sound asleep as well under a pile of Pekinese – took a shower, dressed again and went down to make herself toast and put coffee on. Peth had said he would be there at nine, so at seven she woke Kitty, made breakfast, fed the dogs, and woke Zal.

Thinking, in the silence, of the events of the preceding night.

'It was lists of things.' Kitty widened her eyes at Agent Peth. 'A bunch of pieces of folded-up paper. I only got a quick look at it, and it didn't make sense: "Steinway piano" was one of them, and "victrola". Just random words.'

'It sounds like a code,' remarked Emma, and poured out coffee. 'I thought you put it in your jacket pocket.'

'I *did*!' Kitty sounded as distressed as she did when describing the apocalyptic circumstances which on one occasion or another made her late meeting Frank Pugh for dinner. 'I *know* I did!'

You're *the one who should be writing about the blameless Marianne's travails in Paris, not me,* reflected Emma. Hopeless as her sister-in-law was before the camera, when concocting a story in person, Hermes himself, the god of liars, would have believed her.

'And I can't remember – I think I took the jacket off to help push the boat into the water, because you had to lend me yours—'

'If you would,' said Agent Peth, 'could you write as many of those words as you remember – did you see the contents of this packet at all, Mrs Blackstone?'

Emma shook her head. Eight years with Nanny McIntosh and another dozen at The Misses Gibbs' Select Academy For Young Ladies screamed at her that her falsehood would blazon her face in crimson letters – or turn her into salt, à la Lot's wife. But evidently the two agents were color-blind to such manifestations, because they only nodded.

'You, Mr Rokatansky?'

'I saw something was written in three columns, but I didn't see what it was. I was watching out behind us.'

'Miss Carlyle could not identify Gloria DeMille – as the female agent calls herself – as the woman she saw on the Enterprise lot on the third of May.' The agent – rather bluer around the jaw than at their previous encounter but still ramrod-straight in the black-leather-and-chrome of the living-room chair – sipped his coffee, made an automatic reach for the candy bowl, then stayed his hand.

Emma smiled graciously and pushed the vessel towards him on the glass table. 'Please,' she said. 'You must be exhausted.'

'Thank you, m'am.' He unwrapped a tootsie-roll, meticulously folded the paper and stowed it in his inner pocket as he chewed. 'Miss Carlyle says that the woman she saw on May third was both shorter and much heavier than Miss DeMille, and her hair was lighter, and a little longer. The Bureau is circulating her description.'

'Miss Carlyle may not be able to put them on the Enterprise lot for the murder.' Zal, sharing the modernistic black-and-chrome sofa at Emma's side, ruffled at Black Jasmine's silky mane. 'But one of the cameramen at Big Bear caught three people on film, running away from the burning cabin, and I can have a print of that for you Tuesday, blown up as big as you need.'

The two agents exchanged a startled glance, and Agent Shardborn said, 'Thank you, Mr Rokatansky. Arson is a felony under California state law and will certainly increase the chances of conviction for conspiracy to commit first-degree murder.'

And that, reflected Emma, should satisfy the newspapers, *even if they* can't *get a conviction for killing Mr Zapolya. Everybody will believe they did, which is enough for Mr Jesperson.*

'A packet of Turkish Murad cigarettes was found in Miss DeMille's handbag,' added Agent Peth, reaching for another tootsie-roll – and being careful, Emma noticed, not to disturb Chang Ming, who lay slavishly at the agent's feet with his head on the man's instep. 'The handbag also contained a Browning .38 Super automatic pistol, whose bullets match those found in the railing and deck of the *Marlin*, which was burned in Pyramid Cove last night. Mr Albert Cimino, the *Marlin's* owner, was found unhurt at seven o'clock this morning by the crew of a pleasure vessel –' he glanced at his notes – 'which happened to be passing San Clemente Island.'

He folded his candy-wrapper and made no comment on what a pleasure boat would have been doing at seven a.m. fifty-five miles from the California coast. Possibly someone had told him it was none of his business.

Mr Ricelli must have sent his 'boys' back to look for poor Mr Cimino the moment they got their liquor unloaded . . .

How extraordinarily kind of him!

Emma said, 'Oh,' and poured herself some more tea.

TWENTY-TWO

Zal, Emma, and Kitty drove up into the low mountains that overlooked Los Angeles the following afternoon. They left Zal's Bearcat in Bolton Canyon, and climbed to the encampment in Weid Canyon where – Pete Camora, who brokered jobs for Hispanic extras, informed Kitty – many socialists who had fled Mexico in the Revolution had taken refuge among the laborers working on the new dam. That, he said, was the most recent address he had for Emilio Esparto.

IT WAS THE REDS, screamed the headline of the *Times* that morning. ('Mr Jesperson certainly didn't waste any time,' Emma had remarked over breakfast). NEW EVIDENCE IN ZAPOLYA MURDER, proclaimed the *Examiner*, with an article (plus an editorial and two letters) concerning attempts by a Communist group to interfere with 'a number of Hollywood studios' (unspecified) and Ernst Zapolya's valiant and categorical refusal to have anything to do with such nefarious activities. It was heavily implied that whatever else 'Stalin's Red Death Squad' had done, the murder of Ernst Zapolya could almost certainly be laid at their door.

The *Times* article quoted Frank Pugh and Larry Palmer (at length) on the subject of the arson at Big Bear: an effort to disrupt the filming of the new smash hit *Hot Potato*, which praised the scrappy courage of an American girl.

Emma wondered if that meant that either she or Sam Wyatt would be instructed to drop all current projects and re-write a few new scenes for *Hot Potato* demonstrating Cincinnati Wilder's scrappy courage.

The camp among the straggly oaks in Weid Canyon was almost a little town: tiny houses roughly put together from unpainted lumber alternated with shanties and tents. Small children dashed barefoot in the dust, reminding Emma of her father's descriptions of the Italian and Egyptian villages near his various dig sites. Women hung laundry on lines stretched from house-corners to trees; neat pens had been constructed behind several of the houses to confine goats or, less effectively, chickens. A well had been dug – presumably with the assistance of the Los Angeles Bureau of Water Works and Supply – and outhouses dotted the hillslope behind the camp. The largest of the wooden buildings was apparently a store, with a rough porch in front and an open kitchen – roofed with pine-poles and tent-canvas – to one side, where two women were making tortillas.

Dogs barked. Men's voices argued lazily from inside the store – presumably everyone who was interested in going to church had done so that morning – and from somewhere in the trees came the noise of what sounded like a cock fight. The place smelled of woodsmoke and privies. A very pregnant young woman called out from the thin gray-green shadows of a clump of cottonwoods near the trail, 'You maybe lookin' for somebody?' Her English was good. 'Maybe I help you?'

'We're trying to find Emilio Esparto,' returned Zal in English. 'Pete Camora told us he might be here.'

'He moved on,' she answered immediately. She was, Emma guessed, sixteen or seventeen, though she remembered her father describing the Egyptian and Italian girls as looking older than their years. Her face was intelligent, behind the expression of stolid stupidity, her dark eyes watchful. Emma wondered if she'd been assigned sentry duty because of her English, or her approaching maternity. 'Last month, six weeks.' She shrugged.

'Could you find someone to get word to him?' asked Zal. He kept to English, though Emma knew he spoke Spanish well. 'Tell him Kitty is here to see him, with something from his friend Ernst.'

The girl considered him for a moment more, then turned her head and called to a boy – he looked about eight – who was feeding chickens behind one of the tar-paper dwellings a little further up the trail. The boy ran into the shack. A man came out, unshaven and a little sleepy-looking, heavy-shouldered

and, like many men in Los Angeles, in shirtsleeves with his
shirt unbuttoned. As he came down towards them, the girl
turned back to Zal, explained, 'The contractor boss for the
dam, he says, nobody comes into the camp. I'm gonna go up,
see if anybody knows where Emilio moved on to. The
contractor boss says somebody gotta stay here with you, OK?
This is *mi padre*, Señor Reyes. He don't speak English much,
please, I'm sorry.'

'Quite all right,' said Zal, and gazed innocently off into the
trees as the girl explained something to her father in Spanish,
before she darted away up the path. The older man studied
Zal, then the two young women, with flat, dark, wary eyes,
and Emma was aware of two other men who suddenly loitered
by the fence of the garden where they'd been working a
moment before.

Kitty took her cigarette case from her handbag and offered
it to their guard with a smile. The man returned the smile, and
lit both her cigarette and his own.

She had barely inhaled three puffs when a voice from up
the path called, '*Cara mia!*' and Kitty turned, radiant, and
dropped the cigarette to the ground.

'Emilio!'

She dashed up to meet him – Emma had deduced that, guard
notwithstanding, the 'contractor boss' and his orders were an
invention to keep strangers out of the camp. The dark-haired,
powerfully-built man strode down to meet her, and the warmth
of their embrace informed Emma that Kitty probably knew
Emilio Esparto – a.k.a. Francisco Castillo, a.k.a. (now) Luis
Vasquez – very well indeed.

'You never told me you were a socialist!'

'Hush!' He was laughing, and put on an innocent expression. 'A socialist? I?' Though not handsome, Emma could see
how the fluid power of his movements, the laughter in that
mobile face, would translate very well to film.

'Oh, it's all right.' Kitty waved back to her two friends.
'Zallie and Emma know, and those awful Communists got
arrested for trying to kill us, though I'll bet they come up with
witnesses that they were someplace else when poor Ernst was
shot. Ernst wanted to give you this.'

She held out the little packet of papers to him, re-wrapped in its brown paper; then fished again into her handbag and brought out the Enterprise Films envelope that she'd taken from Zapolya's pocket three weeks ago. 'And this,' she said. 'It's four thousand dollars. And . . .' Another search of the handbag. 'This, too. There's a hundred pesos here. I'm . . . I'm sorry about what happened to Ernst. And that I couldn't bring you all this sooner. But if I had, the Communists would probably have followed me, instead of being locked up in the pokey like they are now.'

'It's all right, *corazòn.*' He looked down into her eyes, half smiling and half sad. 'Ernst was a good friend. And he believed in justice for the people.' And as if he saw something in Kitty's eyes that Emma didn't, he added quietly, 'A man can wish to fight for the rights of the common people, without realizing that each one of them *is* a common person, with the right not to be treated like a film prop. The world is full of such people, *cara.* Many men who would die for the rights of the masses treat individual women like servants without a thought, when they get them into bed. So many mothers treat their children so.'

He placed his palm to her cheek. 'God can work with clay, and with it still bring about good. We can only do what we can, and try not to hate.'

Kitty sighed, and looked up into the dark eyes. 'I guess that's why I'll never be the Leader of The People.'

His smile brightened, and he bent his head to kiss her again. 'People need more than leaders, *cara.* They also need tales of love and light, to get them through the hours of darkness alive.'

Two days later, three lines on the back page of the *Van Nuys News* – beneath two columns carried over from the front page concerning the upcoming arraignment of Pyotr Braeden, Jonas Schechter, and Dora Unger (a.k.a. Gloria DeMille) – mentioned that well-known director Bob Campbell had replaced Erich von Stroheim on Enterprise Films' production of the new smash spectacle *Crowned Heart.* And as Kitty had predicted, Miss Unger claimed she could produce a dozen witnesses as to her whereabouts on May third, 1924.

'Though I'd sure like to see her try,' remarked Kitty, after a very late lunch of omelets and champagne on the high front porch of the pink stucco palace on Ivarene Street. 'I mean, everybody who'd testify for her has got to know they'll get followed all around town for just *weeks* afterwards by the Katzenjammer Kids. I'd think the local commissar is going to just throw the three of them under a bus, rather than have that happen. And serve them right!'

'But that would risk having them turn King's evidence against the commissar,' pointed out Emma. 'Or whatever it's called in the United States.'

'And besides . . .' Nomie Carlyle leaned back in the depths of one of the wicker porch-chairs with Chang Ming panting happily in her lap. 'Miss Unger didn't look anything like the woman I saw behind the cathedral sets.'

She glanced from Kitty's face to Emma's, and Emma saw again how haggard she looked, as if the strain of the past month had eradicated even the relief of vindication. Haggard, and a little puzzled, like a woman who finds that a dish doesn't taste the way she thought it would. *Why don't I feel better about all this?* 'I mean, I only saw her from the back, but she was shorter and heavier than-than Miss Unger . . .'

Below them, the shadows of the little villa's ridiculous roofline lay far advanced across the straggly lawn, already touching the slope where the ground rose to Ivarene Street. The golden air had the glittering quality so prized by directors and cameramen; Emma felt a pang of sympathy for Zal, back in the film building of Foremost running through thousands of feet of negatives in quest of those takes in which Harry hadn't gotten between Kitty and the camera, or Gully Ackroyd hadn't blundered into either the furniture or Ken Elmore, or the lighting had been correct. The air smelled of dust and sage: the scent of the California hills.

'You think that matters to the papers?' Kitty groused. 'She sure tried to murder *me*, and I'll testify all they want to *that*.

Plus there's the footage Alvy Turner got, of the three of them running away from the cabin. The light's not good, but there's about ten frames where you can see them, silhouetted real good against the flames. Did you get a subpoena yet, Nomie? What are you wearing to the courtroom?'

Nomie flinched, and set aside her champagne as if suddenly sickened of its taste.

'Emma, darling, do you think my plum-and-lavender Poiret would look respectable enough, if I wore the diamond earrings? And maybe a scarf at the neck? Or should I get something else? I want to look really respectable, so they'll all believe me and put those nasty Commies in Leavenworth. D'you want to go shopping tomorrow, sweetheart? Nomie?' She looked from one to the other hopefully.

'Aren't you meeting with Mr Palmer at the studio tomorrow about *Crimson Desert*?' Emma reminded her, and Kitty pouted.

'Nertz. You're right. Well, the day after . . . Or, no, I have costume fittings . . . I'll ask Frank about it tonight. Are you going to Peggy's party tonight, Nomie? I just *knew* when I read they'd fired Von, that meant that Jesperson was wrapping up *Crowned Heart* . . .'

The girl shook her head swiftly, and turned her face aside. Zal's tales of von Stroheim's epic rages on the set returned to Emma's mind: his savage bullying of the actors, his perfectionist demands for take after grueling take. How had the director treated this pretty girl – barely more than a child despite her tawdry reputation – whom everyone in Hollywood agreed couldn't act to save her life? 'You're not still worried about the police, are you, Nomie? It sounds to me –' she gestured with the paper – 'as if Mr Jesperson has got what he wants: a culprit to bring the investigation to a close, without anybody looking into what Marina Carver – or her mother – were doing that afternoon. In fact, a trial to take everybody's attention off his studio . . . and to give him all kinds of publicity for *Crowned Heart* and *Broadway Bluebird*.'

Nomie produced a radiant last-reel-of-the-film smile, and shook her head. 'Oh, no. I . . . I'm just tired. And Harry

– Mr Garfield – is picking me up for dinner at the Grove tonight.'

'Oh, dear.' Emma sighed. 'I never did return his bracelet to him, and he'll probably want to give it to you tonight . . . I wonder if it would be bad form for me to just hand it to you now?'

Nomie giggled, looking suddenly more like her old self, and Kitty said, 'You know, sweetheart, you could do a lot worse than marry Harry. Emma can tell you what a nice gentleman he is – well, Roger Clint can, too . . . He doesn't get nasty when he drinks, and he doesn't use cocaine, and he smells nice. And he really does need to marry somebody pretty soon. Frank would give you a contract at Foremost, you know.'

'I know.' The girl ducked her head, as if she would have blushed – but she didn't. In fact Emma thought she looked a little pale. 'But I—' Then she stopped her next words, whatever they would have been, on her lips, and looked away again.

In a more serious voice, Kitty said, 'You think about it, sweetheart. I mean, Emma has Zallie . . . and I'd like to see things turn out well for you.'

Nomie almost whispered, 'Thank you. Maybe they will.'

Kitty went off to Peggy's party – an event, Emma gathered, partly to celebrate the conclusion of shooting *Crowned Heart* and partly to rejoice at not having to put up with Erich von Stroheim any longer – and Nomie walked down to Franklin Avenue to catch the streetcar for that down-at-heels mansion on Third. Shortly after Kitty's departure, Zal arrived, with a late dinner of lo mein and egg fu yung in boxes from Sammy Cho's. Records on the gramophone, a snowstorm of newspaper uproar about Communist plots, and a number of possible – and increasingly absurd – future scenarios involving spies and boat chases, mysterious Mexican villages and piracy on the high seas.

'Didn't Julius Caesar get kidnapped by pirates?' asked Zal a little later, out of sleepy darkness.

'He did. He was outraged that they only charged his family

twenty-five gold pieces for his ransom and said he was worth at least fifty.'

'Sounds like him.'

It was good to lie in Zal's arms.

TWENTY-THREE

And of course, Kitty phoned at nine o'clock the following morning – Zal had left at seven for the studio – begging Emma to meet her at Foremost with her midnight-blue Lanvin gauze, the blue-and-yellow pumps, pearls ('I know they're fakes, dearest, but they're *really* good fakes and at least that old trout Willa Jesperson won't be looking daggers at me anymore . . .'), and assorted undergarments and accessories.

'You're absolutely the alligator's adenoids, darling!'

An ambition I never thought I'd attain cataloging Etruscan inscriptions at Oxford . . .

With the skill of increasing practice, Emma wrapped the Lanvin frock in tissue paper, tucked the ersatz pearls into one velvet box and Harry Garfield's diamond bracelet into another, and sorted deftly through snowdrifts of chemises and step-ins, camisoles and stockings, in the cedar-lined cupboard drawers of her sister-in-law's dressing-room.

And found among the frou-frou of silk, a pair of gloves.

Black gloves, edged in a line of lace. Smudged on one side with white plaster and the brown dust of the back lot. Clean on the other, as if they had been dropped after the explosion that jammed the cathedral door.

She turned them over. The right one was charred a little, as if it had been too close to a gun muzzle when the weapon was fired, and dotted with stiff, tiny crusts.

She licked her finger and rubbed one spot. It came away red.

For some minutes Emma stood, the gloves in hand, while the three Pekinese sat lined up in the dressing-room doorway waiting for their promised excursion to the studio.

Then she replaced the gloves where she had found them, finished packing Kitty's outfit into her Italian leather overnight bag, and went downstairs.

The three boxes of Ernst Zapolya's files which von Stroheim had had sent over from Enterprise still stood stacked in the scullery. With public attention drawn away by the scarlet herring of Communist conspiracy, Emma had felt no great urge to delve into the dead director's secrets. Beyond ascertaining that there were no love letters or threats, she had been more concerned with her friend's innocence and safety, than with who had actually pulled the trigger of that .32 Savage the police had found.

Now she opened the boxes, like her father picking patiently at those twelve crates of finger-sized Etruscan potsherds, and thumbed through the files until she found the one marked, *The Fall of Atlantis*. It was much fatter than the others, plumped out by studio memos concerning the debacle of the corrupt continent's actual inundation. She had to search for some time before she found a single typewritten sheet noting the names of the thirty-five extras who had been hospitalized with crush injuries from falling masonry. At the bottom, three names were listed as 'deceased'.

One of them was Ruth Crumm.

In the Bible, she recalled, Ruth and Naomi had been an inseparable pair of women, facing together an uncaring world. Would a mother name her two daughters after them?

The date of the film's release was 1919 (and it had made a total of $125,000 in its first three months). Filming had taken place from February to October 1918. In 1918, Emma guessed, Nomie Carlyle – only Agent Peth had called her Naomi Crumm – had been twelve.

'Everybody comes to Hollywood from someplace else,' Zal had said. 'You'll never meet so many orphans and strangers in one place again in your life.'

What would become of a twelve-year-old girl – an extremely pretty twelve-year-old girl – alone in a strange city, with no way to buy food or pay her rent, when the older sister who had cared for her was dead?

'Was that what you were going to tell us out on the gondola?' she asked Kitty, later – after the initial meeting with Larry

Palmer and the rest of the cast of *Crimson Desert*, a thrashing-out of potential problems with the scenario ('Could you maybe write in a love triangle, Duchess?'), and a long discussion about where one obtained 200 camels in Southern California and how one transported them to the Mojave Desert. 'That Nomie really had killed Mr Zapolya?'

Kitty nodded. The soft gray of the Los Angeles sky had just begun to dim above the high square silhouette of Stage Two, visible across the dusty plaza through the French windows. 'I felt so bad about dragging you and Zallie into it,' she whispered. 'I never meant—'

'It's all right.' Emma folded her hands on the corner of the makeup table, and realized that it was, in fact, all right.

I could have been drowned that night.

No marriage – to anybody – no money. No expeditions to Egypt, with or without coverage in Screen Stories. *Or Zal could have died, and I lived.*

She didn't think she could have endured that kind of pain twice.

But Ernst Zapolya surviving the Battle of Ravenstark would not necessarily have prevented attempts by Josef Stalin's agents to silence myself and Kitty. And heaven only knows what problems Kitty would have run into complying with his request.

'I knew Ruth,' Kitty went on after a time. 'She and I were extras together in *Cleopatra* and *The Slave Market*; I think she was one of Sennett's Bathing Beauties for a while. I met Nomie once or twice – they had an apartment on Fergusson Alley, a horrible dump, but it was all they could afford. Nomie was just a kid. Ruth called her Nay. She skipped school all the time to work as an extra because they needed the money, but she hated the movies. Hated acting.'

She looked down, her small hands toying with the delicate bottles of nail varnish and pots of rouge that lined the makeup table between them: Egyptian Poppy and Persian Blush. 'After Ruth was killed I lost track of-of Nay. A couple years later I heard about Nomie Carlyle – she must have been fourteen or fifteen then – screwing pretty much anybody who could get

her a part, but I didn't know it was her until she came on the
lot as an extra about a year and a half ago. She said she was
doing fine. That she had promises from a couple of producers.'

The brush-fine brows drew together, the slim fingers stilled
on a bottle of perfume that cost more than Nomie Carlyle's
rent. 'I asked her if she needed help. She said no. And I know
losing somebody like that does something to you. Getting
dropped out on your own, and knowing there's no reason for
you not to do whatever you need to do.'

As Kitty had been, Emma reflected, when her parents –
outraged at her adolescent defiance – had thrown her out of
their flat when she was fourteen.

'I thought it was . . . well . . . Ruth told me once they didn't
have any family. Their dad had been killed fighting in the
Philippines, and their mom died of pneumonia about two years
after they moved to Hollywood before the start of the war.
And if Enterprise gave any of those extras' families a dime
in compensation, I never heard about it. And I was an extra
then, too, so I probably would have heard.'

Emma said nothing for a time, remembering the nurses telling
her, when she'd come out of a week of semi-consciousness,
that her parents had died and the house had already been sold.
'But where can I go when I get out of here?' she had asked.

Recalled, too, the biting letter Jim's parents had sent her,
about how their son had 'betrayed his heritage' by marrying
a *shiksa*.

In time she said, 'I found a handwritten note from Willa
Jesperson in the Atlantis file. It just said, "Do not fear. All is
well. Lukas, Bardy, Bertini signed affidavits, will testify that
you briefed extras. Mancuso paid off".'

'Herb Mancuso was an investigator for the coroner's office
back then.' Kitty looked up from the makeup jars. 'I know
Jeff Bardy was an assistant director at Enterprise – I slept with
him a couple of times to get a featured part in *What About
Lizzie?* – he had a scorpion tattooed on his . . . Well, anyway.
I think Bertini was a cameraman. How do you know it was
from Willa?'

'It was her private stationery,' said Emma. 'It had a little
engraving at the top, of the gladiator statue that stands in her

parlor. She didn't sign the note. And in any case, I should think Nomie would have had to sue the studio for compensation, and that's something a child her age couldn't have afforded, and probably didn't even think of.'

'No.' Kitty sighed. 'Anyway, the minute we came up the cathedral steps and I saw Nomie passed out by the doors, I knew it was her, and I didn't blame her. That's why I grabbed her gloves, because of course they had blood on them and of course they could have traced them through Wardrobe—'

'You knew it was her?'

'Darling, *nobody* faints that gracefully, with their skirt pulled down over their knees. And I guessed then, that she'd put all that work and all that time into staying in pictures, just so she could work herself around to where she could get Ernst alone.'

She shook her head at the recollection. 'She must have seen us coming – Ernst was right there near the stairs, so she could have looked straight out across the square. And when she couldn't get the door open, she flung the gun and the gloves up through the hole in the wall above the door. The gun went up through 'cause it was heavier, but I think the gloves just flopped around and dropped back into the debris. You know how it is, if you try to throw something light like your underwear up out of sight on to a high shelf in a hurry . . . or maybe I guess you wouldn't.' She studied Emma doubtfully. 'But she had to drop down in a faint right there before we got there.'

'And that's why she said she saw a woman in black,' said Emma thoughtfully, and Kitty nodded.

'So if somebody *had* got a glimpse of her, she could say it was somebody else. Please don't tell the police.'

Emma said, 'No.'

Who are these people . . .?

The lovely eyebrows puckered in distress. 'Does that make you an accomplice or something?'

'It makes both of us accessories after the fact. This evening I'm going to go through the rest of Mr Zapolya's files and take out everything that might possibly bear on his connection with communist groups, and send it to the Katzen – send it

to Agents Peth and Shardborn. That should divert everyone's
attention from anything to do with the studio – if there is
anything there in the first place.'

*If Mr Pugh and Mr Jesperson and all the executives at Fox
and Paramount can do it*, she reflected resignedly, *I suppose
so can I . . .*

'Oh, send it to Mr Jesperson,' said Kitty. 'Whatever he
doesn't burn, he'll forward on to them, and it'll make big
points for Peggy – I'll let him know that it was Peggy who
urged you to do it, if you don't mind.'

'No,' Emma sighed again. *I'll bet Euripides never had to
lie to the BOI.* 'I don't mind.'

'You're a doll!' Kitty sprang to her feet, leaned down to
kiss Emma's cheek. 'Thank you! Oh, nertz, it's three o'clock
and I was supposed to be over at Wardrobe . . . Oh, here
comes Larry looking for me—'

And indeed, the stooped, tweedy form of the director
could be seen crossing the plaza outside.

'There's this scene in *Crimson Desert* where I'll be dressed
in this slave-girl costume in chains . . . Yes,' she added,
stooping to ruffle the three Pekes, who had likewise scrambled hopefully up. 'We won't be that long, and then Frank's
taking me to the Biltmore for dinner, and I'm meeting Mr
Crain later for drinks' – she named an elderly oil millionaire
of her acquaintance – 'so you won't mind taking the car
home, will you, sweetheart? It's a real pity Emilio had to
leave town.'

'And did the other three thousand dollars out of that seven
thousand Mr Zapolya had on him go to Nomie?' Emma asked.
'I assume he meant all seven thousand to go to Mr Esparto.'

'Oh, yes.' Kitty had turned from the window for a hasty
check of her makeup. 'But I figured he owed Nomie something – Larry, darling, I'm *devastated*, I'm *so* sorry, for some
reason I wrote down that we were meeting Mary at *four* . . .'

She clung to the director's arm, gazed with smoldering
flirtatiousness up into his eyes, and the man grinned – clearly
dazzled – and shook his head. 'What, you didn't delay so you
could get me here to your dressing room?'

Surrounded by dogs, Emma stood in the French door,

watching them cross the plaza. Admired again her beautiful sister-in-law's playful grace, sometimes a schoolgirl coaxing the director for forgiveness, sometimes a vamp languishing on his arm. Beautiful and glittering and careless, walking the path she had chosen. The path, it seemed to Emma, for which she had been born.

'People need more than leaders,' Emilio Esparto had said. *You must ask yourself – you must* know *– who is this girl? Who are any of us? And which way does* my *path lead?*

'Duchess?' said Harry Garfield's voice beside her. 'Mrs Blackstone?'

She hadn't heard him come along the shaded walk.

'I have something for you.' She dug in her cardigan pocket, brought out the neat red velvet box.

The flat of his hand gently forestalled her. 'Please,' he said. 'Can't I get you to keep it?' The dark eyes met hers, tender and a little sad.

'I thought you might want to give it to Nomie Carlyle.'

A corner of his mouth turned down, and he sighed. 'I tried emeralds last night,' he admitted. 'A pretty nice double string, emeralds, and pearls.' He reached into his own breast pocket. 'They'd look good on you.'

She smiled at him, and shook her head.

'Please?' There was a touch of schoolboy in the quirk of his brows. She'd seen it in the dailies of *Hot Potato* as well. 'The thing is, Nomie's leaving town. She may already have left – she said last night she was taking the train this morning.'

'To where?' She recalled what Kitty had said, about the sisters – Ruth and Naomi Crumm – having no family. *Orphans and strangers* . . .

She recalled the lost look in the girl's dark eyes yesterday afternoon. The look of a woman who wonders why she doesn't feel the way she thought she'd feel.

'Beats me. But she said, now that *Crowned Heart* is wrapped, that she doesn't want to stay in Hollywood. Sounds to me like Ernst's murder spooked her. More than the murder, the way Jesperson was getting ready to hand her over to the cops without a second thought. I told her it would be OK,' he added, shaking his head. A little puzzled, Harry Garfield turning, briefly, into Howie Mellnick, a real man trying to understand a person – not a film star – that he had met and liked.

'She could be good, you know,' he added. 'I could help her along. I mean, she can't act, but she's got that quality . . . She really could go someplace. And I know Frank would sign her if I asked him.'

'What did she say?' asked Emma.

'It was weird,' said Howie. 'I told her all this – what I'm telling you. And I told her with the Reds nabbed and the BOI handling the investigation, she had nothing to be afraid of. And she said, "I'm not afraid. I just don't want to stay. I hate this town. I want real life".' He shook his head again. 'Do you know what she meant?'

'No,' Emma lied. And for a moment she heard, far off, the bells of Oxford on May Morning, like the carillons of a drowned city, ringing beneath the sea.

What does Harry hear? The German guns in the Forest of Argonne?

Some nights, she seemed to hear them, too.

She pressed the jewel case into Harry's hands, smiled across at him.

'I can't talk you into it? Zal knows the score – you know he wouldn't mind.'

'I'd mind.'

She watched Harry go, crossing the plaza towards Wardrobe – presumably to consult with Mary Blanque about slave-boy costumes and more chains? *So where is Real Life? Oxford, and the quest for ancient truths, ancient worlds that were Real Life to all those Babylonians and Etruscans and Romans, who lost those they loved and wore complicated disguises and postured for their living behind jeweled masks? Who sought revenge only to find in its achievement the hollow echo that asks, What now?*

Or Hollywood, the Babylon of Lies – the city of orphans and strangers. Where at least a few people, she knew, lived in truth.

'You'll have to tell the truth,' Kitty had said to Nomie. And Nomie had taken the first train out of town, rather than live in her lies a moment longer than she had to. Seeking a real life at last.

'I'd mind,' Emma had said. And so would Zal.

And Howie – Harry – had at least understood this.

Around her, the dogs sprang to their feet and dashed madly to greet Zal as he crossed the plaza from the film building. Bespectacled and slightly scruffy, and always there when she needed him.

'Haply I think on thee, and then my state/Like to the lark at break of day arising/from sullen earth sings hymns at heaven's gate . . .'

Harry stopped him halfway across the plaza in the gold slant of the afternoon light; the two men exchanged a few words. Then Harry thumped Zal's shoulder in friendly congratulation, and continued on his way. Zal stooped to greet the dogs, then straightening up, quickened his step.

'One day he's going to meet the right girl and make her very happy.' He grinned.

'As long as she isn't in love with someone else.'

They kissed in the French window of Kitty's dressing room – *Aunt Estelle really would take me to task about all this promiscuous kissing . . .*

'You all right?'

'I don't really know. Un-betrothed,' she added with a smile. 'Not for want of lover's pleas. But . . . you heard about Nomie Carlyle?'

'That she left town this morning?' asked Zal. 'I gave her a ride to the station. Or that she bumped off Ernst Zapolya?' And, to Emma's startled look: 'That's what Kitty meant in the boat the other night, wasn't it? I wasn't sure,' he added, 'until this morning, when she told me that she gave her affidavit because she knew *for a fact* that Agent Madame X wasn't the one she saw behind the set that day.

'They'll declare it unsolved, but everybody'll "know" it was the Reds, and that's enough for Jesperson,' he added, turning his head, to look out across the dusty plaza toward the stages. Ned Bergen and his minions formed a little procession, bearing lumber and canvas and Parisian lampposts, to start building sets for the next Foremost Productions opus.

'Nomie's a straight girl,' he went on. 'She'd kill the man who killed her sister – out of carelessness and vanity and just plain not thinking . . . The man who condemned her to six years of the kind of life she's been living. And you know if she'd gone to Chicago or New York or even Oatmeal, Nebraska, at that age you know somebody would have taken advantage of her. Maybe given her a worse time than she's had. But she wouldn't send even a Red agent to the gallows with a lie.'

Emma nodded. 'No,' she said. 'It makes me feel a bit better about letting her walk away scot-free.' *Which I suppose is actually* much *worse than being photographed kissing strange men on the sidewalk in front of the Café Montmartre, or accepting rides home from bootleggers . . .*

'You think she's scot-free?'

'No,' said Emma quietly. 'No.' *Leave her to Heaven*, Hamlet's father had said . . . And trust that Heaven knew her deserving. 'The Jespersons are, though,' she added, bitterness touching her voice. 'And they're as much to blame – probably more – for the past six years of Nomie's life as Mr Zapolya was.'

'If it went to trial back then,' pointed out Zal practically, 'you know neither of them would have swung for it. They probably wouldn't even have done time. As it is, each of them got an arrow through the heart: pain and grief and loss in the place it hurt them the most.'

'Willa Jesperson did,' agreed Emma, remembering the woman's tears. *'You have no idea what a relief that was . . . to see things in terms of the world beyond investments and power . . .' The way she'd half-whispered, 'We were . . .' And turned her head aside, unable to say it.*

Was that pain sufficient retribution, for three deaths and a growing girl-child's six years in hell?

She didn't know.

'But what about Mr Jesperson?'

'Are you kidding? Lou Jesperson lost the quarter-million dollars in budget overruns and production delays that von Stroheim just cost him. That's gotta hurt.'

Emma covered her mouth quickly, but couldn't stifle her laughter. 'Oh, dear!'

'And it's about four times what he'd have paid in fines and compensations – if the judge didn't just get paid off to let him walk away. You gotta take justice where you can find it, in this town, Em.'

The thought of the Austrian director as the agent of heaven made her want to giggle again. Then she sighed. 'I hope she'll be all right.'

Zal put an arm around her waist. 'If she isn't scot-free,' he said, 'at least she's free to walk on into real life, as she said. And who among us is really free?'

A troop of extras went by, gorgeous and incongruous in court dress and powdered wigs, Madge Burdon like a sturdy turnip in a basket of orchids, gesturing as she explained how she wanted them to greet the Thornless Rose of Versailles. Black Jasmine dashed after them, barking final instructions, and Zal strode to scoop him up and bring him back.

'I meant to ask you,' he said, returning. 'How's that broken arm you told me about that night in Big Bear?'

She smiled. 'Healing.'

'Me, too.'